The BIG book of NEW ZEALAND WILDLIFE

Also from Dave Gunson and New Holland Publishers:

ISBN 978-1-86966-198-4

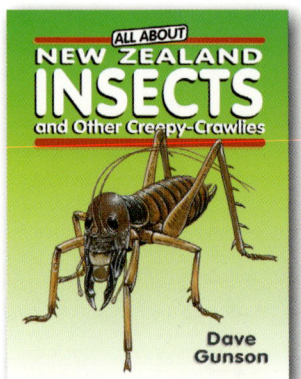
ISBN 978-1-86966-217-2

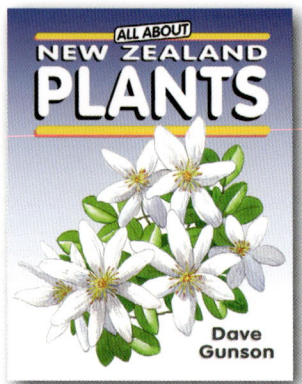
ISBN 978-1-86966-251-6

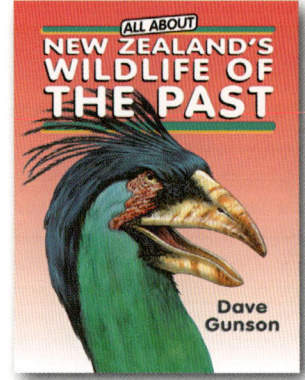
ISBN 978-1-86966-282-0

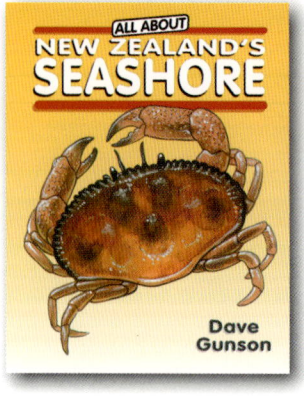
ISBN 978-1-86966-252-3

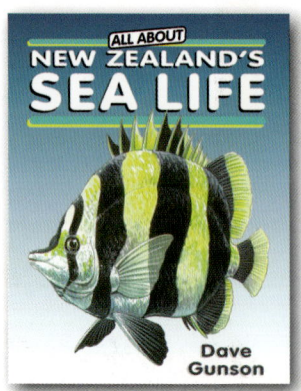
ISBN 978-1-86966-284-4

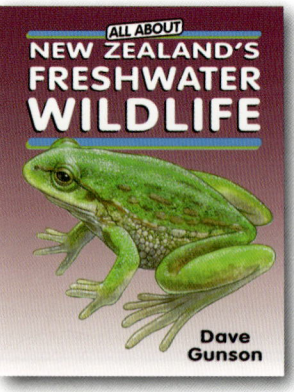
ISBN 978-1-86966-290-5

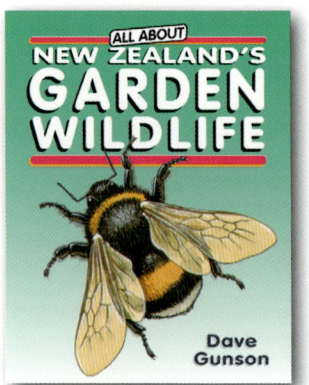
ISBN 978-1-86966-296-7

January 2012

First published in 2011 by New Holland Publishers (NZ) Ltd
Auckland • Sydney • London • Cape Town

www.newhollandpublishers.co.nz

218 Lake Road, Northcote, Auckland 0627, New Zealand
Unit 1, 66 Gibbes Street, Chatswood, NSW 2067, Australia
86–88 Edgware Road, London W2 2EA, United Kingdom
80 McKenzie Street, Cape Town 8001, South Africa

Copyright © 2011 in text and illustrations: Dave Gunson
Copyright © 2011 New Holland Publishers (NZ) Ltd
Dave Gunson has asserted his right to be identified as the author of this work.

Publishing manager: Christine Thomson
Editor: Gillian Tewsley
Design: Justine Mackenzie, Dee Murch and Dave Gunson
Layout: Camille Lowe

Front cover: Fantail, giant dragonfly, kauri tree, pukeko, tuatara
Spine: Huhu beetle
Half-title page: Garden slater, giant centipede
Title page: New Zealand falcon
Contents page: Royal spoonbill
Back cover: Female kauri cone, monarch butterfly, great white shark

10 9 8 7 6 5 4 3 2 1

Colour reproduction by SC (Sang Choy) International Pte Ltd, Singapore
Printed in China by Toppan Leefung Printing Ltd, on paper sourced from sustainable forests.

National Library of New Zealand Cataloguing-in-Publication Data

Gunson, Dave.
The big book of New Zealand wildlife / Dave Gunson.
Includes index.
ISBN 978-1-86966-297-4
1. Animals—New Zealand—Juvenile literature. 2. Plants—New Zealand—Juvenile literature. [1. Animals. 2. Plants—New Zealand.]
I. Title.
578.0993—dc 22

All rights reserved. No part of this publication may be reproduced, stored in a retrieval system, or transmitted in any form or by any means, electronic, mechanical, photocopying, recording or otherwise, without the prior permission of the publishers and copyright holders.

While every care has been taken to ensure the information contained in this book is as accurate as possible, the authors and publishers can accept no responsibility for any loss, injury or inconvenience sustained by any person using the advice contained herein.

The BIG book of NEW ZEALAND WILDLIFE

DAVE GUNSON

NEW HOLLAND

Contents

Introduction — 6

FUNGI
Fungi — 18

PLANTS
Algae — 22
Ferns — 25
Conifers — 28
Higher Plants — 32

ANIMALS

Part 1. Invertebrates (animals without an internal skeleton)
Sponges — 44
Cnidaria — 45
Echinoderms — 48
Worms — 51
Molluscs — 53
Crustaceans — 67
Centipedes & Millipedes — 72
Insects — 73
Spiders & Mites — 92
Tunicates — 96

Part 2. Vertebrates (animals with an internal skeleton)
Fish — 97
Amphibians — 110
Reptiles — 112
Birds — 118
Mammals — 152

Index — 156

Introduction

Where did all our wildlife come from?

Some of our plants and animals are new arrivals from other countries, but many of them have been here since the creation of the New Zealand land mass. It all began hundreds of millions of years ago, when the slow movement of the many plates that make up our planet's crust had created two huge supercontinents: Laurasia in the north, and Gondwana in the south.

Evolution of the islands of New Zealand

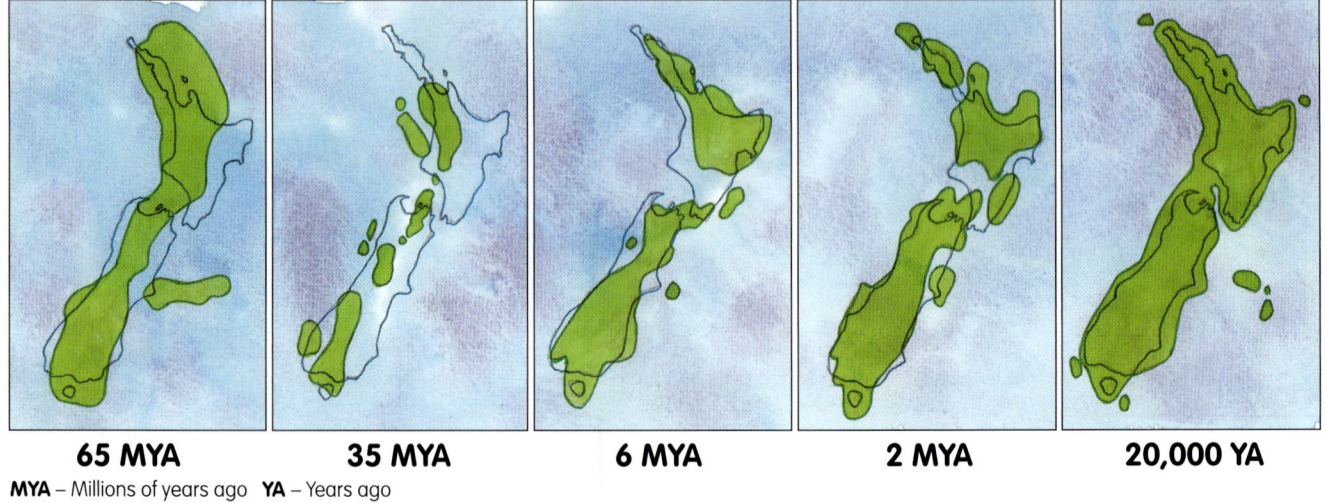

65 MYA **35 MYA** **6 MYA** **2 MYA** **20,000 YA**

MYA – Millions of years ago   **YA** – Years ago

Over millions of years, volcanic activity and the build-up of silt and materials created a new area of land in one corner of Gondwana. As the continental plates continued their slow movements, the supercontinent gradually pulled apart again, and this new corner of land began to break away. By around 80 million years ago, it had separated completely, moving away into the Pacific Ocean. Scientists use the name 'Zealandia' for this breakaway land mass; it was a whole continent in itself and was very much larger than the island chain we now call New Zealand.

Amphibian
This amphibian is one of the most ancient members of all our wildlife. It roamed the land long before New Zealand began its separation from Gondwana, about 250 million years ago. It was about 2 m long, and lived in rivers and lakes where it preyed on fish and other animals.

Though this whole immense period of time was to become dominated by the dinosaurs, many other animals, and early species of plants, had been present on Zealandia before it became separated from Gondwana. As the lands slowly drew apart, so these ancient species became the very first members of our wildlife. For a very long time, animal species were able to cross the muddy shallows of the young Tasman Sea at their leisure. Even as New Zealand was drawn further and further away, it was still relatively easy for new plants and animals to find their way onto our shores.

Cycads
Many millions of years before New Zealand began its slow separation from Gondwana, its forests were dominated by great forests of cycads. There were many different species, ranging in size from a small bush to great trees 18–20 m tall. Although the giant cycads have long since disappeared, many smaller species still exist today around the world.

Early forms of ferns and tree ferns were also present at this time, and even the predecessors of today's conifers – kauri, for example – were making their first appearance.

Eventually, the New Zealand land mass was beyond easy reach, and our dinosaurs, reptiles and all the other animals were then isolated from the rest of the world. Most of them became extinct about 65 million years ago at the close of the Cretaceous period, when great earthwide events brought an end to the reign of the dinosaurs. Although the fossil remains of many marine reptiles – large and small – from this early period have been found in our rocks, it's only been in recent years that similar remains of many land dinosaurs and other very early animals have been discovered.

Allosaur

The allosaur is one of the biggest dinosaur species found so far in New Zealand – around 9–12 m in length – and belongs to a group that includes other fierce meat-eaters such as Tarbosaurus, Spinosaurus, and the celebrated Tyrannosaurus. Fossil remains of many dinosaur types have also been found here, including megalosaurs, hysilophodonts, ankylosaurs and small sauropods.

Freshwater crocodile

About 20 million years ago, New Zealand's freshwater crocodiles, which were about 3–5 m long, lived in swamps and rivers where they caught fish and snapped up any larger animal wading through shallow waters. Crocodiles and alligators are very ancient reptiles – they first appeared over 230 million years ago. They were one of the very few larger species to survive the great extinctions at the end of the Cretaceous period, and have thrived virtually unchanged in habitats all around the world.

With the dinosaurs gone, mammals – previously small, mostly nocturnal or secretive animals – eventually became the dominant land creatures in most parts of the world. New Zealand was different. It had very few land mammals (although the remains of small mammals have been recently discovered), and so birds and insects became the principal animal groups here. Some of them, mostly free from attack by other animal species, became giants of their kind, and some developed unique or unusual lifestyles.

Land mammal
It's only in recent years that fossil evidence has indicated that New Zealand was home to species of land mammals. This rat-sized creature lived in New Zealand about 15 million years ago, and probably preyed on other small animals such as insects and worms. In most of the rest of the world, mammals developed and thrived after the fall of the dinosaurs. It's not yet clear why our own mammals failed to survive, and eventually died out.

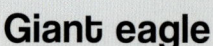

Giant eagle
This bird really deserves its name; it was the largest bird of prey ever to have existed, and had a wingspan of around 3 m. Its talons were the size of a modern tiger's, and it was big and tough enough to prey on even the largest moa – swooping down from the sky on the flightless birds as they crossed open ground.

As the larger flightless birds became more scarce when human settlers arrived, so the numbers of the giant eagle reduced, until it finally became extinct around 400 years ago.

Birds such as the kiwi, for instance, took to nesting on the ground, instead of up in trees or on cliffs.

New animal and plant species – usually by accident of sea currents or fortunate winds – have regularly arrived here over the many millions of years since then.

Hot and cold, large and small

During this long period, the islands of New Zealand passed through a great many physical changes. Some of the newcomer species adapted well and managed to survive even as temperatures and conditions changed dramatically, while some struggled to cope and gradually failed and died out. Sea levels have risen and fallen as warm periods and ice ages have come

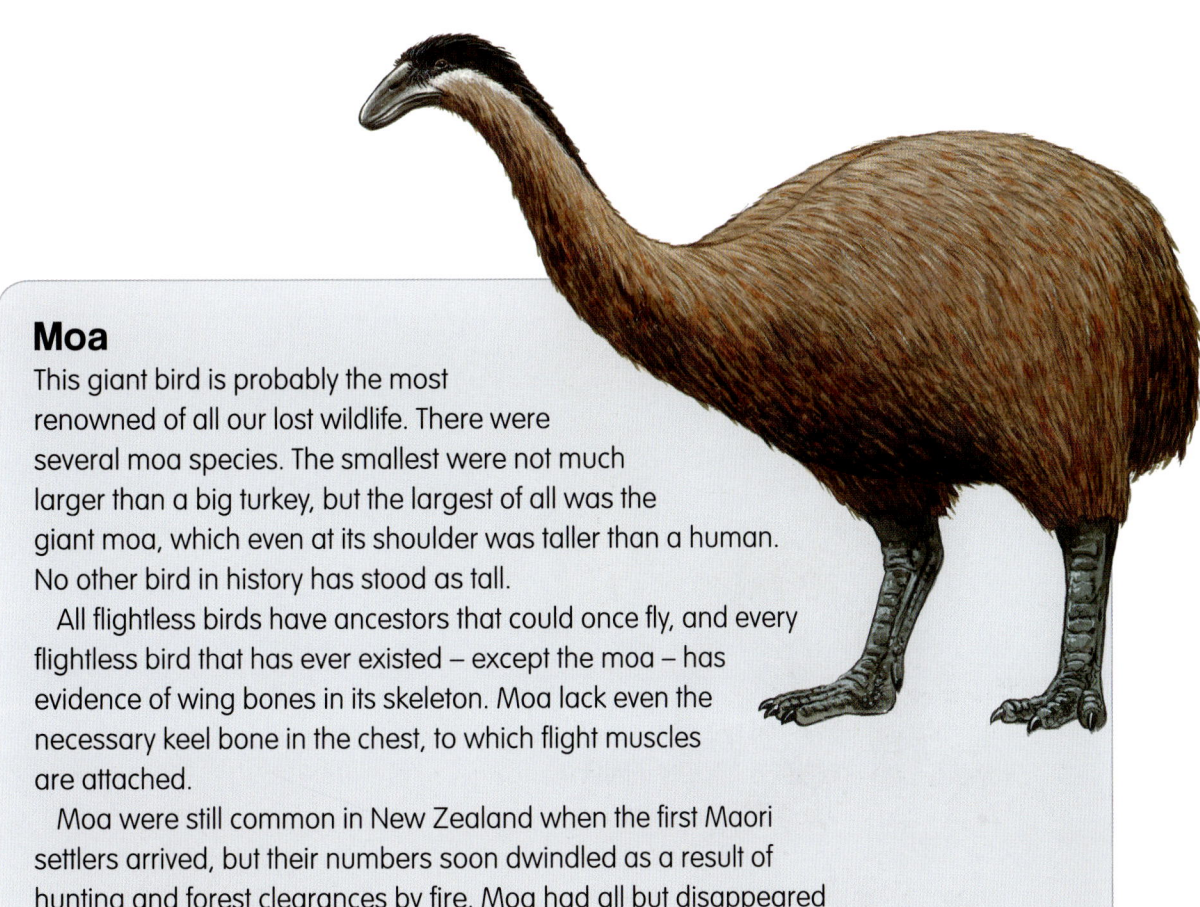

Moa
This giant bird is probably the most renowned of all our lost wildlife. There were several moa species. The smallest were not much larger than a big turkey, but the largest of all was the giant moa, which even at its shoulder was taller than a human. No other bird in history has stood as tall.

All flightless birds have ancestors that could once fly, and every flightless bird that has ever existed – except the moa – has evidence of wing bones in its skeleton. Moa lack even the necessary keel bone in the chest, to which flight muscles are attached.

Moa were still common in New Zealand when the first Maori settlers arrived, but their numbers soon dwindled as a result of hunting and forest clearances by fire. Moa had all but disappeared by the time of the first European settlers.

and gone, and the New Zealand land mass has increased greatly or reduced to just a few small islands in the ocean.

The land has also seen periods of volcanic activity, too, which have helped to shape the country. Most of these have affected only their local areas, but at least one particularly violent event devastated great areas of the central North Island. This was the eruption of 26,000 years ago which spewed up 1200 cubic kilometres of material, creating the huge vent that eventually formed Lake Taupo.

In the last 1.8 million years, New Zealand has experienced about twenty ice age cycles, with many minor periods of cooling and warming between them.

The last major ice age ended about 10,000 years ago, when the sea level was around 130 metres lower than it is today. Conditions have generally been quite stable since then. And despite New Zealand's isolation from the rest of the world, many species of

Laughing owl
This large owl – twice the size of the morepork, on which it sometimes preyed – profited from the arrival of human settlers at first, as the rats and mice that came with them made for extra prey. Its habit of nesting on the ground – in tree root crevices, or in caves and rocks – made its chicks even easier prey for those same rats and mice, and its numbers slowly declined.

Its name comes from its mad, laughing cry, which was last heard sometime in the early 1900s.

Huia

The huia was an unusual bird, in that the male and female had different bills – the female's was long and slender, and the male's was shorter and robust. Both used their bills for much the same purpose, though – for digging through the bark of rotted tree trunks to get at the insect grubs underneath.

Their black and white tail feathers were valued by Maori for decoration, and also became very popular with European settlers – so popular that their numbers suffered as a result. They also suffered from predators such as rats; and though the huia was made a protected bird in 1872, the last live bird was seen in the 1920s.

animal and plant have still managed to find their way here to become well-established by the time that the first human settlers arrived, several hundred years ago.

Nothing else has had as big an impact on New Zealand wildlife as the arrival of humans. Both Maori and Europeans brought new animal species with them, and made great changes to the land, with forest clearances and draining of wetlands, for example. Some long-established native species thrived with the changes to habitat and environment, but many failed to adapt and died out.

Plant and animal pests

Whether deliberately or accidentally released into New Zealand, many plants and animals have become a nuisance in our natural environments; some have spread to become real pests and endanger our wildlife. Many ground-dwelling or flightless birds have suffered from the rats, dogs, mice, cats, weasels and ferrets that have been brought here. Skinks, geckos and insects have been easy prey for these newcomers, too.

Domesticated animals that have become feral (wild) also do a lot of damage. Wild pigs can catch and eat kiwi and native snails. Goats and many species of deer damage young plants. Possums eat the young growing shoots on many tree species. Even the apparently harmless hedgehog is a pest – it eats worms and snails, and takes the eggs of ground-nesting birds, such as the New Zealand dotterel.

Plants, too, can be destructive. Kahili ginger can spread fast and crowd out young growing plants under the forest canopy. Many other plants, such as jasmine, moth plant and blue morning glory, can spread rapidly to smother established trees. Great tangles of old man's beard can strangle even the tallest trees; and species of heather and gorse can spread across the open countryside – sometimes as far as the eye can see.

Feral goat

Hedgehog

Kahili ginger

Jasmine

14

Today's wildlife

The range of wildlife – new, old and ancient – that we have today is unique, and many of our surviving animal and plant species are celebrated throughout the world for the remarkable features that set many of them apart from their relatives in other lands. Some, such as the kauri and the tuatara, have remained practically unchanged since the days of the dinosaurs.

New Zealand's distance from other large land masses means that it has always been difficult for new, and possibly dangerous, species to arrive naturally on our shores, and to establish themselves. In many ways, it's easier today for these invaders to get here. Some small animal species, such as insects, manage to hitch a ride on ships and aeroplanes, and plant seeds can be brought in accidentally by visitors. Government agencies keep a careful watch for these, and are mostly successful in keeping unwelcome immigrants at bay, though the occasional 'nasty' does manage to get through.

New Zealand has a large number of marine parks and national parks, where commercial development is severely reduced and wildlife is protected. Many islands and areas of specially protected bush and forest have undergone successful programmes of pest and predator elimination. Native wildlife has thrived under these protective environments, and many species once at great risk have increased in numbers.

Overall, New Zealand is very fortunate in its isolation and location in the South Pacific. Conditions are temperate and not generally subject to extremes in climate or weather – not quite hot enough to develop tropical jungle, and not quite cold enough for land to be permanently frozen. Our coastline, which measures over 18,000 kilometres in total length, is swept by warm currents from the north and cooler currents from the south, which bring plants and animals to our waters from other parts of the world. The seas are as rich as the land in their diversity of wildlife – and they define our natural world as much as the species on land do, for New Zealand doesn't just finish at the water's edge. The great land mass of Zealandia, much of it now underwater, is around 15 times larger than New Zealand's dry land area, and it stretches from the Kermadec Islands in the far north to the Macquarie and Campbell Islands in the subantarctic seas.

All of our islands – there are over 600 of them, large and small – offer different environments and ecosystems, too. Extensive and varied forests, great swathes of open country, wetlands, great and small lakes in both main islands, complicated river systems, thermal areas, high mountain chains – all these provide homes for our incredibly varied wildlife.

About the entries in this book

The three main and most easily seen groupings, or kingdoms, of the natural world are fungi, plants and animals. New Zealand has many tens of thousands of wildlife species from these kingdoms, and this book provides a good introduction to the main groups in our unique natural world. Most of our more famous and celebrated plant and animal species are included here, plus an interesting selection of some of the odd, obscure, weird and wonderful species that inhabit our islands.

Both the animal and plant sections in the book are divided into their main classes and types, such as ferns, conifers, insects, birds and so on, but their arrangement, and the individual species in each part, follow no particular scientific order.

The section on animals is divided into two parts: invertebrates, which are those animals that lack an internal skeleton, and vertebrates, which are those animals that have an internal, bony skeleton.

FUNGI

Long ago, fungi were thought to be close relatives of plants, because they mostly grew from the ground and did not move about as animals do. But we now know that fungi cannot use water and direct sunlight for growth, as plants can. Instead, they make chemicals that break down dead or living organic material (bits of animals or plants) to use as food. Fungi are a very important part of the general circle of life, as the minerals released from this breakdown are returned to the soil to enrich it, and so provide food for growing plants.

There are more than 20,000 fungi species in New Zealand, and probably around 300,000 worldwide. They range greatly in size: the tiniest are too small to see without a microscope, while the largest are almost too heavy to lift. Fungi come in many different shapes and may have dull or bright colours. Hundreds of species have the traditional mushroom shape of stalk and cap, but others look like potatoes, bowls, cones, sea stars, fans, sea anemones, tiny buttons or leaves. Some are soft and fragile, some are jelly-like, and some are as tough as old leather or wood.

A number of species are used in the making of foods such as cheese and wine, and in medicines. There are many edible species, too – and many more that are harmful and even deadly poisonous to animals and humans. Never taste an unidentified fungus. Even if you have only touched it, make sure you do not put your fingers to your mouth, and make sure that you wash you hands as soon as you can.

Fungi reproduce by releasing fine spores into the air, sometimes with an explosive 'puff'.

The common term 'mushroom' is generally used for fungi that have an obvious stalk topped by a cap of some sort, and the name 'toadstool' is often applied to those with a grainy, warty covering on the cap – probably because this makes them look like a warty toad.

Scarlet flycap

This is probably the most famous mushroom around the world, as it's been illustrated in countless picture books, cartoons, films and advertising materials. It's not too hard to find, either, as its red cap makes it easy to see, and it readily grows in many types of bush and forest around New Zealand, especially around conifer trees. It can also be seen in gardens and parks when conditions are right, towards the end of summer and into autumn. The red cap fades to a metallic bronze as the fungus ages.

The caps of some specimens can reach over 13 cm in diameter, and the mushroom can reach a height of 17 cm or more.

This species probably came to New Zealand in the 1800s with imported tree seedlings from Europe, where it was commonly used as a fly deterrent by placing the red cap in a saucer of milk. Flies who took a taste didn't last very long, apparently.

FUNGI

Blue pinkgill

The bright colour of this little fungus can be a startling find on a forest walk in autumn. It is found mostly in North Island forests, and only rarely in the South Island.

Its strong blue colour often fades as it ages, and becomes more green, and then fades to greeny-brown and ochre. It can grow to a height of about 10 cm, and the cap can be 2–5 cm wide.

The blue pinkgill is also known as the little blue mushroom, or the blue-cap. Other pinkgill species can be seen in grey-brown and orange-brown.

The blue pinkgill has a very special claim to fame, as it's probably the only fungus to feature on a nation's money – New Zealand's $50 banknote.

Green waxgill

The green waxgill can be found among the ground mosses of most types of forests all around the country. It grows to about 5 cm in height, with a cap up to 3 cm across. It has a lumpy covering of slime, which gives it a slightly glassy look. A second type of green waxgill is a much brighter green and has a covering of smooth slime, which gives it a clear, glossy appearance.

Other waxgill species can be found in shades of red, orange and yellow.

Artist's porebracket

There are many species of bracket fungus in New Zealand, but this is one of the largest. It regularly grows to over 60 cm wide and well over 10 cm thick, and some can even reach over 1 metre in width. It appears on tree trunks and fallen logs in all types of forest around the country. Though most forest fungi may last only a few days or weeks, the porebracket can live for several years.

It gets its name from the fact that the darker upper surface can be easily marked, revealing the pale layer beneath. You could make a drawing on it, but unimaginative passers-by usually just leave their initials, unfortunately.

The orange porebracket is much smaller, usually around 6 cm wide, and is – you guessed it – orange. This species is very common and can be found on all types of tree trunks and branches, both in forests and more open situations – even on manufactured wooden products, like pallets and packing cases, that are left outside.

19

FUNGI

Coral fungi
It's easy to see how these fungi get their name, as they closely resemble small stands of sea coral. They come in a wide range of colours – yellow, orange, white, pink – and one that's found in the Auckland region is a strong purple colour. One tiny species earns the name baby-fingered coral as its 5 cm-high stalks end in further stalk divisions that look like tiny hands and fingers.

Coral fungi can be found in all types of forest around the country, usually appearing in autumn. As with many other forest fungi, some also appear at other times of the year, after a warm rain. They usually grow no more than 4 cm in height, but appear in large clumps.

King's pouch
This bright purple fungus is very common in South Island beech forests. It measures up to 9 cm in height, with a cap up to 7 cm wide. It cannot release spores into the air as most other fungi do, but instead seems to rely on being broken and eaten by birds and other animals. The bright fruit-like colour of this and other related fungi may attract birds to eat them. The birds then pass the spores through their droppings, as they regularly do with plant seeds.

There are many other similar pouch fungi, in yellow, orange, grey-green and dull blue. One bright scarlet pouch fungus grows beside miro trees, where it looks just like the tree's fallen fruit.

Common basket stinkhorn
These fungi are quite easy to find in forests and parks around the country, in the damp leaf litter on the ground. They even grow in the mulched leaves in gardens.

The stinkhorn begins as a small egg shape, which opens to reveal the basket structure. The basket then unfolds to its full size –16 cm or more across. It is not fixed, and may roll down sloping ground, or be blown about by the wind. The greenish mass of spores is carried on the insides of the arms and is foul-smelling; this attracts flies, which land and walk through the spores, helping to disperse them.

FUNGI

Velvet earthstar

The body of this forest-floor fungus is usually about 2–8 cm in diameter. The outer layer peels back into a star shape with up to eight 'rays', and reveals the small papery puffball inside. The ball stands on a short stalk and has a small hole at its top. When it is knocked or hit by raindrops, the spores puff out through the opening into the air and are carried away by the breeze.

Like many fungi found in the leaf litter of the forests, the velvet earthstar is most commonly seen in autumn, or after rain.

Lichens can be found in almost every environment around the world, from hot deserts to frozen wastes, rainforests and seashores. And, of course, you'll see them on the branches of trees, or on rocks and on stone walls.

They are actually a combination of a fungus and an alga (a very simple plant) that unite to form one 'compound plant'. This union is usually referred to as a 'lichenised fungus'.
The fungus supplies the alga with nutrients and water, while the alga supplies the fungus with sugars, and both provide each other with some structural protection. This results in a very slow-growing plant that can live for hundreds of years. Some lichens on Arctic rocks are thought to be several thousand years old!

Fructose lichen

Crustose lichen

Lichen

The leaf-like green-grey lichens that you'll see on tree branches are called 'fructose' lichens (and no, they don't cause any damage to the tree). Some have long, pointed growths, while others are more rounded and folded tightly. The flatter, rounded lichen growths that you'll see on rocks, stones and other hard sufaces are known as 'crustose' lichens.

Different species of crustose lichens can be seen in a range of colours – black, grey, yellow, orange and white. The circular growths of these lichens can expand and merge to form great masses on exposed rocks.

21

PLANTS • Algae

Algae are some of the simplest plants of all. Some are found on land, mostly as small pondweeds in rivers and lakes. But the greatest range of algae are those that grow in the salt waters of coastal seas, which we call seaweeds. Of course, they're not 'weeds' at all, but a vitally important part of the ecology of the sea, especially for young fish and other animals that feed on them. Like plants on land, they depend on sunlight to produce food substances, so seaweeds do not grow in dark, deep water.

Seaweeds have no proper leaves, stems or roots like the more complex plants on land. They attach themselves to rocks by means of a 'holdfast', a structure that can be very large and complicated. Without the stiffness of stems and trunks, seaweeds can sway easily with the water surges and currents, which can be very rough around rocky coasts.

Extracts from seaweeds are used in medicine, fertilisers, cosmetics, textiles, and even in ice cream. Seaweeds are also gathered for food in many parts of the world, especially Japan. There are three major seaweed groups: green, red and brown. Greens generally occupy the highest places in the sea and on the shore; the browns are lower down; and the reds (the group with the most species) are lowest of all. It can be difficult at times to tell which group they belong to – reds can be shades of pink and purple, brown, yellow or even green; and some browns can appear to be shades of green. Most green seaweeds, though, are some shade of green.

There are about 600 seaweed species around New Zealand's coasts.

Air cushion weed

Air cushion weed is found all around the coast in mid-tide regions, especially in the more sheltered waters around harbours. It has air-filled bladders and is usually just a few centimetres across. It grows on rocks and on other seaweeds, such as coralline turf, in rock pools. Air cushion weed is also known as the oyster thief, as in some species the weed attaches itself to an oyster. As it grows bigger and becomes more buoyant, it floats away with the oyster still attached.

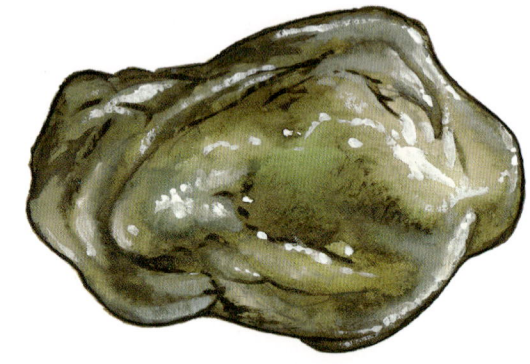

Coralline turf

The rough, pinkish, moss-like turf that lines the ledges of rock pools is a member of the red seaweeds. It looks like a lumpy, scaly growth, or a fine pinkish 'paint' over the rocks. It provides a home for lots of tiny animals and plants. Coralline turf gets its name from its similarity to tiny corals. A build-up of calcium through its structure gives it a tough little seaweedy 'skeleton'.

Venus' necklace

Venus' necklace (or Neptune's necklace) is found all around the coast, especially on rocky shores and in rock pools. It varies in colour from brown to olive-green. The branching fronds can grow to more than 50 cm long, with chains of thick, water-filled bladders that prevent it from drying out during low tide. Animals such as sheep like to eat the tasty young bladders at the ends of the fronds. As with many seaweeds, thick stands of Venus's necklace provide protection and food for small sea creatures such as the common cat's eye shell (page 61).

PLANTS • Algae

Karengo
The purplish-red karengo grows on the rocks of the middle and upper seashore, and is a very hardy plant. When it's exposed to sunlight at low tide, it dries up to look like lumps of purple-black plastic, before it's immersed again in the rising tides. It usually grows in clumps up to 20 cm across. It is just one of many edible seaweeds that are eaten by Maori, and related species around the world have long been used as a food source. When it's dried, karengo makes a good addition to soups, and has even been used as a sort of chewing gum!

Green lettuce
Green lettuce is bright green, so it's easy to see on the lower shore. It grows to around 30 cm across. Like its red cousin karengo, it can be dried and used in soups and other foods preparations. Green lettuce can be a problem in sheltered places such as harbours and estuaries, where the waters are rich in nutrients. It can thrive and spread in these conditions, until great masses of green lettuce clog up the whole shoreline.

Zigzag weed & Flapjack weed
These two seaweeds grow in shallower waters around the coast. They have small, air-filled bladders among the fronds to help keep them upright in the water so they can benefit from the sunlight. Zigzag weeds grow to around 1 m in height, and the flapjack weed is usually a little larger. Dried fronds of these seaweeds can be seen scattered in the driftline at the back of the beach, often with the shells of tiny spirorbis tube worms (see page 52) attached to them.

Flapjack weed

Zigzag weed

23

PLANTS • Algae

Margin weed

Paddle weed

Margin weed & Paddle weed

The margin weed (also known as sawtoothed comb weed) grows mostly around exposed coasts south of Cook Strait. Its strap-like fronds can reach well over 2 m in length.

The paddle weed (or common kelp) is more common in northern waters, at depths of 25–30 m. It is the smallest New Zealand kelp species and is sometimes referred to as octopus weed because of its many 'arms'. Instead of floats, it has a thick, solid stalk to keep it upright in the water. The common sea urchin (page 50) finds the young growing parts of this seaweed very tasty, and sometimes swarms of urchins can be seen munching their way through a stand of paddle weed.

Bull kelp

This is one of the largest of all New Zealand's seaweeds and can form great underwater forests. Bull kelp is usually found off the rocky coasts of the South Island, though it is sometimes seen around the North Island, too. The broad-bladed fronds grow from the rounded holdfast and divide into narrower 'fingers' along their length, which can be up to 10 m. The fronds have an air-filled honeycomb structure inside, which helps to keep them buoyant and lifts them up in the water to the sunlight. The tough fronds are sometimes cut and used as waterproof bags for storing muttonbirds (page 118), or harvested as feed for cattle.

Bladder kelp

This seaweed is common on most coasts around the South Island and is rare north of Cook Strait. In places it can form great swaying forests in the sea. It is one of the world's fastest-growing plants. Off the coast of California in the United States, bladder kelp can grow at a rate of nearly half a metre a day; in just three months it reaches a length of 35 m. In New Zealand it may grow to 25 m or more in length, usually in quite deep water at 20 m down.

The holdfasts that keep the kelp attached to the seabed can become very complicated as the plant grows, like the roots of a great tree. The pear-shaped bladders contain air to help keep the fronds upright.

PLANTS • Ferns

The first small, fern-like plants evolved some 400 million years ago. Over time, these developed into the larger tree ferns that formed vast early forests around the world. Many of those giants have long since disappeared, but a great number of modern ferns are direct descendants, like our own ponga (page 27) and mamaku (page 27). There are more than 200 fern species in New Zealand, and nearly half of them are found nowhere else in the world. They grow in almost every environment – on coasts and mountainsides, in thermal regions and in freshwater swamps. They range in size from just 2 cm to 20 m in height.

A fern may reproduce in one of two ways. Some ferns develop new plants from an underground stem, called a rhizome. Others produce spores in structures called sori on the undersides of the fronds. The spores are released and then germinate to form a new plant.

Kidney fern

The kidney fern (raurenga) has handsome, wide, bright-green fronds. It is one of about 30 species of filmy fern in New Zealand, which are all thin, glossy and transparent. It is mostly found in forests in the North Island, and on the western coasts of the South Island – sometimes in great mats across the forest floor.

The kidney fern grows from a rhizome, and can reach 30 cm in height, with fronds up to 12 cm across. Unlike most ferns, whose fronds are divided into many parts, the kidney fern's fronds are practically of one piece. Though it appears delicate, this fern can withstand dry conditions by curling up tightly to conserve water, and then opening again when conditions improve. It can live for 30–40 years.

Hound's tongue fern

It's not too hard to see how this fern gets its name. It grows from a horizontal woody rhizome which sends up bright green, glossy fronds that resemble a dog's lolling tongue. It is hardy and grows in all sorts of forest locations throughout the country: in the ground, on cliffs and banks, over rocks and stones and even up the trunks of trees. The shape of the fronds varies quite a bit; in exposed places, they become more leathery and more divided.

Hound's tongue ferns can grow up to 60 cm in height and can live for 20–50 years. The young fronds were cooked and eaten by early Maori.

PLANTS • Ferns

Ladder fern

The ladder fern (also known as herringbone or fishbone fern) that's seen in many gardens north of Hamilton is not a native plant, but was introduced to New Zealand quite recently from tropical parts of the world. It is sometimes confused with the native crown fern (piupiu). Both grow from underground runners, but the ladder fern often develops into a continuous mass of fronds, while the crown fern remains as grouped ferns growing from a central trunk. The ladder fern also grows from small, edible tubers. It usually reaches a height of around 1.25 m and can live for 30–40 years.

Hen and chickens fern

The hen and chickens fern (manamana or mouku) grows in forests throughout the country. It bears new growths (the 'chickens') on the edges of its fronds. These take root as the frond droops or falls to the ground, and begin growing as new plants. Mature fronds grow up to 1.5 m in length and 15–40 cm wide. The young shoots were often cooked and eaten by Maori. Today, wild goats and deer find them tasty, as do slugs and snails.

Creek fern

The creek fern (kiwikiwi or kiwakiwa) likes damp conditions, such as along the banks of streams and creeks. It grows in the shape of a multi-pointed star, with fronds drooping on all sides and a few upright in the centre. These fronds can be up to 80 cm in length and 2–4 cm wide. The creek fern contains a natural insecticide, which helps to protect it from insect attacks. Maori used to chew the fronds to relieve the pain of sore mouths.

Kiokio

Kiokio (also known as palm-leaf or cape fern) is one of the most common species in forests around New Zealand. It grows in masses in clay banks, damp and dark places, or full sun. Its fronds are a bright display of greens, pinks and reds, and can be anywhere from 30 cm to 2 m in length. The red colouring of the new fronds is from a chemical that acts as a natural sunburn cream to protect the plant from ultraviolet rays. Maori used the fronds to wrap hangi food and to add flavour.

PLANTS • Ferns

Pikopiko
This fern (also known as shield fern or tutoke) is found in forests throughout the North Island and the eastern South Island. It usually grows individually, rather than in a mass. Fronds can be up to 80 cm in length and 8–25 cm wide. The mature fronds of the pikopiko are tough and leathery, but the young shoots or 'fiddleheads' are a popular food and can be cooked in many different ways.

Ponga
The ponga (or silver fern) is the best known of all New Zealand's tree ferns and has become a national emblem. It is found in forests and scrub throughout the country, except for the southernmost South Island. The name 'silver fern' describes the stalks and undersides of the fronds, which are silvery white. Maori used ponga fronds as floor coverings, and the pith (the insides of the fern) was used to treat skin rashes. European settlers used the trunks to make walls for simple bush huts.

The ponga can grow to 10 m in height, with fronds up to 4 m in length, and can live for up to 60 years.

Mamaku
By far the tallest of the tree ferns, the mamaku can reach 20 m in height. It grows in forests throughout New Zealand, and can live for up to 60 years. It is also known as the black tree fern because of the thick black stalks of its fronds, which reach up to 5 m long. The very distinctive dark trunk shows the circular scars of fallen fronds – other tree ferns have just the left-over bases of the stalks.

Maori had many uses for this fern. Slabs cut from the tough base of the trunk were used as a rat-proof lining in kumara pits, and the new shoots and frond bases were cooked and eaten. They used other parts of the plant to make poultices for cuts and wounds, and as a cure for diarrhoea and upset stomachs.

Mamaku and trunk

Ponga and trunk

27

PLANTS • Conifers

After the ferns, the conifers (cone-bearing plants) were the next major group of land plants to emerge – many millions of years later – and they developed and spread to form huge forests around the world. This group included the ancestors of the larch, cypress, fir, spruce and pine trees. Conifers usually produce two different types of cone: female and male. Tiny spores are released into the air from the male cone to fertilise the female cone, which then opens and breaks apart to release the individual seed cases, which are often shaped like wings. This allows them to be carried great distances if there's a strong wind.

Some pines have seeds that are carried on a soft stem or stalk, rather than on cones. This group, called the podocarps, includes rimu, totara, miro and matai. The podocarps first appeared 190–135 million years ago in the Jurassic period, during the time of the dinosaurs.

Kahikatea

The grey-trunked kahikatea is a podocarp and New Zealand's tallest tree: it can reach 60 m in height. It grows in all sorts of situations around New Zealand, even in swamps and marshes, and can live for 500–600 years. The round, berry-like orange stalks are eaten by native birds such as the kereru, tui, bellbird and parakeets, and were harvested by early Maori. A single mature tree can hold over 800 kg of these fruits. Kahikatea's pale, odourless wood is not particularly good for general building, but the early settlers used it to make butter boxes. Whole kahikatea forests were cut down from the late 1800s to the mid-1900s for this purpose.

Miro

Miro (brown pine) is another podocarp, found in forests throughout New Zealand. It grows to 25–30 m in height and can live for up to 1000 years. The small, narrow leaves lie flat, like a feather, on either side of the stem. It has bright pinkish-red berries that taste bitter-sweet, but this doesn't deter the kereru (page 136), which devours them in great numbers.

The matai (black pine) has similarly shaped leaves and fruit to the miro, but its berries are purplish-black. The timber from both trees is strong and even-grained, and has been used for building, flooring and woodcarving.

PLANTS • Conifers

Totara
Found throughout New Zealand, the totara can grow to 30 m in height and live for 500–1000 years. Maori still use the totara to build meeting houses and other whare, and also waka. A full-sized waka taua, or war canoe, could be carved from a single trunk. Totara is the perfect timber as it doesn't rot, and is quite easy to work and carve. The flaky bark was also used for lining roofs and walls. European settlers used totara for buildings, as well as for railway sleepers, pilings, telegraph poles and fences.

The tiny red berries of the totara are a favourite of many birds, and Maori used to climb these high trees to collect berries by the basketful.

Rimu
The rimu (or red pine) is another podocarp that is found throughout New Zealand. It is a slow-growing tree that lives for 800–1000 years. For such a large and imposing tree – usually 30–60 m in height – the rimu bears surprisingly small flowers and fruits on the ends of its long, prickly-leafed branches. The smooth, warm-coloured timber was used in the past for house-building and furniture-making, among other things. Maori used it to make a charcoal pigment for tattooing, and they used the sap to heal cuts and wounds. Captain Cook's crew and later settlers also made a type of beer from the leaves.

Tanekaha
The tanekaha (or celery pine) is a very unusual tree because it doesn't bear true leaves. Instead, it has branch stalks that spread and flatten out into small fan shapes that look a bit like celery. It is found mostly in the North Island, north of Whanganui, and in parts of the upper South Island. It usually grows to heights of around 20 m and can live for over 200 years. It produces small reddish catkins or soft cones, followed by purplish flowers and fruits. The catkins can be so numerous that great 'puffs' of spores from them may be seen when birds land in the branches.

Tanekaha timber is straight and hard and has been used for general building purposes, wharf piles and mining timbers. A strong red dye can be made from the bark. Young tanekaha saplings were once also cut for use as walking sticks, and sent to London for sale.

29

PLANTS • Conifers

Kairaru

Kauri

This ancient form of conifer is the most celebrated and famous of New Zealand's trees. Millions of years ago, kauri were found throughout the country, but they are now restricted to the upper third of the North Island. These great trees can reach over 40 m in height and live for 1000–4000 years.

Kauri is certainly the most distinctive of all our larger trees, with its thick, clean trunk rising to a crown of huge branches. The tree's bark is regularly shed in great flakes, which prevents climbing epiphytes (plants that grow on other plants) such as rata (page 38) from growing up the trunk. Many other types of epiphytes, however, do manage to find homes in the branching forks higher up.

The fallen bark flakes and leaves around the base of the tree gradually decompose and over time form a great reddish mound called a pukahukahu. This helps to protect and feed the kauri's relatively shallow system of roots.

Kauri have been protected trees for many years now, and giants can be seen in several reserves and forests in the northern North Island. The largest kauri standing today is Tane Mahuta, in the Waipoua Forest. It is over 50 m high, and its girth (around the trunk) is 13.77 m. It is thought to be about 2000 years old.

PLANTS • Conifers

The largest kauri ever officially measured was a supergiant called Kairaru, which stood in the forest at Tutamoe Mountain, near the Kaipara Harbour, until it was destroyed by fire in the late 1800s. This tree was thought to be about 4000 years old. Its girth was over 20 m, and its height (to the first branches) was nearly twice that of Tane Mahuta. There were once other supergiants – a felled tree found near Coromandel Harbour measured over 45 m in length, and a kauri stump in the Warawara Forest, near the Hokianga Harbour, had a girth of 32 m.

Along with totara, Maori used kauri to build the great waka taua (war canoes). Early European settlers felled great numbers of these giants for construction and shipbuilding – in 1861, it was estimated that of the more than 6000 buildings in Auckland, over 5000 were built of kauri. When a kauri is damaged, it leaks a sticky gum, which was used to make paint, varnish and other products. Many trees were regularly cut and 'bled' for this gum. Ancient kauri forests were burned down so that gumdiggers could retrieve the gum deposits in the ground. For a time in the late 1800s, kauri gum sales were worth even more than gold, wool and kauri timber itself. Maori also used kauri gum for burning torches, making soot for dyeing, and as an early form of chewing gum.

Male cone

Female cone

PLANTS • Higher Plants

The higher or more advanced plants include the flowering plants, which were the last major type to develop. They appeared only about 120 million years ago, during the time of the dinosaurs. Flowering plants, which now number nearly a quarter of a million species around the world, include all the garden and wild flowers, most modern trees, flowering shrubs and grasses.

The plants in this group vary tremendously in size, from just 1–2 cm in height to trees measured in tens of metres. Their flowers come in all shapes and sizes, too – from hard-to-see blossoms just a couple of millimetres across, to the foul-smelling, 1-metre-wide flowers on the Indonesian Rafflesia.

Many flower-bearing plants rely on animals to help them reproduce. For instance, insects carry pollen between male and female flowers as they search for nectar and pollen from the blossoms. After fertilisation, the plants produce seeds from which new plants will grow. Sometimes the seeds are simply released by the plant once they've developed, and sometimes they are hidden inside a juicy, tempting fruit (such as apples, tomatoes, berries, etc.). Birds and other animals eat the fruit, then spread the seeds by passing them out in their droppings.

Mangroves

Mangroves form an important part of our ecology. They provide homes for a wide range of animals and other plants, and make a protective nursery environment for shoals of young fish.

Because the mangrove lives in water with a high salt content, and the mud in which it grows has no oxygen, the plant sends up hundreds of short 'breathing' roots to take in air. The mangrove can get rid of any excess salt through glands in its tough leaves.

Mangroves grow on the coast around the upper half of the North Island. They are largest in the far north, where they can reach 10 m. At their southernmost extent they rise only about half a metre from the water. They can live for 200–300 years. Although mangroves produce sweetly scented flowers which are pollinated by bees and other insects, they produce no seeds. Instead, they develop a form of seedling (called a propagule) directly on the plant, which later falls to the water below to be carried away to take root elsewhere.

Propagule

Ice plant

There are two species of ice plant growing around our shores: the Maori ice plant (with pink or white flowers) and the larger Hottentot fig ice plant (with much bigger pink or yellow flowers). Both have thick, fleshy, three-sided leaves, and woody stems that grow in tangles along the ground. They are found growing quite close to the sea, usually just above the high-tide mark. Both plants can live for 20–30 years.

The Hottentot fig ice plant was introduced from South Africa to help stop sand dunes drifing, and now grows freely around the country. The flowers of both plants turn to follow the sun during the day, and have leaves with waxy coatings to help conserve water and stop them from drying out.

PLANTS • Higher Plants

Pingao

Pingao is also known as golden sand sedge (because of its yellowish colour) or sand-binder sedge. It is a primitive type of sedge, with no close relatives anywhere in the world. This 1-metre-tall plant has tough, rope-like stems which sprout new shoots as shifting sands cover them – the more the sand moves, the more this plant reinforces the dune by putting out new growth. Plants can live for up to 30 years, so the stems can form quite a tangle under the sand. Pingao grows all around coastal New Zealand, where it plays an important role. There are over 100,000 hectares of coastal dunes, some of which extend for several kilometres inland, and may reach over 100 m in height, with smaller dunes in front. Stabilising plants, such as pingao and ice plant, help to prevent dunes from advancing further inland and smothering fields and forests.

Flax

There are two flax species. Mountain flax (wharariki) is the smaller; its stems grow to 2 m, with drooping seed pods and yellow flowers. The larger New Zealand or common flax (harakeke) has more erect stems (to 4 m) and darker, reddish flowers. Both species are found nationwide in a wide variety of locations: in the high country, near inland waterways and on exposed coastal cliffs. Flax plants generally live for 10–50 years. Flax is still used by Maori to make many different things: sandals, mats, cloaks, baskets and fishing lines, as well as tukutuku panels. The nectar in the flowers is attractive to birds, especially the tui (page 148) and the bellbird (page 147).

Raupo

Raupo (or bulrush) is a swamp and wetland plant that is found throughout New Zealand. The stems grow to 3 m long, and it can live for up to 50 years. Early Maori found many purposes for it, from food and medicine to construction materials. They used it to thatch their whare, and bound its stems together to make light rafts or canoes. Raupo pollen was gathered to make bread, porridge and cakes – or mixed with crushed manuka beetles to make a nice, tasty beetlecake! The roots and new shoots could be cooked and eaten, too, and were sometimes eaten raw. European settlers also used the fluff from the seed-heads as mattress stuffing.

PLANTS • Higher Plants

Pohutukawa

The pohutukawa, with its spectacular displays of red flowers in early summer, is one of the most familiar trees around the upper third of the North Island. It is a very hardy and adaptable tree – its twisted trunks and branches appear in some precarious coastal cliff-edge sites, as well as in parks and gardens. It's appropriate that its name loosely translates as 'splashed by spray'. The pohutukawa is a member of the myrtle family, which includes the rata (see page 38 for a comparison of their flowers), manuka and kanuka. Other distant members of this family include the guava and the feijoa.

Pohutukawa can live as long as 500–800 years and grow to an impressive 20 m in height. One of the largest and oldest pohutukawa is called Te Waha o Rerekohu ('the mouth of Rerekohu'), at Te Araroa, near East Cape. This tree has 22 trunks, with a total girth of over 20 m, and is thought to be about 600 years old. Another much smaller tree at Cape Reinga may be of similar age.

The tough, durable timber of the pohutukawa (part of its scientific name means 'heart of iron') was used by early European boatbuilders, once they'd dicovered that seaworms could not bore holes in it.

Sundew

This is an insectivorous plant – which means it can 'eat' insects! There are more than 100 sundew species around the world, but only one grows in New Zealand. It's found in swamps and marshes in high country and down to sea level in the far south. In summer, the sundew produces long reddish stems with small white or pink flowers. The leaves are about 7 cm long, with hair-like tentacles that end in sticky droplets. When a flying insect lands on the surface, it becomes trapped in the goo and triggers a chemical reaction in the leaf. The other hairs fold in over the struggling insect, which becomes hopelessly 'stuck'. The insect dies, and the remains are digested and absorbed by the plant through the leaf's surface. When there's nothing left, the leaf hairs open out again to await the next visitor.

PLANTS • Higher Plants

Kaka beak
It's not hard to see how this plant gets its name, as the flowers are shaped like the beak of the kaka! Although it is popular in garden centres, it's now quite rare in natural habitats (the Kaipara Harbour, and parts of the North Island's east coast). Perhaps only 500 or so specimens survive, making it one of our rarest wild plants. Life in the wild is tough for the kaka beak, as it comes under attack from slugs and snails, sheep, goats, cattle and deer, which is why it's now found only in places where these nibbling animals can't get to. If left alone, it can live for about 100 years and grow to 2–5 m in height. As can be seen by its leaves, the kaka beak is a relative of the kowhai (page 39), and is also known as kowhai ngutukaka.

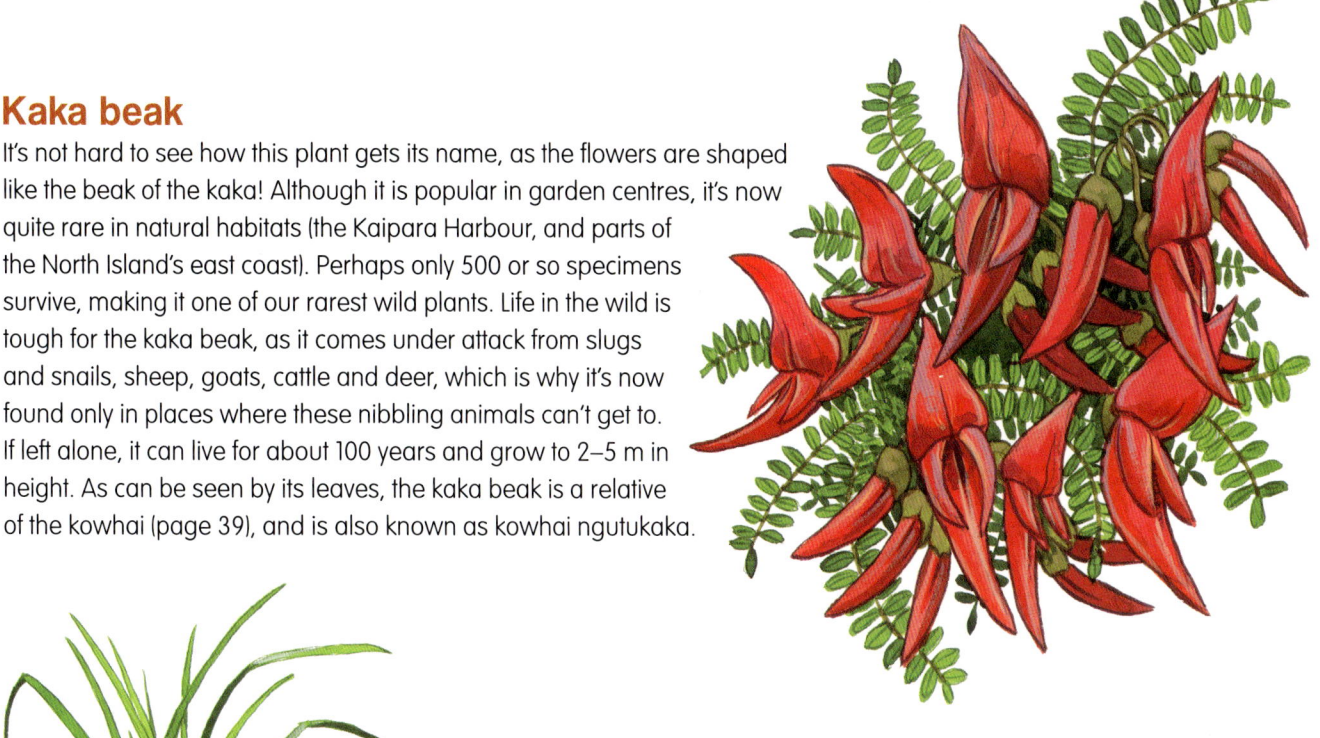

Kiekie
Kiekie grows in forests throughout the North Island, upper South Island and the West Coast. It is a climbing vine. The branches form a jumble around the forest floor, and then grow around and up tree trunks, often to great heights. They can develop into great clumps in the crooks of branches of bigger trees. These plants can live for 20–100 years.

The tough, 1-metre-long leaves were used by Maori to make rain capes, mats, baskets, fish traps and woven tukutuku panels. The kiekie has long, white, spiked flowers in spring, and bears thick fruits up to 15 cm long, which usually appear in bunches of three in autumn or early winter. The fruit is sweet, but the fleshy outer leaves of the flowers are much sweeter, and are said to taste like peaches; they can even be fermented to make a strong brew.

Manuka
This is one of New Zealand's most attractive flowering trees, with its great masses of little white or pink flowers. Manuka is found nationwide. It can live for up to 60 years, and grows 4–12 m in height. Manuka honey and manuka oil both have beneficial health properties. Maori used different parts of this tree to treat aches and sprains, and mouth and throat ailments. The hard, straight wood was used by European settlers for tool handles and wheel spokes. Captain Cook's crew made a passable hot drink from the leaves, which gave the plant its common name of tea-tree.

PLANTS • Higher Plants

Cabbage tree

There are five species of cabbage tree in New Zealand, and many more related species in the southern hemisphere. They are found throughout New Zealand. Some can grow to 20 m or more in height, and they can live for 200–800 years.

The cabbage tree (ti kouka) is one of the hardiest of New Zealand's trees. Cut logs – and even small chips cut from a cabbage tree trunk – will grow again if planted. The cabbage tree has been put to many uses in the past. Maori harvested the leaves to make capes, sandals, bird snares, rope, roof thatching, and medicines for dysentery and diarrhoea. Leaf buds, stems and roots were also turned into food. Captain Cook's crew thought it tasted like cabbage, hence its name. Early settlers even managed to brew forms of beer and rum from the tree's roots.

Clematis

The native clematis (puawhananga) is a climbing vine that entwines itself through and to the tops of forest trees. Its large, scented white flowers up to 8 cm across are often seen displayed over trees such as the manuka (page 35). Clematis plants can live for 20–100 years.

Maori regarded the clematis as a sacred flower that heralded the arrival of spring, though they also wore it as a sign of mourning. Later, during summer, the clematis produces fluffy, greenish seed balls.

There are several other native clematis species, usually with smaller, creamy-yellow flowers. There is also a species introduced from Europe that has become a pest in the bush as it can rapidly smother native plants. It is known as old man's beard, a name shared by an equally troublesome lichen.

PLANTS • Higher Plants

Tawa

Tawa is one of the more common trees in North Island forests, and it is also found in parts of the South Island West Coast. Tawa trees grow up to 25 m in height and can live for 40–80 years. The flowers are green and are very tiny for such a substantial tree – barely a couple of millimetres across. The fruits, though, are large, purplish berries that are a favourite of birds and humans alike. They were gathered by Maori, who prepared the kernels (the hard 'nut' inside the berry) by roasting or steaming. Dried kernels could be kept in storehouses for some years before being heated and prepared. The flesh of the berries could be added to other food or eaten raw.

Tawa timber is straight-grained and brittle when dry. Maori used it for bird spears, and European settlers used it to make kegs, barrels and boxes. It is also a popular timber in furniture-making.

Kawakawa

Kawakawa (also known as the pepper tree) is a shrub-like tree that is found in lowland forests throughout the North Island and in the upper half of the South Island. It grows to around 6 m and can live for 20–30 years. It bears bright orange fruit spikes, 4–8 cm in length, which are eaten by birds such as kereru. Maori sometimes added them to other foods after sifting out the small, hard seeds.

Kawakawa leaves could be used to make a form of tea. The leaves often have holes, where they have been eaten by caterpillars. The reddish wood of the kawakawa has a bamboo-like appearance, with obvious 'joints' at intervals.

Rewarewa

Also known as New Zealand honeysuckle, the rewarewa is actually a member of the protea family. It is found in forests throughout the North Island, and in Marlborough. It can grow to 40 m in height and live for 100 years or more. The shape of its leaves changes as it grows – very long and slim when young, then becoming shorter and broader as the tree matures. Its great bunches of red flowers are renowned for their nectar, which attracts honeybees (page 81) and many birds. When the flowers fall, they cover the ground surrounding the tree in a dark red carpet. The long, red-brown seed pods are very distinctive, too; when mature, they split open to reveal the winged seeds, which are carried off on the breeze.

The attractively speckled timber of the rewarewa has been used for furniture-making and picture framing.

37

PLANTS • Higher Plants

Rata

There are several species of rata, and all are close relatives of the pohutukawa (see page 34 for a comparison of the flowers). The two main species are the southern rata (15 m in height), from the South Island and lower North Island, and the northern rata, or giant rata (40 m), found mostly in the North Island. Both can live for more than 300 years. Southern rata grows from a seed into a tree, but the northern rata takes its time before becoming a proper tree – it usually starts as a vine, growing in the branches of another tree (such as rimu or kahikatea), and then it grows roots and branches until the host tree is smothered, and eventually the rata is substantial enough to become a tree in its own right. Some other rata species stay as small vines, without developing into trees, and some bear white flowers instead of the usual bright red blossoms. Rata nectar is popular with many birds – and possums, too, which also eat the new leaves and often kill the plant by continually eating each year's new growth.

Whau

This tree prefers the open, sunny country of coastal regions and lowland forests, especially in the North Island and upper South Island. It can grow to 6 m in height and lives for around 20–30 years. Whau is a unique tree in several ways. After showing its large white flowers, it produces seeds in a tough, spiked case – the spines can be up to 2.5 cm – and it's the only New Zealand tree to do so. The spiked cases are a bright greenish-yellow at first, then darken to purplish-brown as they split open to reveal the bright orange seeds. The timber of the whau is even lighter in weight than balsa wood, which makes it one of the lightest woods in the world. Maori used whau wood as floats for fishing nets, and for rafts.

Seeds

Karaka

The karaka is a very hardy tree, usually found in coastal locations around the North Island and the upper half of the South Island. It can grow to 20 m in height and live for 30–100 years. It is a very distinctive tree, with its smooth, strong trunk and glossy, deep-green leaves. The bright orange–yellow fruit that appears towards the end of summer is attractive, but poisonous to humans. However, it was a favourite food of Maori, who would discard the poisonous pulp and keep the hard kernel inside, which was prepared by baking and soaking in water for many days. Kereru have no problem with the berries, though, and happily gorge themselves on the fruits with no ill effects!

PLANTS • Higher Plants

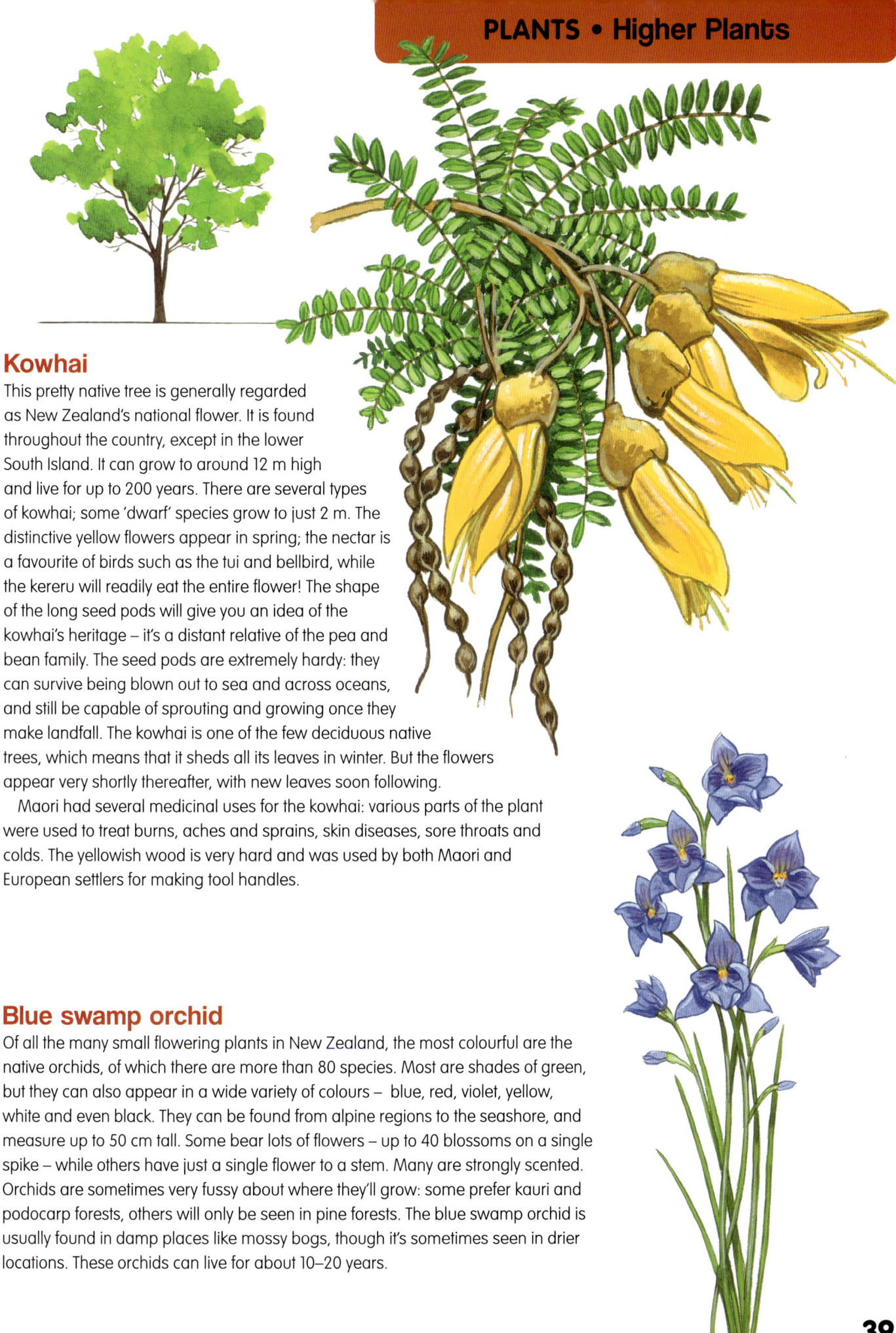

Kowhai

This pretty native tree is generally regarded as New Zealand's national flower. It is found throughout the country, except in the lower South Island. It can grow to around 12 m high and live for up to 200 years. There are several types of kowhai; some 'dwarf' species grow to just 2 m. The distinctive yellow flowers appear in spring; the nectar is a favourite of birds such as the tui and bellbird, while the kereru will readily eat the entire flower! The shape of the long seed pods will give you an idea of the kowhai's heritage – it's a distant relative of the pea and bean family. The seed pods are extremely hardy: they can survive being blown out to sea and across oceans, and still be capable of sprouting and growing once they make landfall. The kowhai is one of the few deciduous native trees, which means that it sheds all its leaves in winter. But the flowers appear very shortly thereafter, with new leaves soon following.

Maori had several medicinal uses for the kowhai: various parts of the plant were used to treat burns, aches and sprains, skin diseases, sore throats and colds. The yellowish wood is very hard and was used by both Maori and European settlers for making tool handles.

Blue swamp orchid

Of all the many small flowering plants in New Zealand, the most colourful are the native orchids, of which there are more than 80 species. Most are shades of green, but they can also appear in a wide variety of colours – blue, red, violet, yellow, white and even black. They can be found from alpine regions to the seashore, and measure up to 50 cm tall. Some bear lots of flowers – up to 40 blossoms on a single spike – while others have just a single flower to a stem. Many are strongly scented. Orchids are sometimes very fussy about where they'll grow: some prefer kauri and podocarp forests, others will only be seen in pine forests. The blue swamp orchid is usually found in damp places like mossy bogs, though it's sometimes seen in drier locations. These orchids can live for about 10–20 years.

PLANTS • Higher Plants

Beech

Almost half of the native forests in New Zealand are made up of beech trees. There are several species: silver beech, hard beech and red beech; all have similar-shaped (but different-sized) serrated leaves, while black beech and mountain beech have plain, rounded leaves. Many beech trees can live for more than 300 years. Most are tall trees, reaching up to 30 m in height. The mountain beech is generally the smallest – it grows to about 15 m in mountain forests.

all shown actual size

Silver beech

Hard beech

Red beech

Black beech

Mountain beech

Though different species of beech can be found around most of the country, the South Island has the largest beech forests, and these are quite different to the mixed forests of the North Island. Few plants are able to grow in association with beeches, so their forests are far more open and spacious. Beech timbers have been used for making furniture, barrels, railway sleepers, bridges and wharves; and Maori used the timber of the black beech to make a slate-black pigment for staining weaving materials.

Kohekohe

Sometimes referred to as New Zealand cedar, the kohekohe is a distant relative of mahogany, the famous hardwood used in furniture-making. It can be seen mostly in the coastal forests of the North Island, and in the upper South Island. Trees can reach 15 m in height and live for 20–80 years. Kohekohe produces masses of small, creamy-white flowers, which grow straight out from the trunk or branches in long sprays. The large leaves have a vaguely onion-like smell, yet possums find them very attractive to eat! They contain a natural curative, and a preparation made from the leaves was sometimes used by Maori as an antidote to poisoning from karaka berries (page 38).

PLANTS • Higher Plants

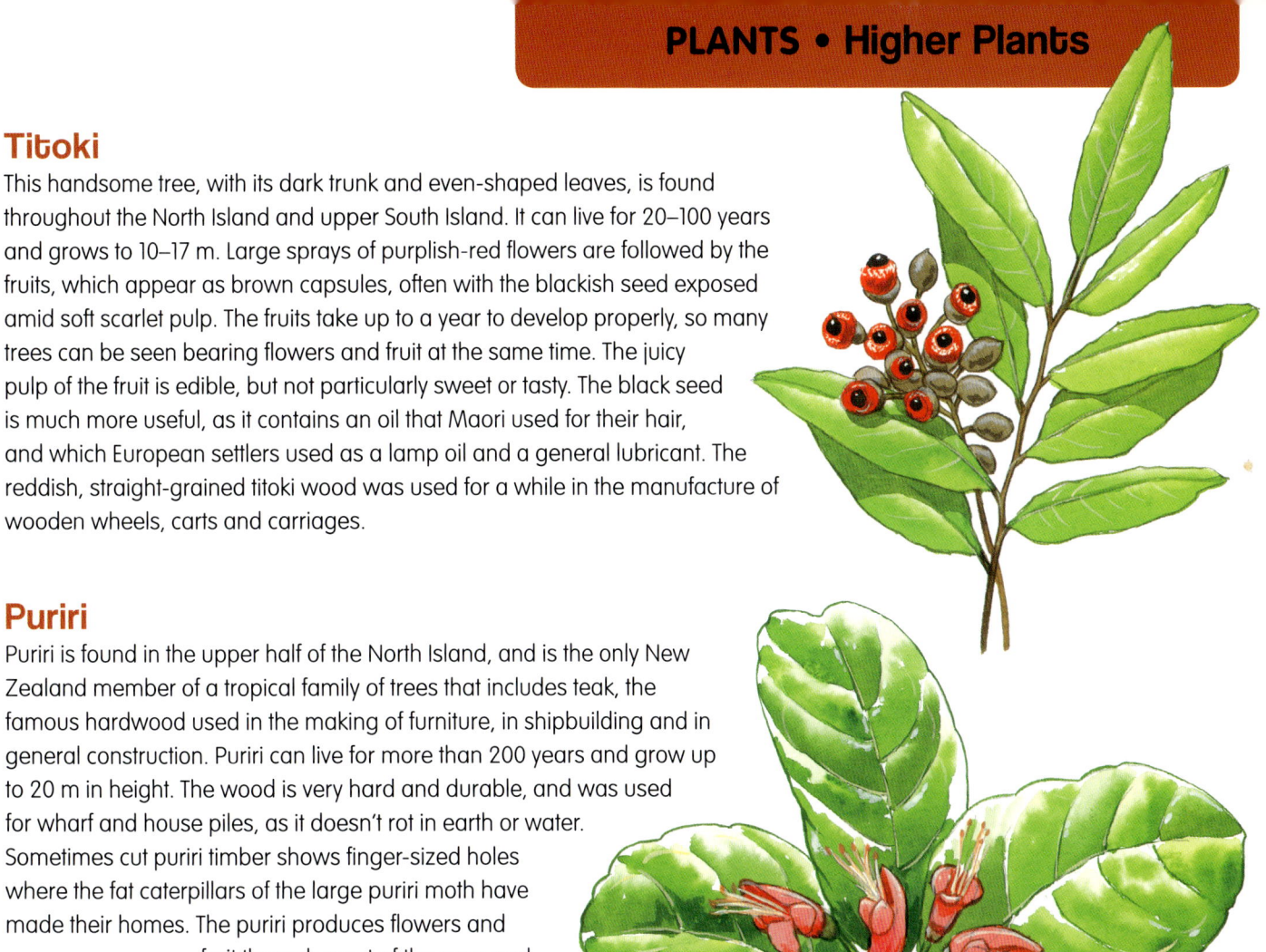

Titoki
This handsome tree, with its dark trunk and even-shaped leaves, is found throughout the North Island and upper South Island. It can live for 20–100 years and grows to 10–17 m. Large sprays of purplish-red flowers are followed by the fruits, which appear as brown capsules, often with the blackish seed exposed amid soft scarlet pulp. The fruits take up to a year to develop properly, so many trees can be seen bearing flowers and fruit at the same time. The juicy pulp of the fruit is edible, but not particularly sweet or tasty. The black seed is much more useful, as it contains an oil that Maori used for their hair, and which European settlers used as a lamp oil and a general lubricant. The reddish, straight-grained titoki wood was used for a while in the manufacture of wooden wheels, carts and carriages.

Puriri
Puriri is found in the upper half of the North Island, and is the only New Zealand member of a tropical family of trees that includes teak, the famous hardwood used in the making of furniture, in shipbuilding and in general construction. Puriri can live for more than 200 years and grow up to 20 m in height. The wood is very hard and durable, and was used for wharf and house piles, as it doesn't rot in earth or water. Sometimes cut puriri timber shows finger-sized holes where the fat caterpillars of the large puriri moth have made their homes. The puriri produces flowers and fruit through most of the year, and the bright red berries are a favourite food of tui, kereru and other birds. Maori used to boil the leaves as remedies for ulcers, sore throats, and general aches and sprains.

Nikau
The nikau is New Zealand's only native palm tree, and can be found down to the upper half of the South Island – farther south than any other palm in the world. There are also nikau palm species in the Kermadec Islands and Norfolk Island, and it's a close relative of the tropical coconut palm and the date palm. The nikau is very slow-growing – it may take many years before the young tree develops a proper trunk – and doesn't flower until it's about 30 years old. It can grow to 10 m or more in height and live for more than 100 years. The pink–purple flowers appear on large, multi-branched spikes, and then bear fruit a year or two later. The red berries are eaten by birds such as the kaka and the kereru. The palm leaves, up to 3 m long, were used by Maori for roof and wall thatching and for making bags.

PLANTS • Higher Plants

Vegetable sheep

The vegetable sheep must be one of our oddest-looking plants. It gets its name from its appearance: when several are seen on a high-country hillside, they look just like a small flock of grazing sheep. This plant is actually a member of the daisy family, but instead of producing a bold show of flowers on long stems, it forms a dense, tightly-packed cushion of furry leaves and tiny flowers. This mat formation gives the plant protection against cold, wind and grazing predators. It also guards against drought, as the water in the soil below the packed leaves is slower to evaporate, and a more even temperature is maintained in the soil.

There are several species of vegetable sheep, with different-coloured leaves and flowers. Some form small mats just a few centimetres across, while others grow to sheep-sized hummocks, and larger. They can live for 150 years or more.

Mt Cook lily

This handsome white flower is not actually a lily but a giant buttercup, closely related to the little yellow buttercup that you'll see in your own garden. It is probably the largest buttercup in the world: it can reach 1.5 m in height, and the leaves are easily as big as a man's hand, and often much bigger! It can live for 20–50 years. The Mt Cook lily likes to grow in high, sunny valleys in among the protection of tussock and other long grasses, though grazing deer have eliminated it altogether from some locations. It's found in mid South Island mountain regions, and on Stewart Island. There are several, smaller high-country buttercup species in alpine regions, but none is as large or as impressive as the Mt Cook lily, which has been celebrated in many books and on postcards and postage stamps.

Hebe

There are more than 100 hebe species, which makes it one of our most numerous types of flowering plant. They can be found from the seashore to alpine regions over 3000 m above sea level, which is the highest elevation for any flowering plant in the country. The alternating leaves are a distinctive feature of the hebe's structure, though some species reduce their leaves to tight, scale-like structures when growing in harsh high-country locations. They appear in a wide range of sizes: at sea level, some species can grow to around 6 m in height, while some alpine hebes measure just 10 cm. Many hebes can live for 10–50 years. The hebe's flowers can change with the different species, too – they are generally larger at sea level, and can be showy, with large, simple petals, or with densely packed flower 'spikes'.

PLANTS • Higher Plants

Penwiper plant
This unusual-looking plant is a member of the mustard plant family. It was given its name by early European settlers, who thought that its leaves resembled the felt pads used to wipe quill pens clean. It grows in South Island mountain regions north of Otago, among the small, loose stones of scree slopes. Not many plants can make a home on these unstable surfaces, but some species of lobelia, willowherbs, and even some buttercups as well as other smaller plants are able to join the penwiper in its precarious home. Penwipers usually grow to around 25 cm in height and can live for about 2–3 years.

Mountain daisy
Daisies make up one the largest plant groups in New Zealand, with well over 100 species in just about all environments and situations around the country, from coastal regions to high in the mountains, where most daisy species are found. The example illustrated is typical of the many mountain daisies. Some daisies have developed into tree forms, growing to heights of around 7 m, while others are tiny and hug the ground. Flower size also varies enormously; some daisies – like the vegetable sheep, on the opposite page, have flowers much smaller than a fingernail, while others may measure 12 cm or more across. Leaves can vary greatly in colour, and in shape – from thin leathery straps to broad 'plates'. Rangiora is also a member of the daisy family, and has leaves large enough to be used as notepaper (using the white undersides), or even for emergency toilet paper while tramping in the bush!

Tussock
There are many different species of tussock grass. They can withstand great ranges of conditions, from sub-zero temperatures to burning days of 40°C or more. Many tussock species can grow to 2 m or higher, and some can live for up to 300 years.

Before land was cleared for farming by early European settlers, great areas of the central North Island and large areas of the eastern South Island were essentially tussock country. Natural tussock areas are now probably only one-tenth of their original size. These large, dense grasses appear in a wide range of colours – brown, green, gold, red-brown and so on. They provide cover for many smaller plants which grow in and around the base of the plants, and this also makes a protective environment for insects, lizards and other animals.

ANIMALS • Sponges

Although they may look like some sort of plant, sponges are actually colonies of very tiny animals. They can appear in many shapes, such as cups, vases, leaves or organ pipes. Size can vary from well over 1 m in height to minuscule boring sponges, which leave seashells pitted with masses of little holes where they have made their homes.

Sponges feed by drawing water in through lots of small holes in the body of the sponge, sieving out food particles, and then expelling it again through larger holes. Some species in other parts of the world are even capable of catching live prey.

Sponges have remained unchanged for many hundreds of millions of years. They are very long-lived; some species can live for 50 years or more. There are nearly 500 different species of sponges living in New Zealand waters, and around 10,000 known species in the world.

Finger sponge

You often see pieces of finger sponge washed up and tangled in the seaweed along the driftline at the top of the shore – sometimes still attached to a shell or stone. The finger-like bodies vary in shape, thickness and number. Some can be nearly a metre in length, with quite complicated structures – sometimes with the 'fingers' joining up and separating again. Though they are usually shades of grey or brown when washed up on the shore, they are often brightly coloured – such as purple, yellow or red-brown – when they're alive.

Golf-ball sponge

Golf-ball sponges (or globe sponges) are often found below the overhangs of low-tide rock pools. They often appear as misshapen blobs, but sometimes can grow into a proper ball shape. The orange golf-ball sponge usually grows to about 4 cm across, while the pink golf-ball sponge is slightly smaller and prefers slightly deeper waters. Both types can live in a great range of coastal environments – in harbours, on wharf pilings, on open and rocky shores; all they need is a solid, protected surface to establish themselves.

Breadcrumb sponge

The breadcrumb sponge spreads itself like a small carpet over rocks and shells. It has exit holes which are raised from the main body of the sponge and look like lots of little volcanoes. Similar encrusting sponges come in a wide variety of colours including yellow, purple, orange, red, pink and grey. The related slaty sponge – coloured in dirty greys and purple-blacks – can form enormous growths and sheets over the rocks below low tide. When the sponges die and are cast ashore, they give off the most awful smell.

ANIMALS • Cnidaria

Cnidaria is the name given to all those groups of animals that have tentacles armed with poisonous stinging cells – jellyfish, sea anemones, hydroids and corals. These cells are activated when a small prey animal blunders into them, and the tentacles then draw the stunned captive into the mouth.

Cnidaria all live in water, most of them in the seas. Some, like jellyfish, can float and swim freely through the water, while others, like corals, remain fixed to hard surfaces, and can form great colonies on the seabed.

Common jellyfish

By far the most common jellyfish in New Zealand waters is the 20 cm-wide common jellyfish or petipeti, which is also found worldwide.

Like all jellyfish, it has tentacles armed with stinging cells, but it's quite harmless to people. It's often washed up on the shore in large numbers, especially in northern waters. The four lilac panels in its body are the reproductive organs, and the fringe of the disc has eight eye notches.

Jellyfish propel themselves through the water by contracting the main body, or 'bell', which pushes out water and provides lift. The jellyfish relaxes the bell to allow water in again, then repeats the action.

Portuguese man-o-war

The Portuguese man-o-war (or bluebottle) drifts on the surface of the sea, with long tentacles trailing in the water to snare prey as it passes. It's often washed up on the shore in large numbers. It's not a true jellyfish, but a colony of tiny animals called hydroids. Groups of hydroids have different duties: some form the tentacles and stinging cells; some operate as the digestive system; and others construct the bladder of air which keeps the whole colony afloat. The bladder can be as large as 12–15 cm long, and the tentacles may grow to be several metres long.

The stinging tentacles can inflict quite a painful shock to humans even long after the jellyfish has apparently 'expired', so if you find one on the shore, don't pick it up.

By-the-wind sailor

The by-the-wind sailor is another bright blue jellyfish that is actually a hydroid colony. At only 5 cm across, this species is much smaller than the Portuguese man-o-war, and is practically harmless to people, though its stinging tentacles are still quite deadly to small prey. It, too, is often washed ashore in large numbers on western coasts of New Zealand. Like the Portuguese man-o-war, this hydroid colony cannot move of its own accord, but depends solely on its inflated 'sail' to catch the wind and be blown along.

ANIMALS • Cnidaria

Olive beadlet anemone

Red beadlet anemone & Olive beadlet anemone

These are two of our most common species of sea anemone. Anemones snare any tiny food scrap or animal that comes too close to their stinging tentacles. They are quite safe for humans, however – all you might feel if you touch one is a slight 'stickiness'.

The red beadlet resembles small blobs of dark red jelly when it is exposed on the rocks at low tide, but then it opens up again when the water returns. The olive beadlet anemone is usually seen in more protected positions, such as below the overhangs of rock pools, where it may gather in large numbers.

Red beadlet anemone

Speckled anemone

Speckled anemone & Camouflaged anemone

The speckled anemone can also be found in the dark crevices at the bottom of rock pools, where it covers itself with small pieces of shell, sand and stones to hide from possible predators, and to disguise itself from its own prey. It grows to about 5 cm across.

The camouflaged anemone is about twice this size, but despite its name, it is not quite so adept at disguising itself with shell pieces and stones. It, too, is quite common around rocky coasts, where it lives in the deeper recesses of rock pools.

Camouflaged anemone

Wandering sea anemone

This is one of our largest species, growing up to 15 cm long. It loosely attaches itself to seaweeds in coastal waters, and can release itself to float free until it finds a new and better location.

Larger sea anemones like this are capable of snaring and digesting small fish, shrimps and shellfish that come within reach of their tentacles. The harder, indigestible parts of their prey are later disgorged.

Wandering sea anemones are very hardy creatures, and can be found in all depths from rock pools to deep oceans. Their lifespan ranges from just a few years to 50 years.

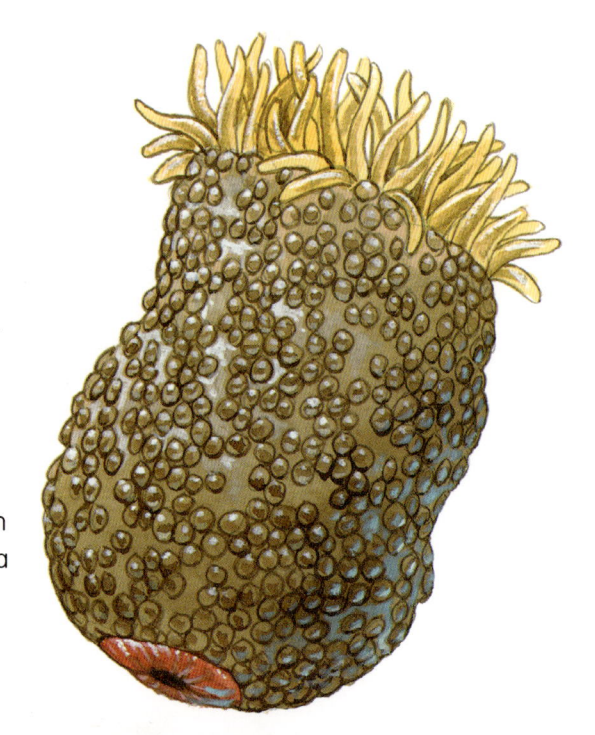

46

ANIMALS • Cnidaria

Fan coral

Our waters are generally too cool for corals to appear in numbers great enough to create the large reefs that can be seen in tropical seas, such as in Australia's Great Barrier Reef. Even so, plenty of corals can be seen in our warmer northern waters, especially around the Poor Knights Islands.

There are more than 20 species of coral in New Zealand waters, one of the most common being fan coral. It grows to about 2 cm in width. It secretes a limestone substance around itself, in the form of a cup, which protects it and binds it to the rock underneath. Fan corals look very much like sea anemones – they have many arms, which they extend into the current to catch tiny animals and plants.

Other forms of harder coral can be found around the coast at varying depths. Some are shaped as cups or fans, and some colonies even form many-branched 'trees', which are tough enough to snare fishing nets. Some brittle stars (page 49) entwine themselves in the branches of these tree corals to feed on the individual polyps.

Dead man's fingers

This type of coral is known as soft coral, because it doesn't secrete a hard covering. Instead, it relies on its structure to stay erect in the water. However, those species that live in very shallow waters just fall down to become jelly-like blobs when uncovered by a low tide. Dead man's fingers is one of the most common of this coral type, and usually attaches itself to rocks and the shells of molluscs. It's actually a colony of many coral polyps, rather than an individual organism like the fan coral. It grows to look rather like a discarded rubber glove, 15 cm or more in height, and sometimes appears in large numbers in the same area.

ANIMALS • Echinoderms

The group of animals called echinoderms includes several marine invertebrates such as sea stars (starfish), brittle stars, feather stars and urchins. Typically, echinoderms are divided into five equal parts, with the mouth in the centre. The animal is protected by a hard outer skeleton, called a test. Most echinoderms are mobile seabed dwellers, and are found on most shores and in deeper waters. Most feed on small particles of organic matter, though some are capable of engulfing their prey of larger animals.

Cushion star

The cushion star is one of the most common sea stars in New Zealand waters. It lives mostly in rock pools and the shallow waters of tidal flats. It comes in a wide variety of colours – green, grey, black, brown, orange, yellow, red or blue – and it may be plain or flecked with other colours. It measures up to 10 cm across and usually has five arms, though sometimes it has four or six – or more.

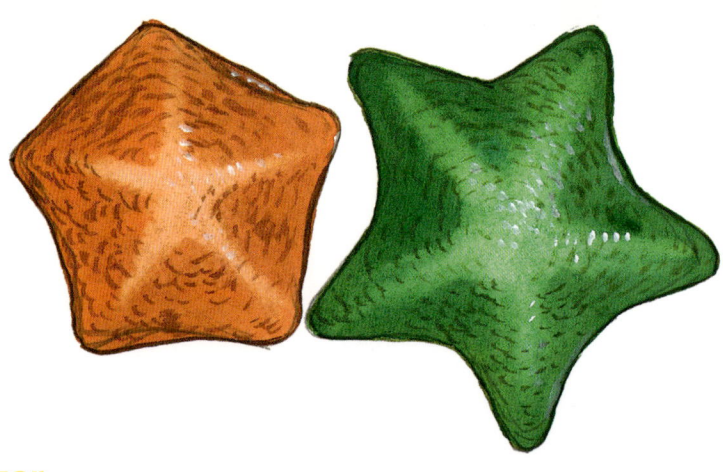

Reef star

The reef star, at over 35 cm across, is one of our largest sea stars. It has 10–12 arms, and can be found on rocky coasts all around the country. Sea stars like this crawl over rocks and seabed, using hundreds of tiny tube-feet under their arms and bodies, until they find food such as scallops, mussels and other bivalves. The reef star pulls the two halves of the shell apart and then devours the animal inside. Some of the larger sea stars, such as the giant seven-armed star, which can grow to over 50 cm across, will also eat sea urchins, chitons, paua, crustaceans and even smaller sea stars. Most are quite hardy animals, and some larger species can live for over 40 years.

Sand star

The spines of the sand star (also known as the carpet star) are flattened at the top and expanded, giving the animal a tiled or carpet-like appearance. It usually lives half-buried in the sand below low tide, where it searches out small crustaceans and shellfish. At more than 20 cm across, it's large enough to eat its prey whole, and it even attacks its own kind when really hungry. Like many sea stars, it doesn't strictly follow the five-part body rule, but can have seven or more arms. Many sea stars can lose arms to escape predators, and these are regrown later, so individuals can have full-sized arms and small stubs where new arms are growing.

ANIMALS • Echinoderms

Firebrick star

This is one of the more common sea stars seen in reef waters off Northland and around the Bay of Plenty. It lacks the usual spiny top that most sea stars have; instead it is covered in small knobs and lumps, like a cake decorated with 'hundreds and thousands'. It patrols the reefs to seek out small animals, especially sponges.

The firebrick star is not the only sea star with an unusual or attractive appearance. There are around 150 different species in New Zealand waters, and they come in a wide variety of bright colours and strange shapes – some look like odd biscuits, or combs.

Mottled brittle star

There are over 160 species of brittle star. The mottled brittle star, or mottled sand star, is one of the most common. It grows to 15 cm across and lives at the bottom of lower-tide rock pools. At night it comes out to feed on tiny food particles in the sand. Brittle stars are generally more mobile and quicker than sea stars. Their feet are set to the sides of their arms, rather than underneath, so they can scuttle along using a rowing action rather like that of an octopus.

If disturbed or roughly handled, the brittle star can throw off one or more of its arms, broken into sections. Each piece will thrash about briefly to confuse a predator, while the brittle star wriggles off to safety. The arms can be regrown later.

Feather star

There are about 25 species of feather star in our waters. They have 20 or more very thin, feathery arms. Very small organic particles floating through the water are caught on the sticky tube-feet on the arms, and is then passed to the mouth in the centre.

Feather stars begin life attached by a small stalk to the seabed or a hard surface. As they grow, they break away and become free-living animals. Closely related to these animals are the sea lilies, which are mostly found in deep waters. Some remain permanently attached to their stalks, which can reach a height of 1 m and an arm spread of 70 cm.

ANIMALS • Echinoderms

Common sea urchin skeleton

Common sea urchin

The common sea urchin, also known as kina or sea egg, is one of the most numerous of all the sea urchins around New Zealand, and pieces of its external skeleton are often found on the shore. This species feeds mostly on seaweeds, but also on sea anemones and sponges. It travels by using its hundreds of stiff spines, together with a series of long, tube-like feet. It has been a favourite food of Kiwis for generations; and it is also eaten by some sea stars, large shellfish and fish.

The usual lifespan of the common sea urchin is 7–8 years, though some can live for up to 15 years. It grows to 12 cm wide and can weigh over 1 kg.

Cake urchin

The cake urchin is also called the sand dollar or snapper biscuit. It lives under the surface in fine sand around the low-tide area, where it sifts the sand for tiny food particles. It's usually about 8 cm in diameter. Pieces of its flat test are often found on the shore. These broken segments show its very complicated structure, which seems to leave hardly any room for the animal to live inside.

There are about 20 species of sea urchin around the seashore. They live either well down in the sea below low tide, or buried in the sand and mud of softer shores.

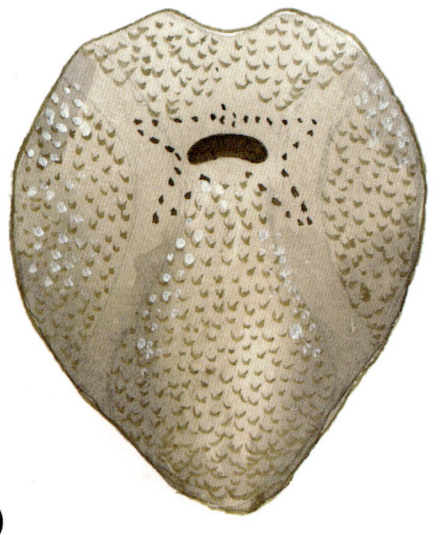

Cake urchin segment

Heart urchin

This sea urchin is usually about 5 cm long. It's found in the mud below low tide, where it burrows along well below the surface, sieving for food particles. Unlike most other sea urchins and their close relatives, the sea stars, which all have a five-part body structure, this species has become essentially 'two-parted'. Its test is very thin and fragile, so it's rare to find one unbroken. Even if you do find one intact, a gentle touch is sometimes sufficient to crumble it.

Heart urchins can congregate in near-uncountable numbers in the mud of the larger harbours around the country.

ANIMALS • Worms

Worms are one of the most numerous types of animals on earth – there are probably more than 45,000 different species. Segmented worms, such as aquatic and land earthworms, alone number about 12,000 species.

Worms of various kinds have made their home in every one of New Zealand's habitats – in the sea, buried under the sand and mud of the seashore, on land (and under it), and in many freshwater environments. There are even tiny worms that live inside other animals.

Earthworm

There are over 200 different types of earthworm in New Zealand. About 19 of these have been introduced by European settlers to help enrich soil of farms and gardens. The worms do this by pushing and pulling themselves along under the ground, and by leaving their faeces, called casts, on the surface. This effectively aerates the soil, and brings nutrients up near the surface.

Native earthworms live in all sorts of environments – some shuffle through the leaf litter on the forest floor; others can climb into the forest canopy. Some are giants, too; one species from Northland measures up to 1.4 m long and burrows nearly 3 m below the surface.

Many native earthworms have adapted to a water environment and spend their lives in streams and rivers; some bury themselves in sediment, and others swim like eels to seek out small particles of organic matter in the water. Some of these can reproduce by simply breaking apart, and the two pieces then develop into separate individuals.

Flatworm

There are several species of flatworm. Some are up to 20 cm in length, but most are about 2–5 cm. They can be found in damp places under rocks and leaf litter and under stones in streams, rivers and lakes or on shores. They feed on small animals, such as crustaceans, snails and even other worms.

These creatures are quite simple in construction, with no blood circulatory system and with only very simple body organs. Even a small body part of a flatworm can regrow itself into a new, complete individual.

ANIMALS • Worms

Leech
There are several species of marine, land and freshwater leech in New Zealand. Most are not much longer than about 10 mm. Some are predatory, but many are parasites that will attach themselves to other small animals, such as snails or other worms, to bite and draw blood. Some marine or freshwater species attach themselves to the feet of wading birds, or to fish. In searching for a host, the leech travels across stones and plant stems by 'looping' along like a caterpillar, using the suckers at each end of its body.

Tube worms
The tiny spirorbis tube worm constructs a small spiral shell to live in – this is often seen attached to seaweed cast up on the shore. Like many worms, the spirorbis build their tubes from body secretions. Other worms glue fine particles of sand and silt together to make their homes.

Populations of tube worms live inside old shells, on rocks and in pools, where they extend their feathery tentacles to catch fine food particles in the water. Depending on the species, these tentacles can be red, black, blue or orange. Some larger tube worms live buried in the sand.

Spirorbis

Peripatus
The peripatus, or velvet worm, is one of the strangest and oldest creatures of the natural world; fossil remains show that it has stayed virtually unchanged for the last 550 million years. It's an odd sort of missing link – it has the appearance of a caterpillar, a segmented body like a worm, and clawed legs similar in style to many insects. The two species in New Zealand have quite different ways of reproducing: one gives birth to live young, while the other lays eggs!

Peripatus live in the damp leaf litter of forests and feed on small animals such as insects. They catch prey by shooting out sticky saliva from glands around the mouth to trap the prey, and then biting into it and sucking out its insides.

The New Zealand peripatus measures around 5 cm in length. There are about 70 species found around the world, and some can measure up to 15 cm or more.

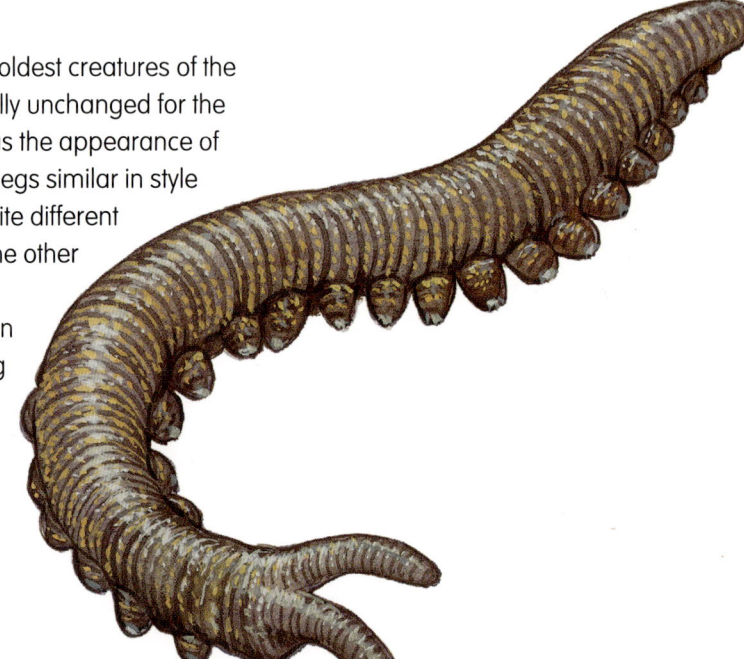

ANIMALS • Molluscs

In general, molluscs have hard shells either inside or outside their bodies. There are about 100,000 species around the world, and they include squid, octopuses, slugs and snails, and all kind of shellfish. There are about 3000 species of mollusc in New Zealand waters, most of which are found nowhere else in the world.

The shellfish that you'll see on the shore are mostly divided into two main groups – bivalves and univalves.

The bivalves get their name from the pair of shelly valves that are secreted by the animal to protect its soft body. The two valves are usually hinged to allow the animal to close them tightly for protection against predators, or to prevent the animal from drying out if it is exposed to the air between tides – for example, mussels attached to mid-tide rocks. Most bivalves have a pair of tube siphons through which they breathe water in and out, and as water passes over their gills, they filter out plants and animals. They all have a strong, muscular foot, or 'tongue'.

Many species of bivalve living on rocky shores are quite easy to see when the tide is going down, because they live permanently attached to the rocks.

Horse mussel

The largest of all the shore bivalves is the horse mussel (also known as the fan mussel or hururoa). It's not unusual to find specimens 15–20 cm in length, and some are up to 40 cm.

These giants live buried 'point down' in the mud or sand of low-tide shores, to depths of 45 m, with just the top part of the shell exposed above the surface. The sharp end of the shell is anchored to a hard surface, such as a stone, by means of a group of fine threads called a byssus. Younger shells have short, hollow spines around the end of the valves to help keep them anchored in the sand. The valves are iridescent inside, just like the inside of a paua shell, and they are very brittle, so it can be difficult to find one intact.

Many plant and animal species can find a home on the outside of these larger shells. The horse mussel shown here carries a seaweed holdfast, tube worms, barnacles and sea squirts.

ANIMALS • Molluscs

Freshwater mussel

Most freshwater molluscs are very small, but some mussels can grow to nearly 10 cm long and reach an age of 50 years. They live buried in the fine mud or sand at the bottom of lakes and streams, where they filter out fine food particles.

The larva of some mussels attaches itself to the skin of a small fish, such as the bully (page 108), to feed on fluids and particles of body tissue. Later, it releases from its host to sink and continue growing into an adult.

Freshwater mussels are also known as kakahi, and were a favourite food of early Maori. The shells were often used to scrape kumara – and also for shaving!

Green-lipped mussel

This 20 cm-long species is more common in warmer northern waters. It is grown and harvested commercially for food (you'll see it in tanks in the supermarket). Maori used the shells to make fish hooks.

Sea stars like to eat the green-lipped mussel, and they can pick up a crab for dessert, as the tiny pea crab sometimes makes its home just inside the mussel's gape.

Little black mussel

There are about 18 species of mussel in New Zealand; the little black mussel is the smallest at just 3 cm long. It can appear in densely packed colonies on rocks and stones high on the shore, all around the country. In the north it can even be found in great numbers on the breathing roots of mangroves (as shown in the illustration), and often in the company of barnacles and rock oysters. Like other mussels, the little black mussel is attached to the rocks by a series of threads called a byssus. Some species can push against the rock with their foot to break the threads, and then move to a new location.

ANIMALS • Molluscs

Rock oyster
The 8 cm-long rock oyster is usually found around the mid-tide zone of the North Island and the upper South Island. It lives with one valve permanently fixed to the rock and the other valve free to open and close. Often the colonies are so densely packed on the rocks that the shape of an oyster's shell is determined by whatever small space may be available, and so many become quite distorted.

There are four oyster species in New Zealand, including the Pacific oyster, which is up to 12 cm long and is farmed commercially. The best known is the Bluff oyster – around 10 cm long – which is an all-time favourite on restaurant menus.

Jingle shell
The jingle shell, like the rock oyster, lives permanently attached to hard surfaces. It's found under stones or on other shells, from the low-tide zone down to deep water. The delicately crinkled, coloured valves are often cast ashore, and people collect them for decoration or to make hanging mobiles. They are usually about 5 cm across, though sometimes larger ones are found. The valve that's attached to the rock is always plain, and has a hole by which the animal fixes itself to the rock. The opening valve is nearly always brightly coloured, often golden orange or yellow.

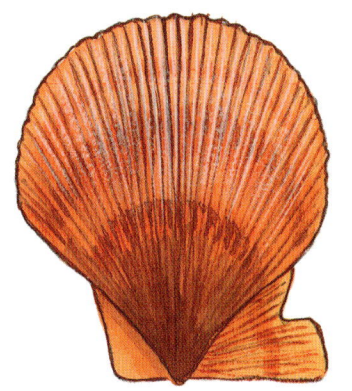

Fan scallop
The fan scallop, or fan shell, is found off rocky shores all around the country. Those in the north are about 3 cm across, while those in the south are larger, at about 5 cm. Northern species attach themselves to rocks and other hard surfaces, while southern species sometimes embed themselves in living sponges.

They have a rough surface, and appear in a great range of colours – red, yellow, orange, pink, grey, white and purple, sometimes with strong colour bands or markings.

Common scallop
This shell, also known as the queen scallop, must be the most famous symbol of the seashore. It can be 12–16 cm across and live for up to 5 years. It moves freely around the low-tide zone of sandy shores, and deeper. The two valves are quite different: one is curved, with well defined ridges, and the other is flat and smooth. When resting, with the valves slightly open, it displays a row of bright blue eyes around the rim, to watch for movement nearby. If endangered, the scallop can swim off jerkily through the water by opening and closing the two valves quickly to create a backward jet-thrust of water.

ANIMALS • Molluscs

Common cockle
The common cockle is found in harbour mudflats and muddy sand environments all around the country, where it lives in great numbers just below the surface from mid-tide downwards. It is a good food source for humans (and many other animals). This shellfish has a very distinctive purple rim on the inside of the valves, and usually grows to about 3–5 cm across. Though known as a cockle, this shellfish is actually a member of a group of bivalves known as Venus shells.

Large dog cockle
The large dog cockle lives in the sand or in gravel, well below the low-tide zone. The thick, heavy valves of this shellfish, measuring up to 8–10 cm across, are often cast up on the shore, usually damaged or deeply eroded and pitted, and sometimes with worm shells on the inside (see tube worms, page 52). Many tribal societies around the world, including Maori, have used this species as a food source, and also for carving and wearing as pendants.

Morning star shell
Another member of the Venus shells is the very pretty morning star shell (also called tawera, or zigzag shell). This shell is quite common on sandy shores from low tide and below, all around the country. It grows to about 2.5 cm across. This is a good shell to use in crafts, and for children to collect, as no two shells ever have the same pattern.

Triangle shell
Sometimes, after a storm, hundreds of 7 cm triangle shells can be washed up on the sandy shore. They live buried just under the sand, beyond the low-tide zone, with their siphon tubes stretching to the surface. Though the valves are thick and strong, the hinge between them is quite weak, so it's rare to find them still attached to each other. They are a favourite food of crabs and seabirds.

These shells are members of a group called trough shells, of which there are about 10 species in New Zealand waters. Many are larger than the triangle shell, at 9 cm or more, though not as 'sharp' in shape.

ANIMALS • Molluscs

Tuatua & Pipi

Tuatua live all around the country and generally prefer to make their home in the sand of the mid-tide zone. Sometimes these 8 cm-long shellfish are found in such numbers that they are tightly packed together in great expanses on the shore.

The pipi is similar in size to the tuatua, and may likewise be found in the more protected waters of estuaries and harbours. It too occurs in vast colonies, with individuals tightly packed together.

Pipi and tuatua have short siphons, and so they live just under the surface. This makes them easy prey for crabs and sea stars (and for humans, too, of course).

Pipi and tuatua shells were used by Maori for a variety of purposes besides food: for scraping flax, scaling fish – and tied together in small bunches as rattle-tails on kites.

Pipi

Tuatua

Toheroa

The toheroa is by far the largest of this famous shellfish trio – it grows up to 15 cm in length and can live for over 15 years. Toheroa usually live deep in the sand of the mid-tide zone, and are found all around the coast, though they only appear in large numbers in a few locations, such as on the North Island's west coast. The population of a single beach can range from a small handful to several millions! Though once harvested in their tens of thousands at a time, their numbers have greatly reduced over the years. The toheroa is now a protected species, with strict conditions on collecting. They move fast if disturbed by predators, and can even bury themselves down into the wet sand faster than human hands can dig after them!

ANIMALS • Molluscs

Shellfish with only a single valve or shell are called univalves, or gastropods. They form the largest shellfish group of all, with over 75,000 species worldwide, and about 2000 around New Zealand. The group also includes univalves that live in fresh water and on the land.

Most univalves have a similar structure, with a strong, muscular foot containing all their vital organs, and a defined head with eyes and tentacles.

Many can retreat into the shell's interior and close off the entrance with a small shell 'stopper', called an operculum. Some have a small remnant of shell on their body, or inside; and some, like some species of slugs or squid, have no shell at all.

Most univalves live for about five years, and some larger specimens can live for 20 years or longer.

Garden snail

Of some 30,000 species of land snail around the world, more than 1000 species are present in New Zealand. The most common by far is the common garden snail. This animal was introduced by European settlers over 100 years ago and has spread to most parts of the country, where it has become a general nuisance to gardeners. It feeds on plant material by rasping back and forth with its rough tongue, which is studded with rows of hundreds of hard, angled teeth.

As is the case with many snail species, garden snails are hermaphroditic, which means that both sexes are present in each animal. Nevertheless, snails pair off and mate to transfer sperm from one to the other. The white eggs are laid under the surface of the soil. The eggs – and the snails themselves – are eaten by many animals, including humans.

For an animal with only one foot, the snail is a fast mover: it can cover 5 m or more in an hour.

Flax snail

The flax snail doesn't feed on flax – it gets its name from the fact that it's sometimes found near flax plants in Northland. It is vegetarian, and prefers to munch on the fallen leaves of the karaka (page 38) and kohekohe (page 40). The shell usually measures up to around 8 cm in length. Some flax snails are thought to munch on the discarded shells of dead snails, in order to strengthen their own.

There are three species of flax snail. None of them travel very far, once they've found a suitable environment to make their home. They can live for more than 10 years.

Like other larger native snail species, flax snails are eaten by many introduced animals, including rats and wild pigs, despite ongoing conservation efforts.

ANIMALS • Molluscs

Kauri snail

The kauri snail (pupurangi) is found in kauri forests in the north, but not usually near kauri trees. It hunts in dark, damp places for small animals and earthworms, which are its favourite food. The snail's muscular foot is very strong and it is quite capable of climbing up tree trunks, or travelling long distances at good speed. Kauri snails can live for 20 years and measure over 7.5 cm across.

There are several other giant land snails living in our forests, with similar-shaped shells, measuring up to 10 cm across. They come in a range of browns, yellows and gold, and some are striped, with bold markings. All are carnivorous.

At the other end of the scale are the hundreds of very tiny, delicate native snail species. They are a wide range of shapes – flat spirals, long spires, heavily ridged, and sometimes covered in fine hairs. Some are not much wider than a cotton thread and can pass through the eye of a needle.

Radiate limpet

The radiate limpet is one of the most common of New Zealand's 35 limpet species. It measures up to 5 cm in length.

Limpets can be seen attached to rocks throughout the mid-tide zone. They have a simple, flattened shell, which is sealed tightly against a rock while the tide is low. Then, when the rocks are covered by seawater again, the limpets roam over them to scrape off tiny growths of algae.

Limpets usually return to exactly the same place each time, and can wear away a depression in the rock. No one knows just how they manage to find their way back, as the animals cannot see, and don't appear to leave any trail by which they can retrace their 'steps'.

Freshwater limpet

There are several species of freshwater limpet in New Zealand, usually around 3–4 mm in length. The largest, at 11 mm long, is the black limpet. It's found only in the rivers and streams of the North Island, where it lives attached to the undersides of stones and rocks. Like many of its shore relatives, the limpet leaves its chosen spot on the rock to graze the local area for algal growths, then returns.

The black limpet is one of only two luminous freshwater land animals in New Zealand – the other is the glowworm. If the limpet is disturbed, cells in its body surface emit a glowing bright green secretion.

ANIMALS • Molluscs

Paua
It might be said that the paua lives under its shell rather than inside it – just like the limpets. Paua is found all around New Zealand's coasts. It lives on the seabed, below low tide. The shell is famous for its iridescent colours, but the paua animal itself is usually black. Paua is a popular food, as are related species elsewhere, such as abalone. Paua can grow to more than 16 cm in length and live for up to 7 years. It's a good traveller, too – it can cover 1 km of seabed in just 24 hours.

There are two smaller species: the pink paua, also called the silver paua (it's coloured a silvery pink!), which grows up to 10 cm; and the virgin paua, which grows to about 7 cm. Both of these species are more common in southern waters.

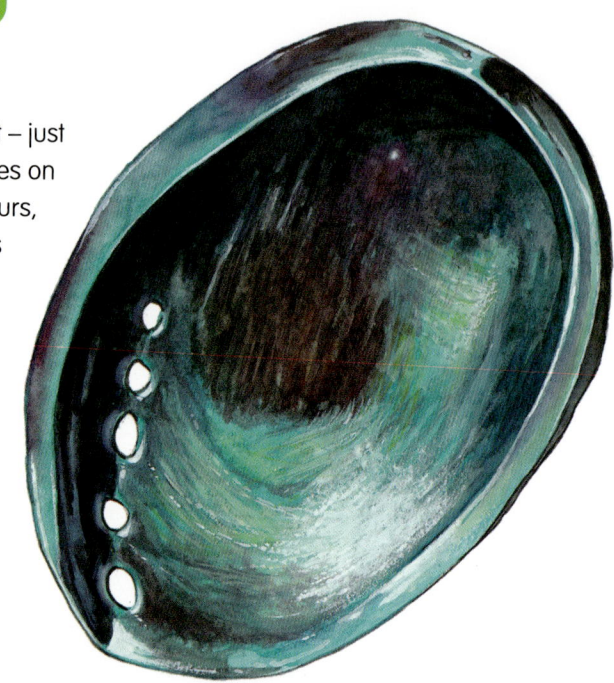

Spotted top shell
There are about 1000 species of top shell around the world, and nearly 100 species live around New Zealand coasts One of our most common is the 3 cm-wide spotted top shell, also known as pupu mai, or the common or dark top shell. It can be seen on rocky shores all around the country, roaming around the rocks in the mid-tide zone, as it searches for food in rock crevices. It has a very tough shell, which allows it to withstand rough waves and currents.

Wheel shell
Another common top shell is the pretty, 2 cm-wide wheel shell, which can be found on most sandy beaches, especially after storms or heavy swells. It lives just below the surface of the sand at low tide, and filters tiny food particles from the sand. Sea stars like to eat the little wheel shell, but it's quick to escape by performing a series of fast somersaults.

Cook's turban shell
This shell was first noted during Captain Cook's explorations around New Zealand. It has a rather heavy, thick shell, and can take much rough treatment before breaking up. For this reason, shells cast ashore are usually in poor condition, even though they're still intact. The dark brown outer covering of the shell, known as a pericostratum, is often mostly rubbed away to reveal the silvery-pearly layer beneath.

Cook's turban shell grazes on seaweeds below the low-tide range of rocky shores all around the country. The shell measures about 9 cm across. There are more than 20 species of turban shell in New Zealand waters.

ANIMALS • Molluscs

Common cat's eye shell
The common cat's eye is another member of the group known as turban shells. It crawls around the rocky shore eating small plants that it scrapes from the rocks. It especially likes Venus' necklace seaweed (page 22), and is also commonly seen around stands of mangroves (page 32), grazing up and down the plants' breathing roots. The young of this species are easy to distinguish, as their small shells have three very marked ridges around the spiral. Its operculum (stopper) looks like a cat's eye and is popular for use in craft work. The cat's eye shell can grow to 7 cm across. It's quite hardy and can live for up to 25 years.

Ostrich foot shell
There are about six species of these shells in New Zealand waters. Some small, brown species are common around the North Island, while the larger ostrich foot shell is found on shores all around the country.

The name comes from the heavy-lipped opening, which resembles the two-toed foot of the ostrich; this is sometimes cast ashore, broken off from the rest of the shell. Ostrich shells are variously marked in yellow, grey, brown, red or purple, and measure around 8 cm in length. They live below the surface of the sand and filter through it for fine food particles.

Maori commonly wore these shell rings as pendants; and they make good wind chimes.

Speckled whelk
Up to 80 different species of whelk – large and small – can be found all around the country on a variety of shorelines. One of the most common everywhere except in the far south is the 7 cm-long speckled whelk, also known as the large spotted mud whelk.

Like many whelks, it is a scavenger (eating almost anything that it can find) and a carnivore (hunting down other animals), and attacks smaller shells to eat their insides. It often appears in large numbers, and many will gather to attack the same prey.

Trumpet shell
The large trumpet shell can measure around 24 cm in length, and is found around much of the coast. There are several species, usually coloured in mottled dark browns and reds, though deeper species are paler and some are near-white. Within the shell, the animal itself is usually a bright orange and white.

The trumpet shell hunts for sea stars, sea urchins and other shellfish on the seabed from low-tide waters to depths of over 100 m. It captures them by drilling through the victim's shell or outer covering with its tongue and injecting venom.

The shell has been used for centuries by Maori as a trumpet (usually called a putarara or putara). The pointed top is cut off, then a wooden mouthpiece is fitted and tied in place.

ANIMALS • Molluscs

Spiny murex
There are several species of murex shell found in New Zealand seas, from shallow waters to depths of 150 m or more. The most spectacular is the spiny murex, which can grow to about 6.5 cm in length.

The murex feeds on small shellfish and barnacles. It drills a hole into its prey's shell, then inserts its toothed tongue to take the meal.

The largest murex in the world can reach more than 15 cm in length, with spectacular spines, and these are keenly sought after by collectors. In ancient Carthage and Rome, murex were much favoured for the rare purple dye that was produced from them, and tens of thousands of murex were regularly harvested for this purpose.

Oyster borer
Despite its size, the little (3 cm) oyster borer is probably more aggressive than most of the other carnivorous shellfish. It preys not just on oysters, but also on barnacles and mussels. It bores its way through their shells to reach the soft animal inside. Using its tough tongue, or radula, an oyster borer can cut through the tough shell of a rock oyster in around 45 minutes. When food is scarce, it even hunts in large marauding 'killer packs' which swarm over their prey. This species can be found near rocky shores around most of the country.

Turret shell
There are about 16 species of turret shell (or screw shell) in New Zealand waters. The 8 cm-long shell usually lives in the more protected environments of harbours and bays, sometimes in such great numbers that it packs the shallow seabed to the exclusion of most other shellfish. It can live in deep water, too, at 90 m or more.

The turret shell filters out food from the passing sea currents by means of fine hairs around the edge of the operculum or opening.

Tun shell
The tun shell is one of the largest shellfish in our waters; the very biggest specimens can reach up to 25 cm in length. There are about eight species to be found on the seabed around much of the upper North Island coast, to depths of 100 m or more.

Tun shells crawl around the seabed on a large, spade-like, brown 'foot'. They probe the sand with their proboscis (a long, tubular mouthpart) to find buried shellfish, crabs, sea stars and sea urchins, which they attack by drilling a hole in the victim's shell to get at the animal inside. The tun's own shell is quite thin, and broken pieces are often found cast ashore on northern beaches. Because of their fragility, whole shells are eagerly sought by collectors.

ANIMALS • Molluscs

Mud snail

Mud snails can be seen trundling around on estuary and harbour flats all around the country. They appear to be continually eating their way across the mud to strain out bacteria and tiny plant material, and trailing a near-continuous line of muddy poos! It's reckoned that a mud snail can work through twice its own weight in mud in an hour. They measure about 3 cm across the shell.

Unlike their full marine cousins, mud snails are air-breathers, but can survive being covered by the tide by taking in air before closing the shell off with the operculum.

Veined slug

Slugs can manage without the protection of a full shell. Some live in the water; others on land. Some of the land slugs have a small shell 'cap' on their back, but others, like the veined slugs, have practically no shell remnant at all. There are about 24 species of veined slug in New Zealand. They get their name from the leaf-vein pattern of their body markings. Most live in the damp and dark of bush and forest, but some are found around flax and other plants in swamps and other wetlands. Some species even manage to find a home under stones high up in the mountains. They are usually about 5 cm in length and appear in a range of colours – cream, brown, orange, yellow or green.

Sea slug

The bright colours of sea slugs are a warning to potential predators that they will make a very unpleasant meal. Some types can eat jellyfish and store the jellyfish's untriggered stinging cells within their own body, so that these become another form of defence for the sea slug.

Sea slugs have a wide range of body shapes: some are simple and smooth, and some have knobs and projections. Many sea slugs carry their breathing gills outside the body in a fan or rosette structure at the rear. Like their cousins on land, many sea slugs have two pairs of tentacles: one large pair for smell, and a smaller pair for touch and feeling.

Most sea slugs grow to between 3 and 10 cm in length, though some species can reach 30–50 cm.

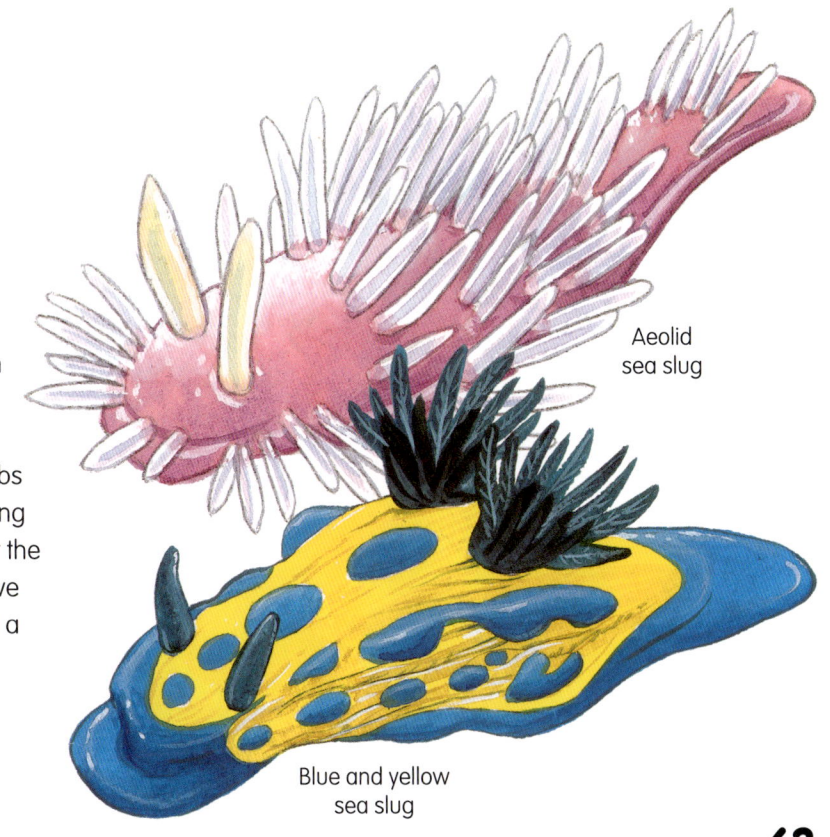

Aeolid sea slug

Blue and yellow sea slug

63

ANIMALS • Molluscs

Snakeskin chiton

Chitons (or coat-of-mail shells) are another type of shellfish. The animal's soft body is protected by eight tough plates, which are bound together by a scaly mantle, or covering.

When the tide is out, chitons can be seen clinging tightly to the undersides of boulders and rocks from the high-tide zone down to shallow waters. When they become covered by seawater, the chitons roam over the rocks to scrape off any tiny plant growths that they can find, and will usually return to the same resting spot each time as the water retreats again. Sometimes, the chiton eventually wears away a slight depression in the rock, allowing it to cling even more tightly to its home base.

By far the most common species is the snakeskin chiton, which can easily be seen on shore rocks around most of New Zealand. It has a snakeskin-like pattern on its mantle and usually grows to about 4–5 cm in length.

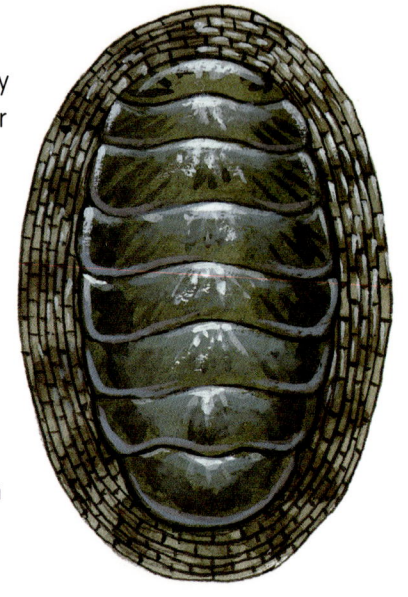

Common octopus

The octopus has excellent eyesight and is reckoned to be one of the most intelligent of all the invertebrates (animals without backbones). Experiments show the octopus is able to learn and to solve problems – such as working out how to escape from its tank and climb into the one next door, where it can see some potential prey!

The most common species in our waters is the common octopus, which measures up to 2 m across the spread of its arms. It lives quietly among the rocks and reef crevices by day, and emerges at night to search for prey such as shellfish, crayfish, crabs and fish.

Like squid, the octopus has a strong, bird-like beak; it holds prey with its tentacles while the beak makes short work of the meal. Also like squid, the octopus can change skin colour and patterning at will, to blend in with its surroundings and to display its mood. It can also release a cloud of dark fluid into the water to confuse any predator, which then usually attacks the inky cloud while the octopus escapes. The young of some species of octopus can attach the stinging cells of jellyfish to their tentacles for added protection from predators.

ANIMALS • Molluscs

Ram's horn shell
Though it looks like a small shellfish or the home of a tube worm, this is actually the flotation device of a small squid. It is the only evidence anyone ever sees of this species, as it lives out in the deep seas in great numbers. This little squid measures only about 7–10 cm in length. The squid can control the air in the shell's chambers to allow it to dive during the day, and then surface at night to feed on plankton (tiny plant and animal organisms).

Like the octopus, squid have eight 'standard' tentacles, but they also have another two that are longer than the others. All are equipped with suckers.

A squid moves by drawing water into its body and then expelling it through a moveable siphon, so that it can take off at great speed in nearly any direction.

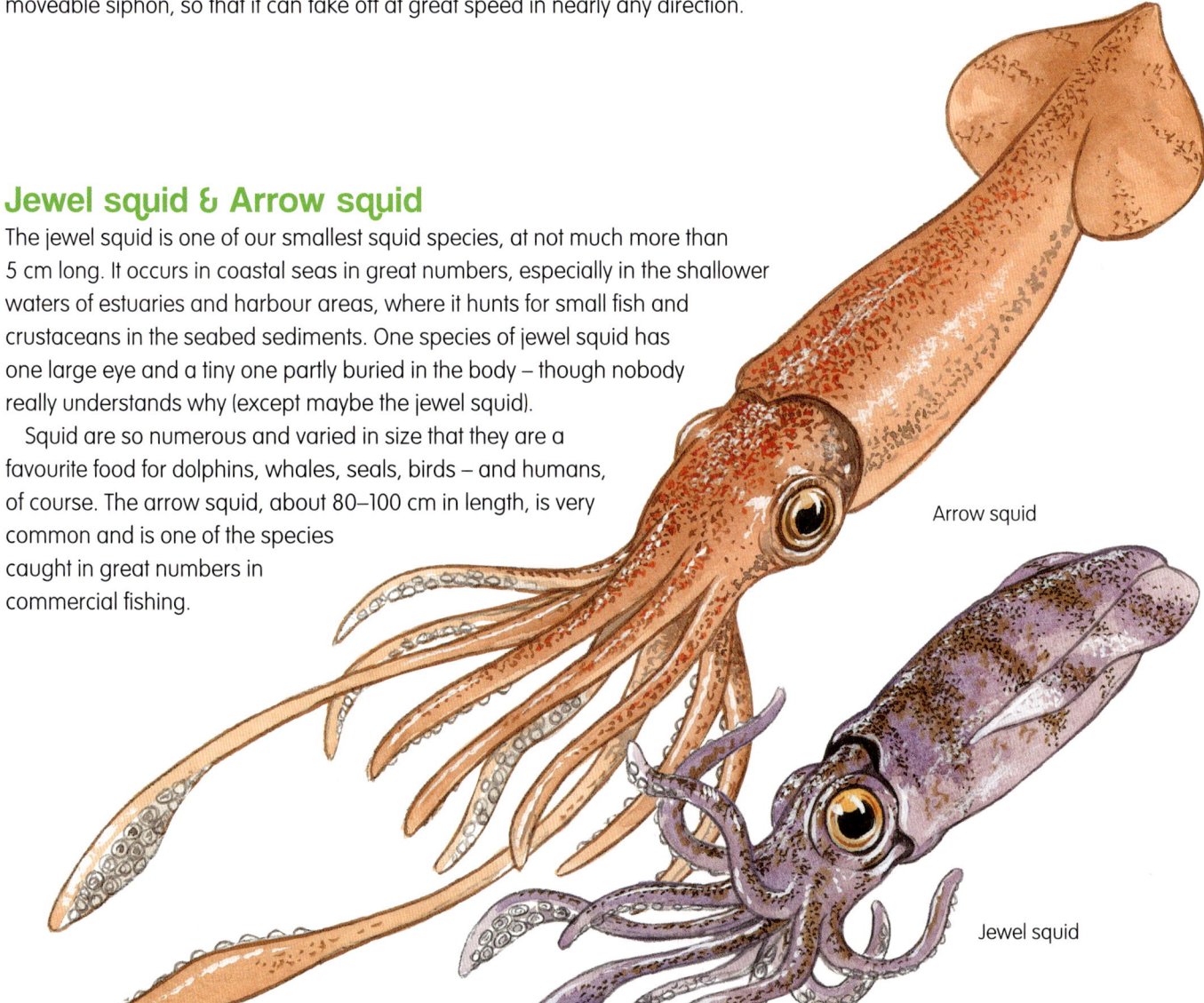

Jewel squid & Arrow squid
The jewel squid is one of our smallest squid species, at not much more than 5 cm long. It occurs in coastal seas in great numbers, especially in the shallower waters of estuaries and harbour areas, where it hunts for small fish and crustaceans in the seabed sediments. One species of jewel squid has one large eye and a tiny one partly buried in the body – though nobody really understands why (except maybe the jewel squid).

Squid are so numerous and varied in size that they are a favourite food for dolphins, whales, seals, birds – and humans, of course. The arrow squid, about 80–100 cm in length, is very common and is one of the species caught in great numbers in commercial fishing.

Arrow squid

Jewel squid

65

ANIMALS • Molluscs

Giant squid & Colossal squid

There are several species of giant squid living in the deep, gloomy depths of the oceans around New Zealand. The mantle (main body) of these animals may only be 2–4 m or so in length, but the huge tentacles, and especially the two extra-long grasping tentacles, can give these beasts an overall length of 20 m or more.

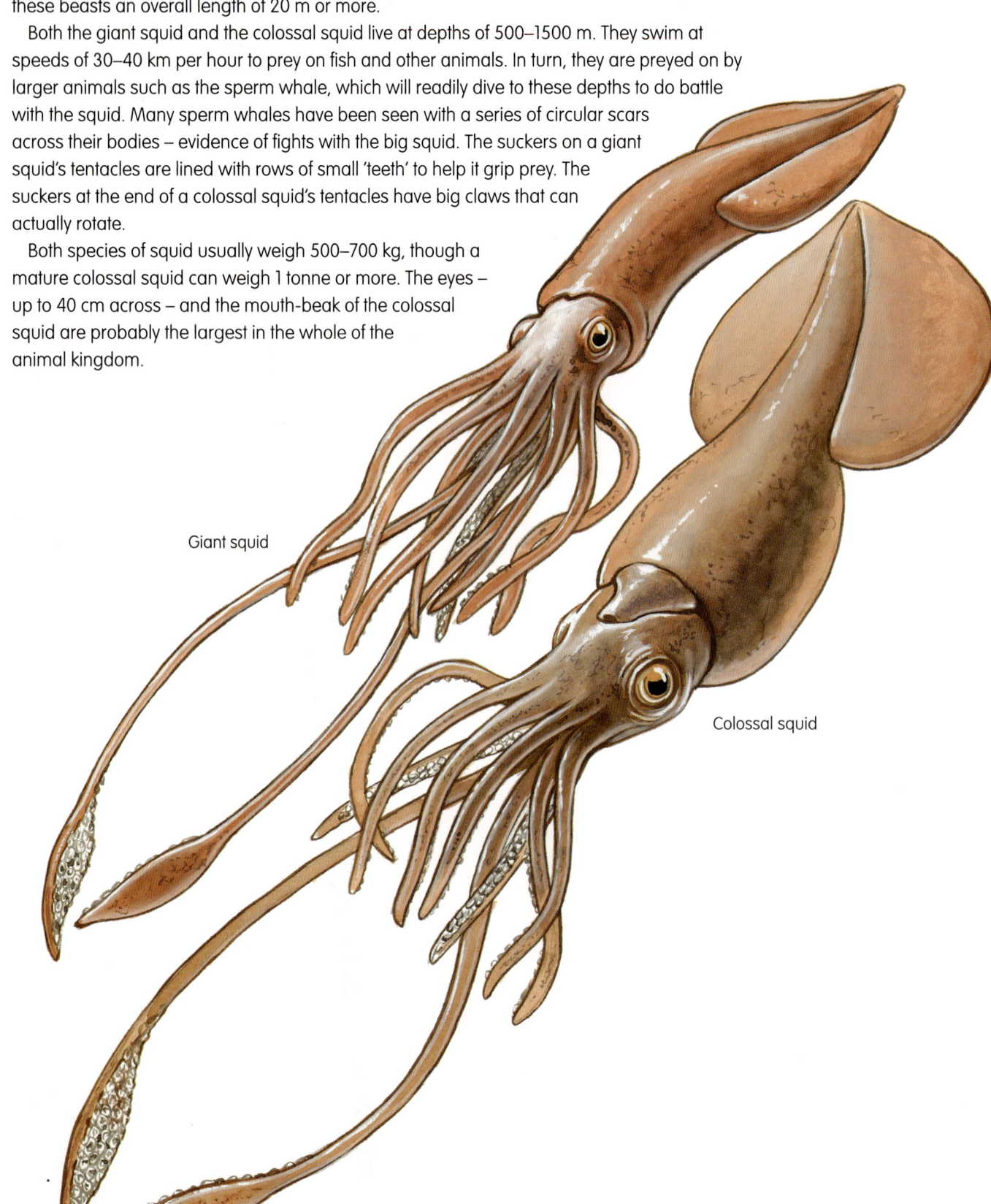

Both the giant squid and the colossal squid live at depths of 500–1500 m. They swim at speeds of 30–40 km per hour to prey on fish and other animals. In turn, they are preyed on by larger animals such as the sperm whale, which will readily dive to these depths to do battle with the squid. Many sperm whales have been seen with a series of circular scars across their bodies – evidence of fights with the big squid. The suckers on a giant squid's tentacles are lined with rows of small 'teeth' to help it grip prey. The suckers at the end of a colossal squid's tentacles have big claws that can actually rotate.

Both species of squid usually weigh 500–700 kg, though a mature colossal squid can weigh 1 tonne or more. The eyes – up to 40 cm across – and the mouth-beak of the colossal squid are probably the largest in the whole of the animal kingdom.

Giant squid

Colossal squid

ANIMALS • Crustaceans

Crustaceans are a group of animals that have jointed 'armour' covering and supporting their limbs and bodies, instead of having an internal skeleton. They usually have two pairs of antennae, or feelers, and they have eyes on stalks. Their abdomen ends in a tail-like extension, which is sometimes folded back under the body.

They can have just a few pairs of legs, or many legs. Their legs have a variety of functions as well as just walking – legs with claws for defence or for handling food, with gills for breathing, or with paddles for swimming.

There are about 40,000 crustacean species around the world, including barnacles, crabs, crayfish, shrimps and prawns. They come in a wide range of sizes, from giant crabs and crayfish down to creatures no more than 1 mm long.

Barnacles

There are several species of barnacle to be found on the shore, from hide tide to low tide zones. Some are wide and flat, and some like stacks of small columns. The modest barnacle, which measures only about 2-3 mm across, is one of the most easily seen. It can appear in great numbers on shore rocks, and on mangrove roots and trunks in northern waters. Its shell mantle is made up of four distinct parts, which make a little white star shape on the rocks

The barnacle lives permanently attached inside its little shell home, which it builds around its body. The animal stays permanently attached within the shell, which it can open or close, and sieves plankton and fine food particles from the water with its long, curled legs. The barnacle has been described as 'a crustacean fixed by its head and kicking food into its mouth with its legs'.

Barnacles will attach themselves to just about anything that doesn't move, and also to a few things that do. Typically, several different species live on rocks, shells, wharf piles, moorings and ships' hulls, but they've also been found attached to whales, crabs, turtles and even on penguins' feet!

Some have gone even further, and have actually managed to settle themselves on the backs of the very animals that prey on them, including crayfish, and even the shell of the oyster borer (page 62).

Modest barnacle

Columnar barnacle

Stalked barnacle

Plicate barnacle

ANIMALS • Crustaceans

Garden slater

Slaters are easy enough to find – you only have to move a stone, look under a plant pot or disturb some leaf litter to see a few of them scuttling away.

There are over 40 species in New Zealand, most of them native. Some of them have very decorative and sculpted plates along their backs, unlike the relatively plain look of the garden slater. They are also known as woodlice, and though they appear to be insects, they are members of the crustacea group called isopods.

Slaters are mostly forest-dwellers, and most are scavengers – they will eat rotting wood, leaves and vegetation, and sometimes fallen fruit. The female slater produces up to 200 eggs, which she carries in a pouch under her abdomen while the young hatch and develop, and then emerge as tiny versions of the adult. Slaters can live for about a year.

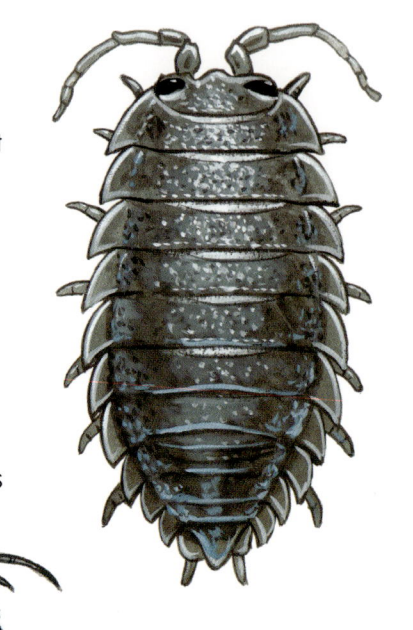

Sandhopper

Sand louse

Sandhopper & Sand louse

If the tangle of dried seaweed and driftwood at the back of the beach is disturbed, sandhoppers will go bouncing and hopping away across the sand. There are several species; the largest can reach 2.5 cm in length. They feed on rotting seaweed and on decaying fish and other animals. If you pick one up, it will tickle as it tries to burrow between your fingers to escape and hide. Other hopper species can be seen in freshwater environments, forests and urban gardens.

The little creatures that scurry away from the same disturbed spot, rather than bouncing and leaping away, are sand lice, also known as sea lice or beach slaters. These 1 cm-long animals are closely related to the garden slaters. They'll burrow and shovel their way through silt and sand, and can curl up into a ball if threatened.

Freshwater shrimp

The freshwater shrimp is found throughout the country, often in waterways near the coast where the water is a little salty. It is pale in colour, and usually 2–2.5 cm long. It feeds on decaying plant and animal material among the waterweed and other vegetation. The young shrimp develops in an unusual way: it grows into a male shrimp, which later changes into a female!

Very similar marine species can easily be seen in rock pools all around the country.

ANIMALS • Crustaceans

Freshwater crayfish

There are two species of freshwater crayfish, or koura, around New Zealand. Both measure about 16 cm in body length. Unlike the sea crayfish, they have large pincers to defend themselves, if threatened.

Like the sea crayfish, the adult needs to moult (shed its hard shell) about once a year in order to grow. Before moulting, the crayfish softens the existing shell by withdrawing lime back into the body to help form the next shell. It takes about 10 days for the new shell to harden, but only about 5 days for the pincer limbs to harden, as they are needed quickly for defence and for catching food.

Crayfish feed mostly at night, coming out to scavenge for small water animals and plants. They are preyed on by fish such as trout (page 109) and eels (page 100). By day, they burrow into soft, sandy streambeds to hide themselves; rocky streams provide decent hiding places, too. Even old cans or rubbish can be used for shelter.

Common crayfish

There are two crayfish that live in shallower coastal seas: the common crayfish (or red rock crayfish) and the packhorse (or green rock) crayfish. The green rock crayfish is the larger of the two and can sometimes weigh over 15 kg – twice the size of its more common red-brown relative.

Like crabs, crayfish are known as decapod crustaceans, which means that they have 10 legs and a hard outer body armour. As a crayfish grows, from time to time it sheds the outer shell. This allows it to expand its soft body to a slightly larger size before the new outer armour develops into the tough, protective shell. These moults take place several times a year until the crayfish reaches maturity at about 5–7 years. After that, it needs to moult only once a year for the rest of its life, which can be up to 50–60 years. Crayfish are at risk from predators such as large fish, marine eels (page 100) and octopus (page 64) at moulting time, so they try to hide in caves and crevices until the process is complete.

Crayfish are great walkers and can travel hundreds of kilometres on the sea floor around New Zealand.

ANIMALS • Crustaceans

New Zealand has nearly 200 crab species, but of these only a couple of dozen are seen regularly around the shore. Shore crabs are very sturdy animals and can spend a long time out of the water. They are great scavengers, and will eat practically anything, whether animal or plant, alive or dead.

A crab has 10 legs, and its soft body – head, thorax and abdomen – is protected by a single flattened shell, or carapace. As they grow larger, crabs need to shed their protective covering from time to time, to allow the next one to develop and harden. These empty, cast-off 'moults' can sometimes be found intact on the shore, but more usually individual claws or legs will be found. Males generally have larger claws than females.

Mud crab

Harbour mudflats can appear to be riddled with hundreds of small holes when the tide is out. Most of these are the homes of mud crabs, and a patient wait will see them emerge to filter tiny food particles from the wet mud and to tidy up their front doorstep. These little crabs (carapace width is usually no more than 2 cm across) have excellent eyesight, and will scurry back into their homes at the slightest movement nearby. They need to stay alert, as gulls and kingfishers will make a point of patrolling these flats for prey at low tide.

Mud crabs are highly territorial, and if one strays into another's area they stand on 'tiptoe' to grip each other's pincers, and then blow bubbles at each other until one admits defeat and scuttles away.

This crab is also known as the short-eyed mud crab or the tunnelling mud crab.

Common rock crab

This distinctive crab is one of the best known of all the species on the shore. Its carapace can measure up 4 cm across. It's common around wet rocks and pools in the mid-tide and high-tide zones. Though small, it can be quite aggressive if disturbed.

All shore crabs naturally breathe through the water, but can spend many hours in the open air, so long as their breathing gills remain wet. Males can be distinguished from females by the size of the abdomen plate on the underside. If it's narrow, the crab is male, but if it's very broad, then it's female – this is where she carries her eggs. Most male rock crabs also have larger claws than the females.

Common swimming crab

When waders feel a nasty nip on their toes while paddling in the water, they've probably disturbed the common swimming crab. The ends of this crab's back legs are expanded into little paddles, which allow it to swim through the water. In times of danger, it can use the paddles to dig backwards quickly into the sand to bury itself. The carapace can measure over 10 cm across, and the long claws are strong enough to crush bivalve shellfish. Pieces of the carapace and parts of the legs are often washed up onshore.

ANIMALS • Crustaceans

Hermit crab
If you observe the inhabitants of a rock pool for a few moments, you will see what looks like a very mobile and unusually fast-moving shellfish scuttling through the water: it's undoubtedly a hermit crab. This crab has a soft, unarmoured abdomen, so its uses the empty shells of univalves for protection. Facing out of the shell, it uses the first two pairs of legs for walking, and the other pairs for keeping a tight hold on the inside of the shell. As the crab grows, it exchanges the shell for a slightly larger one each time (but only after carefully examining the new one to make sure there's no one else already in residence!).

Large shore crab & Red rock crab
The large shore crab is a very mobile species that roams over exposed rocky coasts looking for food. The carapace is about 7–8 cm wide, and with its long legs outspread the crab can measure over 22 cm across. If it's disturbed, it will retreat into a rock crevice and face out, with sharp nippers at the ready – so it's definitely a species to be seen but not handled.

This rule also applies to the fast-moving red rock crab, which is similar in size but with bright red bars on its legs. It has a sharply jagged carapace, and it will readily trap an inquisitive finger between the legs and the edge of the carapace. This crab is normally seen at dusk, when it comes out to forage for food among the rocks.

Red rock crab

Large shore crab

King crab

King crab
There are several similar species of king crab that live on the sea floor of deeper waters (at 800–1200 m) around New Zealand. Nearly all are shades of bright red or red-brown. Some measure 20–30 cm across the carapace and have a leg spread of over 1 metre. They are common around much of the world's deeper oceans, sometimes in numbers great enough to be a commercial fishing catch. They are also known as giant crabs, spider crabs and stone crabs.

The largest of all these giant species is the Japanese spider crab, with a carapace 50 cm long and legs around 1.5 m in length, which can give it a total leg span of 4 m or more.

ANIMALS • Centipedes & Millipedes

Centipedes and millipedes are a very successful group of small animals: fossils show they have remained virtually unchanged for 400 million years. There are about 3000 centipede and 10,000 millipede species known around the world. The name 'centipede' means 'having 100 legs', but they never do; instead, they may have as few as 14, or as many as several hundred.

Centipedes are fast-moving carnivores, with strong jaw pincers. They have one pair of legs for each body segment; the last pair of legs is always much longer than the rest.

Millipedes are entirely vegetarian. Although they have two pairs of legs to each body segment, they are relatively slow-moving.

Garden centipede

There are a number of small centipede species that might be seen around the garden. Most are active only at night; they will scurry for cover if disturbed from their resting place, such as under stones or dense undergrowth, during daylight. Most measure 1–3 cm long and eat small insects such as cockroaches, beetles and flies.

Most of the other centipede species in New Zealand are forest dwellers and are rarely seen. They can appear in a variety of shades of red-brown, brown, green and black, with colour markings. Most feed on worms, insects and larvae.

House centipede

This centipede is found mostly around the Auckland area. It differs from other centipedes in having long, delicate legs – usually 30 – which increase in length further back along its body. Most of the other 30 or more centipede species in New Zealand have legs of near-equal length right down their body. The house centipede prefers warm, damp places – often in houses – where it can catch and feed on small cockroaches, flies and insects. It grows to around 3 cm in length.

Giant centipede

The native giant centipede grows to 25 cm in length, and is large enough and strong enough to hunt substantial prey such as geckos, skinks, worms and large spiders. It has tough jaws that can deliver a bite more painful than a wasp sting – though this doesn't deter rats from making a meal of it. It can be a fast mover, and will even climb trees in pursuit of prey. It can live for about 5 years.

Some large centipedes in other countries are very poisonous: the yellow and black striped tiger centipede from South America, up to 30 cm long, is even agile and venomous enough to catch mice and frogs.

Millipede

The millipedes are distant relatives of the centipedes. They do not have 1000 legs as the name implies, but they do have a lot of them. There are several hundred millipede species in New Zealand, and they eat plant material and fungi.

Like most centipedes, the majority of millipede species prefer to live in the damp, deep leaf litter of the forest floor. Some are extremely small – for example, a species of tufted millipede that lives in the litter of beech forests measures barely 3 mm in length and grazes on tiny algal growths.

ANIMALS • Insects

Insects evolved from the very first creatures that crawled from the sea to live on land many hundreds of millions of years ago, long before the first dinosaurs appeared.

There are more species of insect than there are of any other type of animal. Over a million insect species have been discovered so far, with perhaps another 30 million still to be found. New Zealand is home to about 20,000, and some 90 per cent of these are found nowhere else in the world.

Three things identify the typical insect. Although it may be hard to tell at times, an insect's body is in three distinct parts: the head, with mouth, eyes and a pair of antennae; the thorax (middle section), with three pairs of legs, and often one or two pairs of wings; and the abdomen (rear section).

Eggs

Caterpillar

Monarch butterfly

This is perhaps the best known of all the butterflies in New Zealand. It first arrived here in the late 1800s – probably a few stragglers blown across the Pacific Ocean from North America. It's very much a butterfly of gardens and cultivated areas, and is hardly ever seen in bush or forests. Its wingspan is about 8–9 cm.

The monarch is a very sturdy butterfly: you can feel its strong grip when it lands on your hand.

The female lays tiny, white eggs – usually on swan plants – and out of these hatch the distinctive black, yellow and white striped caterpillars. If these caterpillars get the chance to develop fully (they are preyed on by several species of bugs and wasps) they create a chrysalis around themselves. Inside the chrysalis they change into an adult butterfly over 2 weeks or so, and break out when they are fully developed.

The adult butterfly can live for about 2 months, though some can hibernate over winter if they emerge from the chrysalis in late autumn.

Like all butterflies, the monarch has no proper mouthparts; instead it has a long, curled tube-tongue, which it uses to suck up nectar from plants.

Chrysalis

73

ANIMALS • Insects

Red admiral butterfly

There are about five admiral butterfly species to be seen around New Zealand, all with similar markings, though with different colour patterns. The undersides of the wings of these butterflies are dull-coloured, to help disguise the insect from predators while at rest. Wingspans of admirals range from 4.5 to 6 cm.

There are about 350 species of admiral butterflies around the world. Most are found in Australia, but this red admiral is found only in New Zealand. Its Maori name of kahukura means red cloak.

Like most butterflies, the red admiral is most active during the summer months, and hibernates during winter.

Cabbage white butterfly

This butterfly first arrived in New Zealand in Napier in 1929, probably carried with vegetables aboard a cargo ship. It has since spread widely, and its small green caterpillars have become a common pest in gardens and vegetable crops – especially cabbage.

The cabbage white is the only butterfly of its type to live in New Zealand, but there are about 1200 species of white butterfly worldwide.

The wingspan of the white butterfly is around 3.5 cm. The female butterfly has two dark spots on each forewing, where the male has only one. The female lays over 300 eggs under a vegetable leaf, and after a few days the caterpillars emerge to chew rapidly through the plant, often reducing each leaf to a skeleton of stems and veins.

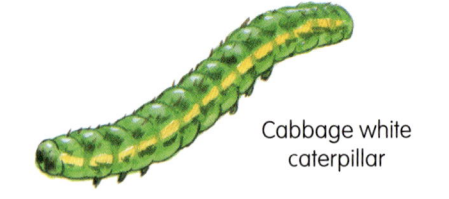

Cabbage white caterpillar

Blue butterfly

The blue butterfly is probably the most common of all the butterflies in New Zealand – and also one of the smallest, with a wingspan of about 2.5 cm. During the summer, varieties can be seen flying close to the ground in warmer, drier places all around the country, both by the seashore and inland.

These butterflies are typically blue-grey or blue-purple above, and silvery-grey underneath. They rest with wings slightly open, and if approached will take to the air again in a flitting, stuttering flight.

The little green caterpillars feed on a range of plants including broom, clover, lucerne, sweet pea and herbs, and sometimes occur in enough numbers to become a crop pest.

ANIMALS • Insects

Tussock ringlet butterfly
There are about 2400 species of tussock ringlet butterfly worldwide. In New Zealand, there are three very similar species that live in the grasslands and tussocks of the South Island.

Like many butterflies, the tussock ringlet has spots on its wings – this is thought to be effective in stopping birds from attacking when the 'eyes' are flashed in defence. Unlike most other butterflies, though, it doesn't fly in the daytime, but waits until the evening.

The tussock ringlet's wingspan is 3.5 cm. When it is at rest, with wings held together, the silvery streaks of its underwings are exposed, and this blends with the general background of tussock and grass stems, making it harder for birds to spot.

Puriri moth
This is the largest of all New Zealand's flying insects, with a wingspan of up to 15 cm. It lives only in the North Island, and is large enough to be mistaken for a small bird. It has variable wing patterns and markings, which are usually in shades of green, brown and yellow. The large caterpillars can live for up to 7 years in tunnels bored into puriri and other trees. But the adult moth lives only for a few days; just long enough to mate and for the female to lay her fertilised eggs – up to 2000 of them.

The adult puriri moth has no mouthparts and doesn't eat for its short life. Cats, rats and other predators can catch the moth while on the ground, and moreporks catch it while in flight.

Magpie moth
Most moths are active at night, but the magpie moth can be seen flying around gardens during the daytime, and is often mistaken for a butterfly.

When they are not walking across lawns and paths on the way to new feeding grounds, the furry caterpillars – known as 'woolly bears' – can be seen on the leaves of ragwort, groundsel and cineraria. These daisy-like plants contain an alkaloid poison, which the caterpillars and adult moths retain in their bodies to make them unpalatable to birds and other predators, though the shining cuckoo (page 139) doesn't seem to mind the taste of the caterpillar and eats them with no trouble.

Magpie caterpillar

ANIMALS • Insects

Cinnabar moth
Like the magpie moth (page 75), this brightly coloured moth is often mistaken for a butterfly, as it flies during the daytime. It was introduced here in 1929 to help control the spread of some noxious plants, and is now common in early summer around the lower North Island and the upper South Island. It has a wingspan of around 3.5 cm. Like the magpie moth, the bright colours of the wings are an advertisement to possible predators that it is very unpleasant to eat.

Tiger moth
There are eight tiger moth species in New Zealand – this group also includes the cinnabar moth (above) and the magpie moth (previous page). Varieties can be seen in the higher country of the South Island and the lower North Island.

It's easy to see how this moth got its name, with its orange and brown colouring. Its wingspan is 3.5 cm.

The females are secretive and mostly flightless, and hide away under rocks and in undergrowth. The caterpillars live on low-growing grasses and plants such as herbs – sometimes after first eating their mum!

The male tiger moths are generally very fast flyers, and can be seen zipping low over the ground in the daytime during summer months.

Gum emperor moth
This handsome, furry moth was first found in Whanganui in 1915 – probably accidentally introduced from Australia – and is now established throughout most of the North Island and the upper South Island. There are two species of gum moth in New Zealand, and about 1200 worldwide.

The gum emperor prefers to live around gum trees and pepper trees, where it lays eggs in summer. When the spectacular green caterpillar emerges, it eats the leaves of the tree until it is big enough to spin a large, hairy, gall-like cocoon in which it hibernates through the winter.

The 'eyes' on the moth's wings are there to startle and deter predators, such as birds, when the wings are suddenly opened and exposed.

Gum emperor caterpillar

ANIMALS • Insects

Huhu grub
(actual size)

Huhu beetle
This is our largest and heaviest member of the beetle family, at around 5 cm in length.

It spends most of its life – about 3 years – as a large grub hidden in old tree trunks and rotten wood in bush and forests. It lives as a beetle for only a couple of weeks or so – just long enough to mate and lay eggs. During this short existence, the adult beetle does not eat at all.

The huhu is a member of the longhorn beetle family. There are about 180 related species in New Zealand, and about 30,000 known around the world. The large, fat grubs of these beetles are a traditional food for people in many places.

Lemon tree borer
Like the huhu, this native species is a member of the longhorn beetle family. It usually measures around 2–3 cm in length. It deserves its name, because it bores into the branches of trees to lay eggs, and especially likes lemon and other citrus trees. The grubs that hatch from the eggs live for about 1 year in the tunnels they create by chewing through the wood. The tunnels can sometimes be extensive enough to seriously weaken the branch, which may even collapse and break. The adult beetle emerges in spring.

Sand scarab beetle
This large, black-brown coastal beetle is found mostly from Canterbury northwards, and there are several smaller, related species on New Zealand's shores. It lives buried deep in the sand above the high-tide mark during the day, and emerges in the evening to forage for food such as leaves, roots and other vegetable material.

Although it can fly, with a droning, clattering sound, it much prefers to walk. Its strong, stout legs leave distinctive tracks in the sand.

The plump grubs are up to 7.5 cm long. They live for a couple of years under roots and driftwood before developing into an adult.

ANIMALS • Insects

Eleven-spotted ladybird

Steelblue ladybird

Ladybirds

Ladybirds are a type of beetle, and all can fly, though their wings are hidden from sight under strong, round wingcases. There are about 40 species in New Zealand; about half of these were brought here to help control insect pests such as scale insects, mites and aphids – a single adult ladybird can eat up to 100 aphids in a day! Female ladybirds often lay their eggs close to aphid colonies, so that the larvae have a good source of food nearby when they hatch.

There are lots of colour variations in ladybird species – for example, black spots on a yellow body, or orange spots on black.

Cosmopolitan ground beetle

There are over 400 species of ground beetle in New Zealand. Their size ranges from just 2–3 mm up to about 4 cm. Nearly all are black and shiny, with lines and grooves on their wingcases. They are mostly active at night, when they come out to hunt for prey such as small insects. During the day, these beetles rest under rocks, stones and logs. In suburban gardens they can often be found in dark, hideaway places – for example, under plant pots or leaf litter.

Some larger ground beetles emit a foul smell to deter attackers and, if that fails, they can deliver a very strong bite with their jaws.

Tiger beetle

Tiger beetle grubs live in small, neat holes in bare ground or in earth banks. They stay in the 15 cm-long holes for a year or more, and snatch up any small passing prey and haul it inside to be eaten. After the larvae pupate, they emerge as adult beetles.

There are about 12 species of tiger beetle. They can be seen all around the country on warm, sunny days on open ground, banks and coastal sand dunes. They run and fly short distances as they hunt for other, smaller insects and catch them in their strong, sickle-like jaws. At night, the beetles burrow under the soil, and then dig themselves out again in the morning.

ANIMALS • Insects

Diving beetle

At 2.5 cm long, this is New Zealand's largest freshwater beetle. It moves through the water by rowing with strong, oar-like back legs as it hunts for its prey of small water insects. The jaws have a special covering that allows the beetle to seize and eat a victim without taking in any water.

The beetle keeps a layer of air trapped under its wingcase, and occasionally returns to the surface to take in a new supply before diving again. It is a strong flyer and will fly noisily from one water source to another.

There are about 16 similar species of water beetle in New Zealand.

Elephant weevil

This 2 cm-long weevil obviously gets its common name from its stout shape and its long proboscis, or snout. It is usually found in forests around trees such as beech, kauri and rimu. Although it's a capable flyer, it's often seen crawling about to feed on tree sap and plants.

The weevil grubs live in tunnels bored into dead trunks and branches, where they are sometimes parasitised by the giant ichneumon fly. This fly has a very long ovipositor (egg-laying spike) with which it can drill right through the wood of the tree trunk and into the grub's body, where it lays its eggs.

Giraffe weevil

At up to 8 cm long, the odd-looking giraffe weevil is New Zealand's longest beetle. It chews and bores into tree trunks to lay eggs, and the hatched grubs live in tunnels in the wood. They emerge as adults after about 2 years.

Giraffe weevils sometimes congregate in large numbers – up to 60 individuals have been found on just one tree. Males sometimes fight, using their long noses to battle. The females are much smaller than the males, and have their antennae set further back from the tip of the snout, so that they can bore further into dead wood to lay eggs.

79

ANIMALS • Insects

Crane fly

Crane flies form the largest group of flies in the insect world, with about 15,000 species. Of these, 500–600 live in New Zealand. They are sometimes called daddy-long-legs, and are often confused with the daddy-long-legs spider (page 95).

The crane fly is attracted to lights and often blunders into houses, but it is quite harmless and never bites or stings. The wingspan is about 3 cm.

Different species of crane fly are found all around the country and in a wide variety of environments such as swamps, farmland, tussock, native forest and the seashore. They may be coloured grey, green, brown, red or black. The wingspan is about 3 cm.

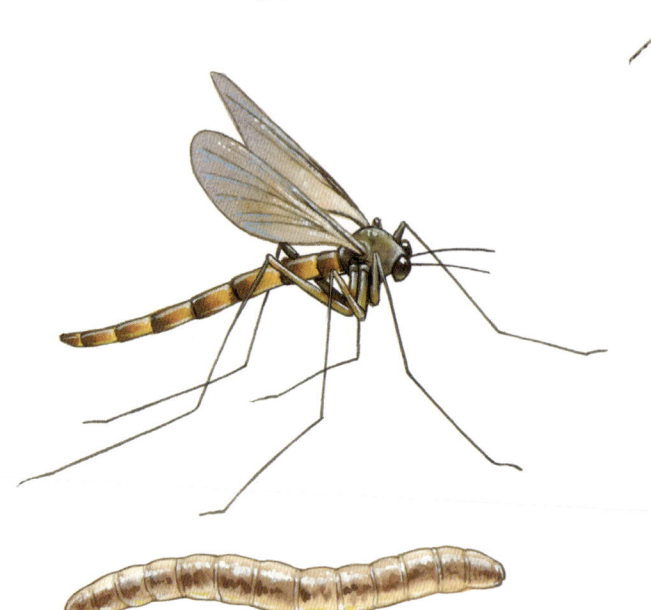

Glowworm

This insect is not a worm, but the larval stage of a small, mosquito-shaped fly. The adult fly lives only for 2 or 3 days, and lays about 80 eggs in any dark, damp place, typically the ceiling of a cave or an overhang.

After hatching, the 2.5 cm-long larvae find cracks or crevices where they can build a silky, slimy 'sleeve' or hammock. From this, they suspend about 70 long 'fishing lines' covered in sticky droplets – the lines can be anything from 5 to 40 cm long.

The larva has a light organ at the end of its abdomen, and when flying insects are attracted to the light, they blunder into the sticky lines and are trapped. The larva then hauls up the line to eat its catch.

Glowworm larva

Mosquito

There are 16 mosquito species in New Zealand; about 12 of these are native, and all are harmless to humans, though they can be very annoying!

Only the female mosquito bites, as she needs to suck blood from other animals – such as lizards, birds, other insects or humans – to help her eggs to ripen and develop.

Mosquitoes breed by stagnant water, where the young aquatic larvae (called wrigglers) develop and are food for ducks, frogs and beetles.

Many mosquitoes are active during the day, but the high, whining flight often heard at night is that of the vigilant mosquito, though it is rarely seen.

ANIMALS • Insects

Black fly
Anyone who has visited the coasts of Westland or Fiordland during warm, sunny weather will remember the bite of these annoying little flies – though they can be found all around the country. They are also known as sandflies, and can appear in dense numbers under ideal conditions, such as in high humidity.

Only the female black fly bites, to suck the blood she needs to help her eggs to mature; and while some species prefer to bite seals, or penguins and other birds, humans are obviously a very handy pit-stop.

There are about 13 species of black fly in New Zealand, but only four of these will bite humans.

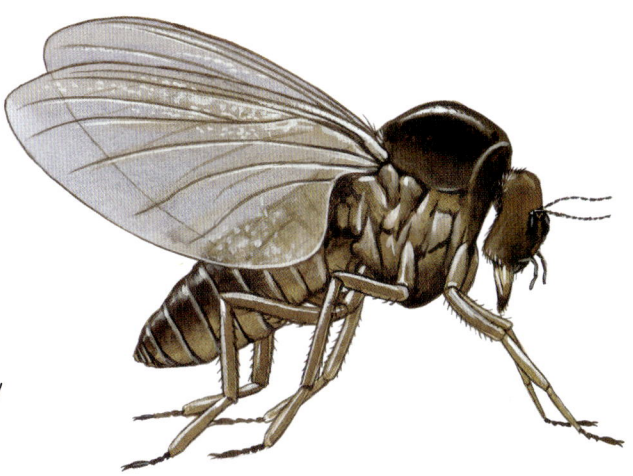

Housefly
Of more than 2000 different species of fly in New Zealand, the most common is the housefly. This fly probably came to New Zealand in the form of maggots in ships' food stores in the 1800s.

The housefly has no proper mouth, but feeds by vomiting on its food to soften it, and then sucking the mess up through a tube-like mouthpart. It likes sweet or rotting food, and breeds in animal dung, food waste or rotten plant material. It can spread disease by carrying 100–300 million bacteria on its body as it travels. It lives for 2–12 weeks.

Honeybee
Honeybees were brought to New Zealand from Australia in 1839, to begin a trade in cultivated honey and crop pollination. The native bees were too small to pollinate the flowers of the new crops.

In the wild, honeybees build a hive in a hollow tree trunk or branches. A queen bee rules the hive, and she lays 2000–3000 eggs every day. The eggs are cared for by thousands of worker bees, which also construct the many wax cells in the hive – the honeycomb – where pollen, nectar and honey are stored.

When a bee finds a good source of nectar and pollen, it returns to the hive and performs a special dance, which tells the other bees exactly where to go.

ANIMALS • Insects

Bumblebee

This bee is social, like the honyebee (page 81), but it lives in much smaller colonies of just a few hundred individuals. The nest is built underground, deep in old trees, or under rocks or thick undergrowth.

The hives are not tidy ranks of honeycomb cells, but just a haphazard collection of pots and cells to house eggs, larvae, pollen and nectar.

The bumblebee is much larger than the honeybee, and its flight is heavier and noisier. Sometimes its legs and body are so pollen-heavy, it's a wonder it can take off at all! The sting is not barbed like the honeybee's, so it doesn't lodge in the skin but can be used again and again.

Wasps

Most wasps are solitary hunters and do not live in colonies or build large nests. The ones that do live in colonies are all introduced species. The two wasps most likely to be seen are the German wasp and the common wasp – both relatively recent arrivals in New Zealand. They are very similar in appearance, with black-and-yellow body markings. The other two wasps of this type are the Asian paper wasp – which is also black and yellow, but much smaller – and the brown and slender Australian paper wasp. All of these wasps can deliver a painful sting.

Some wasps will even carry off large caterpillars, such as those of the monarch butterfly (page 73), as food for their young.

Ants

New Zealand is home to about 40 ant species. Of these, only around 10 are native.

Between 100 and 1 million individuals live in an underground colony. Each colony has a queen ant, which lays eggs to produce new members of the colony. A worker ant may live for 2–3 years, and a queen for 20 years or more. Many ants feed on honeydew, which is a sweet liquid secreted by aphids (page 89); and some ant species actually keep little 'farms' of aphids, and care for and protect them.

A typical ant is about 2–5 mm long, though the large native ant from the North Island can measure up to 1 cm.

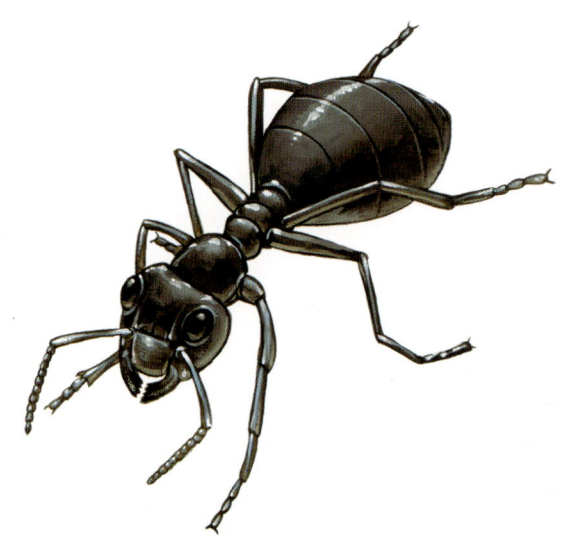

ANIMALS • Insects

Dobsonfly
With its 8 cm wingspan, the dobsonfly could at first be mistaken for a small dragonfly (see below), but the dobsonfly's very short body makes it easy to identify. It also holds its wings back over its body when at rest, rather than out wide like a dragonfly; and it is active mostly during the evening and at night, when it might blunder into lights in a slow, lazy flight. It's also known as the alderfly.

The fly is the adult form of a small, centipede-like larva that lives under rocks in streams. The adult dobsonfly doesn't eat at all during its life of just a few days.

Dobsonfly larva (actual size)

Giant dragonfly
There are about 11 dragonfly species in New Zealand. The giant dragonfly is the largest, with a wingspan of up to 13 cm. It is also known as the devil's darning needle, though it has no sting and is quite harmless. It can be seen anywhere near water in native bush and forests.

Dragonflies are strong flyers, and some reach speeds of nearly 60 km per hour. They can fly vertically up or down, hover like a helicopter, and even fly backwards as they search for their prey of other flying insects, which they can catch in flight.

Dragonflies rest with their wings outstretched, unlike their close cousins the damselflies, which rest with their wings 'closed' vertically.

Damselfly
Brightly coloured damselflies can be seen flitting and swooping through the air by streams and lakes, and zipping over the water's surface as they snatch up small flying insects. There are six species in New Zealand, and in most of these the male and female are different in colour. The 3 cm-long male of the redcoat damselfly is red and black, and the female is bronze, orange and black. Largest is the blue damselfly, with a body length of about 45 mm. Males are bright blue and black, and females are greener.

Damselflies always rest with their wings held vertically together over the body.

ANIMALS • Insects

Stonefly

There are about 2000 species of stonefly found around the world, with over 100 known in New Zealand.

The nymphs are usually coloured bright green, orange-green, yellow or brown. They live in the clear water of stony streams and lakes for 3 years or more, foraging for small insects. Then they emerge as winged adults.

The adult stonefly measures up to 3 cm in length. It's a reluctant and weak flyer, and it can often be seen resting near the water with its long wings folded back along its body. It lives for only a few weeks.

Mayfly

The mayfly gets its name from the time of year in which it appears in great numbers in the northern hemisphere. Adults mate while in flight, after which the female flies close to the water's surface to wash off the eggs from the end of her abdomen; she is often caught by fish as she does so. Because they appear in such large swarms during mating, these flies are an important food source for other animals, such as birds and other insects.

Though the wingless nymphs live in the water for up to 4 years, the winged adult lives for only a very short time indeed – some for a few days, and some only for an hour or so. Wingspan is around 4 cm.

Green vegetable bug

The 1.5 cm-long green vegetable bug, which comes from Europe, is often seen around the garden feeding on the stems of vegetable plants. It has piercing mouthparts which it uses to suck sap from plants, juice from fruit – and even body juices from caterpillars and other insect prey. It is sometimes called the stink bug, because it emits a strong, foul smell if disturbed or handled. It flies with an audible buzz.

This bug has a row of three spots across its back, which makes it easy to tell apart from the very similar (and spotless) New Zealand vegetable bug, which is not a pest on vegetable plants but instead lives mostly on native plants.

ANIMALS • Insects

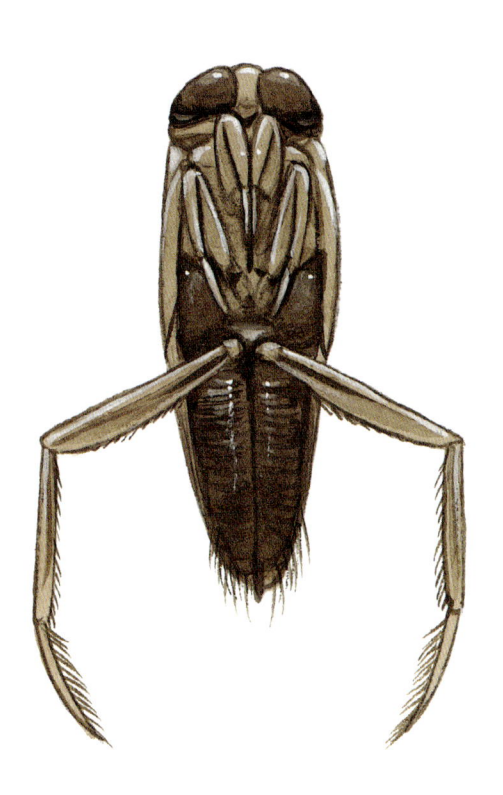

Backswimmer
There are many small insects that can be seen scuttling on or near the surface of the water in quieter ponds and lakes. One of the strangest is the backswimmer. Measuring only 7–9 mm long, it swims just under the surface, on its back! It uses its long rear legs as oars, and the other two pairs are held tightly against its upside-down body, ready to snatch up any prey, such as small insect larvae and tiny crustaceans. Its large eyes allow it to see 'down' to spy any potential prey. It breathes with the help of special hairs that trap a bubble of air against its body, and it breaks the water's surface from time to time to renew the bubble. Some backswimmer species are strong flyers, and some are wingless.

Pond skater & Water boatman
There are two insects that are so small and light, they can travel on top of the water without breaking the surface tension. They can be seen in any water environment where the water is undisturbed.

The pond skater, just 2–3 mm long, scurries quickly about in search of even smaller flying insects that may have become caught on the water's surface.

The slightly smaller water boatman is probably the most common of these little insects. Like the backswimmer, it has long rear legs which are used like oars to propel it through the water. The middle pair of legs are even longer, and it uses these to hang onto the stream bottom or vegetation while the front legs scrape up algae and other small plant food. The water boatman, like the backswimmer, carries a small bubble of air as it swims about.

Both of these insects can be seen with tiny red dots attached to their bodies: these are parasitic water mites (page 95).

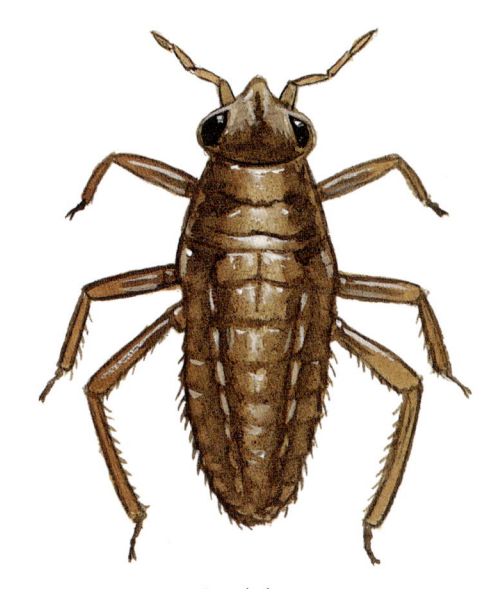

Pond skater

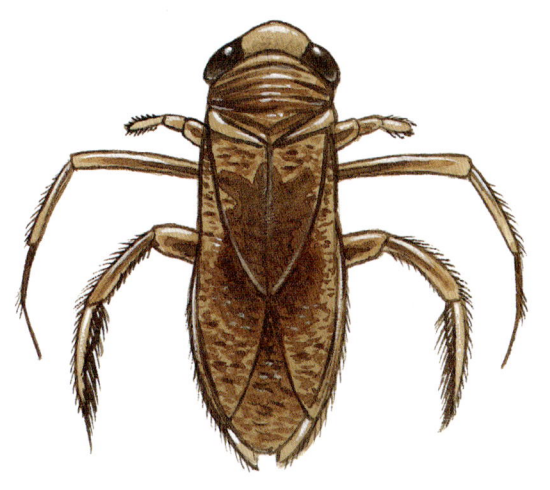

Water boatman

85

ANIMALS • Insects

Tree weta

This member of the weta family can be seen in gardens and forests all around the country. During the day, the weta hides quietly in holes in trees and old logs and other secluded spots, but it ventures out in the evening to seek out food, such as new plant leaves and small insects. In turn, tree weta are often prey for birds and ground predators such as rats.

The discs on the weta's front legs are actually its ears. If disturbed or handled roughly, the weta can scratch with its long, spiny hind legs, or deliver a painful bite with its strong jaws. There are about 7 species of tree weta, and most can live for 8 years or more. Their body length is around 7 cm. The long tail spike seen on some weta is not a weapon, but an ovipositor, which the female weta uses to deposit her eggs in any damp place, such as in rotten tree bark.

Giant weta

Though weta are not unique to this country – there are hundreds of species around the world – nowhere else do they reach the great size of our own giant weta. There are at least 9 species, of varying size; the heaviest – at around 70 g – can weigh as much as a thrush or blackbird. It's body length can be 8 cm or more.

Like most other weta, these giants are active mostly at night, when they come out of hiding to feed on fresh leaves and foliage. Giant weta are not especially aggressive, and don't have large, imposing jaws. They are not as agile or lively as the smaller weta types, so they are easy prey for rats and other ground predators. They are now mostly restricted to offshore islands or high country. Body length can be 8 cm or more, and most giant weta live for 3–4 years.

ANIMALS • Insects

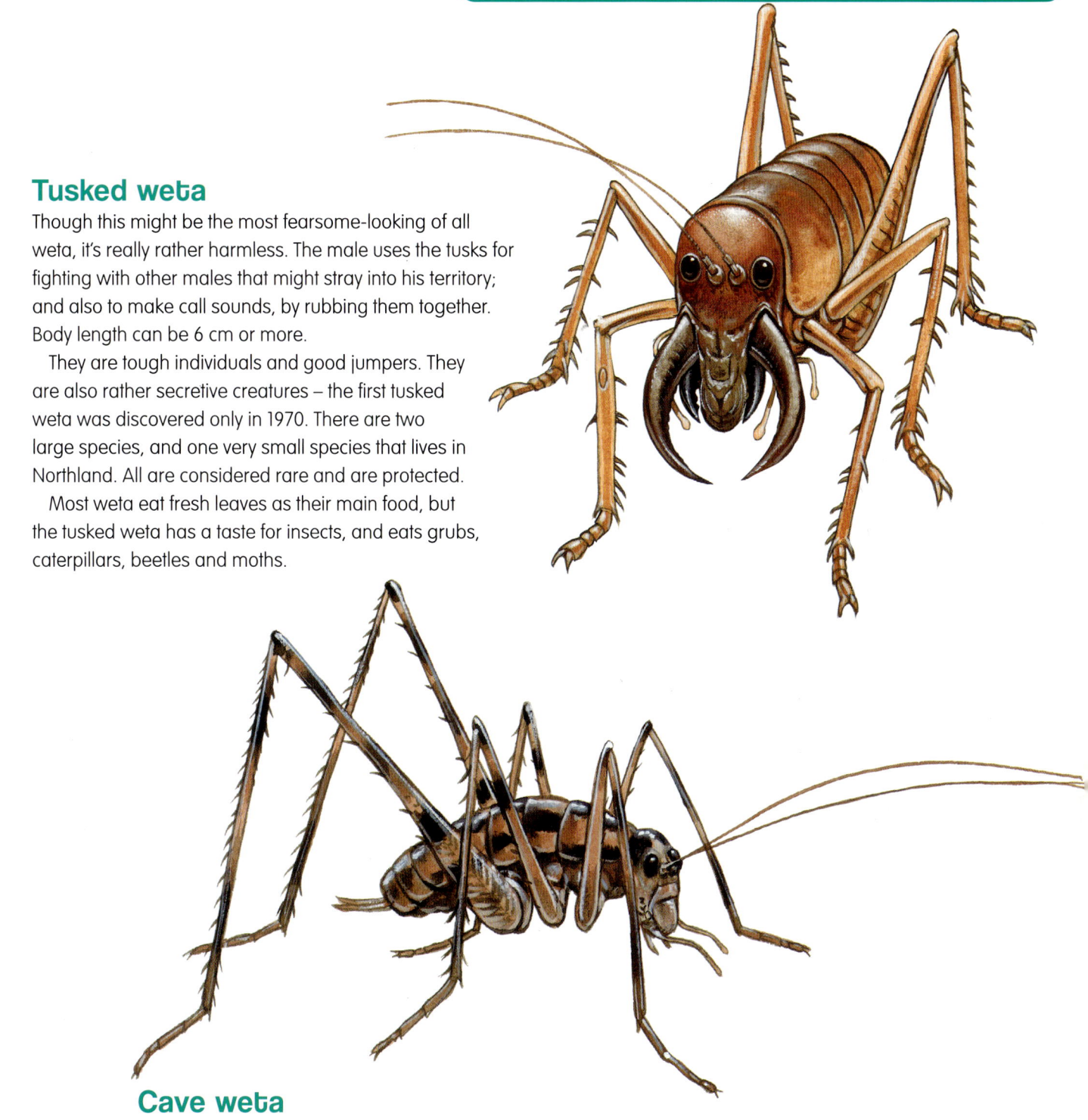

Tusked weta

Though this might be the most fearsome-looking of all weta, it's really rather harmless. The male uses the tusks for fighting with other males that might stray into his territory; and also to make call sounds, by rubbing them together. Body length can be 6 cm or more.

They are tough individuals and good jumpers. They are also rather secretive creatures – the first tusked weta was discovered only in 1970. There are two large species, and one very small species that lives in Northland. All are considered rare and are protected.

Most weta eat fresh leaves as their main food, but the tusked weta has a taste for insects, and eats grubs, caterpillars, beetles and moths.

Cave weta

This is the largest of all the weta groups, with over 50 species in New Zealand and more than 500 around the world. Cave weta live in the cool, damp, dark environments of caves and abandoned mines, where they sometimes gather in great numbers on the walls and upside down on the ceilings.

Compared with other, smaller weta, their bodies are small, and only lightly armoured, but they have especially long antennae and legs. One cave weta was measured with a body length of only 2.5 cm, but a total length of over 35 cm from antenna tips to its hind feet. The giant cave weta can measure about 45 cm overall.

All cave weta are very good jumpers (some can leap 3 m in one go). They eat decaying plant material as well as new, young plants, and will sometimes turn cannibal and dine on their own kind!

ANIMALS • Insects

Passionvine hopper & Green plant hopper

Like green vegetable bugs (page 84), plant hoppers like to pierce plant stems and suck the sap or juice from them, and can become quite a pest in gardens and crops.

The passionvine hopper is easily found, as it rests with its wings outspread like a little moth, often in large groups on the stems of plants such as kiwifruit, jasmine and (of course) passionfruit vine. If disturbed, the whole group will often prefer to walk daintily around the stem out of the way, rather than taking to flight with a sudden 'snap'.

Their young nymphs have a distinctive bunch of hairs on their rear ends, which earns them the name of 'fluffy-bums'.

The green plant hopper is not quite so easy to spot – it rests with wings closed, and at first glance resembles a large, green thorn or small leaf on the plant stem. It will more readily fly off if disturbed . . . but often only to return to the same plant within seconds!

Passionvine hopper

Green plant hopper

Cicada

It's hard not to notice this insect in late summer, as it appears by the thousands and calls in a great, deafening chorus that can sound just like heavy rain. The sound is made by the males drumming special body chambers, or clapping their wings against a hard surface. The noise is made to attract a female to mate.

Once they have mated, the female lays her eggs in the bark of a tree or in plant stems. In spring, the tiny nymphs hatch and drop down to burrow into the soil, where they live for several years, feeding on plant roots. The older nymphs emerge in summer, climb up the tree trunk and anchor themselves there. The outer skin then splits, and the adult cicada struggles out, leaving the empty nymph case clinging to the bark.

There are about 40 different species of cicada in New Zealand, and they live in a wide variety of environments – in coastal dunes, forests, and even high up in the mountains.

Cicada nymph

ANIMALS • Insects

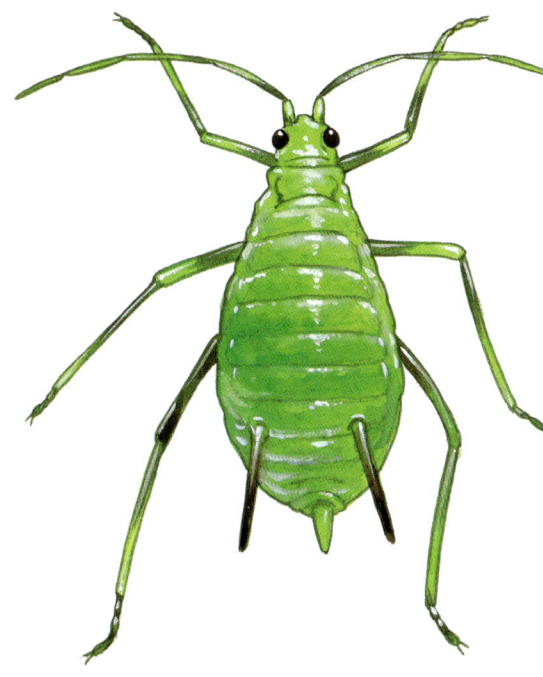

Aphid
Aphids are usually seen as a pest insect in the garden and in some crops, as they can damage plants by sucking juices from the growing stems with a sharp proboscis – a needle-like mouthpart.

There are nearly 100 different species in New Zealand. They come in a variety of colours – usually green, pink, black or brown – and they are about 2–3 mm long.

Aphids secrete a sugary fluid known as honeydew, which is sometimes harvested by ants and bees – it's been estimated that the aphids on just 1 hectare of vegetation can produce 2 tonnes of honeydew in a day! Aphids are eaten by birds, and by other insects such as the praying mantis, wasps and ladybirds.

Grasshopper
There are about 15 species of grasshopper in New Zealand. They can be found in grasslands, high-country tussock and mountain environments. They range in size from 1 to 5 cm.

They feed mostly on various grasses, and they are generally very good hoppers and jumpers. Some types are flightless, so they need good strong legs to get from place to place!

Grasshoppers come in a wide range of colours – grey, brown, green, and even orange or pink, all interwoven with bars and darker marks. Together, these 'camouflage' markings can make the grasshoppers very hard to see when they are at rest against the usual background of grasses, undergrowth and rocks.

Katydid
The katydid's bright green colouring and leaf-like shape make it hard to see as it rests on plants in the garden. Even its wobbly, hesitant walk could be mistaken for the movement of a leaf in a slight breeze. It measures about 4 cm in length.

The katydid makes a *zip-zip* call, which is often heard on quiet summer evenings. The name comes from the call of an American species, which sounds like 'Katy did, Katy didn't'.

There are about 6000 katydid species worldwide, with 4 species known in New Zealand. All are relatives of the grasshoppers.

Katydids feed on young leaves, buds and fruit, which can sometimes give a pinkish tinge to the usual green body colour.

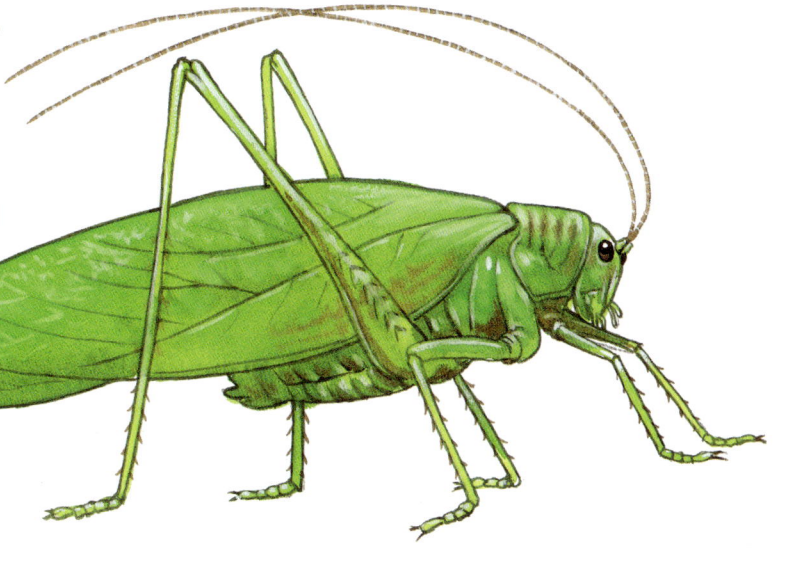

ANIMALS • Insects

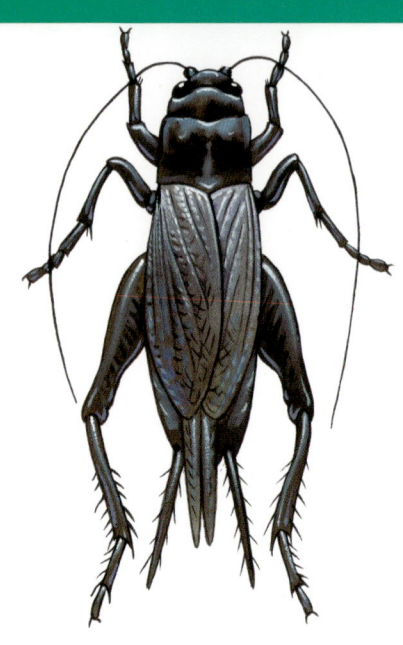

Black field cricket
These little crickets are often seen in the suburban garden. They are very common around the country, except in the lower two-thirds of the South Island. Sometimes they can become so numerous that they are considered a pest on farmland and grasslands, where they eat grass leaves, seeds and flowers.

The black field cricket is about 2.5 cm in length. The males make a loud, high-pitched song by rubbing their hind legs together.

There are about 4000 species of cricket around the world, and about 8 in New Zealand. People consider them a tasty snack in some countries.

Stick insect
There are about 16 species of stick insect in New Zealand, and they come in quite a variety of sizes, colours and shapes – grey, brown, green, or mottled black and white; and smooth, rough, or covered in short spines.

They eat plant leaves, mostly at night, and can be seen in the branches of manuka, kanuka and pohutukawa in the daytime.

The body length can be up to 15 cm. The male is usually much smaller and slimmer than the female, and some species appear to have no males at all – the female just produces more females.

The smooth-bodied and bright green (or brown) common stick insect is found nationwide.

Praying mantis
The 4 cm-long praying mantis holds a pose with its long, spiny front legs held up together 'in prayer' as it waits for prey. When flies or beetles pass close enough, it lunges out in a flash with the front legs to trap the victim.

There are two types here – the bright green New Zealand praying mantis, which is a native species, and the green-and-brown South African praying mantis. The New Zealand mantis usually waits for prey on top of green leaves, while the African one prefers to wait underneath the leaves.

Both types make substantial pale, 'zippered' cases for their eggs, and these are often seen on rigid vertical surfaces such as the side of a house, posts or trees. When the young hatch, they emerge as very tiny versions of the adult.

ANIMALS • Insects

American cockroach

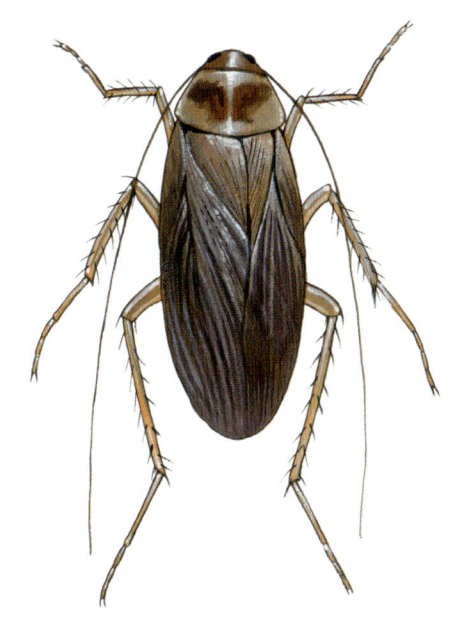

The American cockroach is thought to have first arrived here on Captain Cook's ships in 1769 and later voyages, and is regarded as a disease-carrying pest, unlike most cockroach species. It likes warmth and dirt, and so can often be found in unclean areas of kitchens, bakeries and so on. Though it has wings, this cockroach tends to run fast rather than fly, if disturbed.

Most cockroach species prefer natural environments to buildings, though the native bush cockroach and the winged bush cockroach – similar in appearance, but about half the size of the American cockroach – will sometimes stray into houses or be brought in with firewood. Body length is around 3 cm.

Gisborne cockroach

Cockroaches are a very ancient form of insect – they've been around for 300 million years (they appeared long before the dinosaurs). There are about 4000 species around the world, with over 30 known in New Zealand – most of them native.

The rather handsome Gisborne cockroach is a recent arrival: it first arrived in Gisborne (from Australian cargo ships), and has now spread around the North Island and to the top of the South Island. It is flightless and up to 3 cm long.

The native black cockroach is similar in size and distribution. It is black all over, and it gives out a foul smell if disturbed.

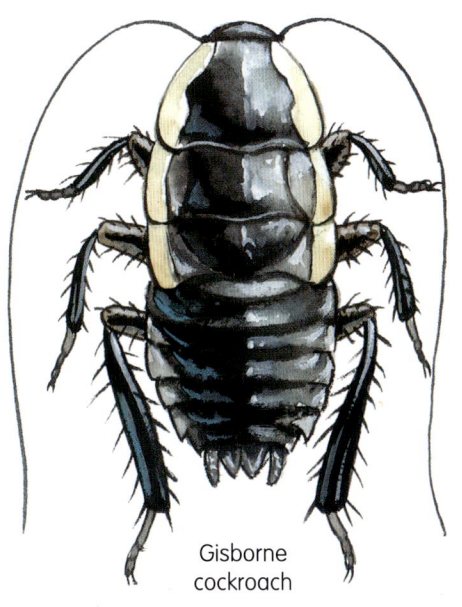

Gisborne cockroach

Earwig

There are about 20 species of earwig in New Zealand. One of the largest is the shore earwig, at nearly 3 cm in length. It can be seen foraging among the seaweed and general shore litter above the high-tide mark.

Earwigs eat plants and fruits, and also hunt and eat slaters and small insects, often using their rear nippers to catch them.

It can be a risky business being part of an earwig family. When the young earwigs hatch from their eggs, the first to emerge may eat the other eggs or the smaller hatchlings, or they might eat their mother – or she might eat them.

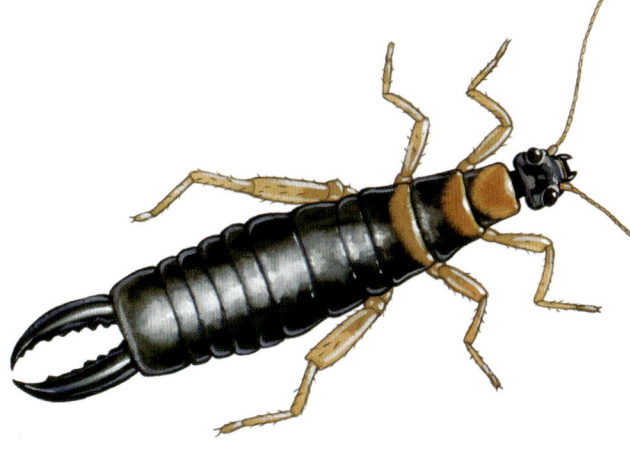

Cat flea

Many different animals – for example, cats, dogs, birds, rats and humans – have their own individual type of flea living on them. Both male and female fleas suck the blood of their host, and the female can lay up to 500 eggs.

There are about 35 different species in New Zealand, with around 3500 known around the world. The common cat flea obviously prefers a cat as its host, but is quite happy to transfer to humans and bite them, too!

Fleas are known for their impressive strength and jumping ability – some can leap to heights of over 30 cm, and at a speed greater than any human could withstand.

ANIMALS • Spiders & Mites

The fossil evidence shows that spiders are an even older form of life than insects – they go back more than 360 million years. They belong to a group of animals called arachnids, which also includes scorpions, harvestmen, ticks and mites.

All have two main body segments, with four pairs of legs, and most have eight eyes. Some are scavengers, but the majority of spiders are hunters of live prey.

There are 75,000 species of arachnid found worldwide. Although spiders are probably the best known examples, species of mites and ticks are actually far more numerous. There are estimated to be around 2500 spider species in New Zealand, in all sorts of environments – in forests, swamps, gardens, mountains, thermal areas, caves, high in the mountains, on the shore, even under the water . . . and floating on top of it, too!

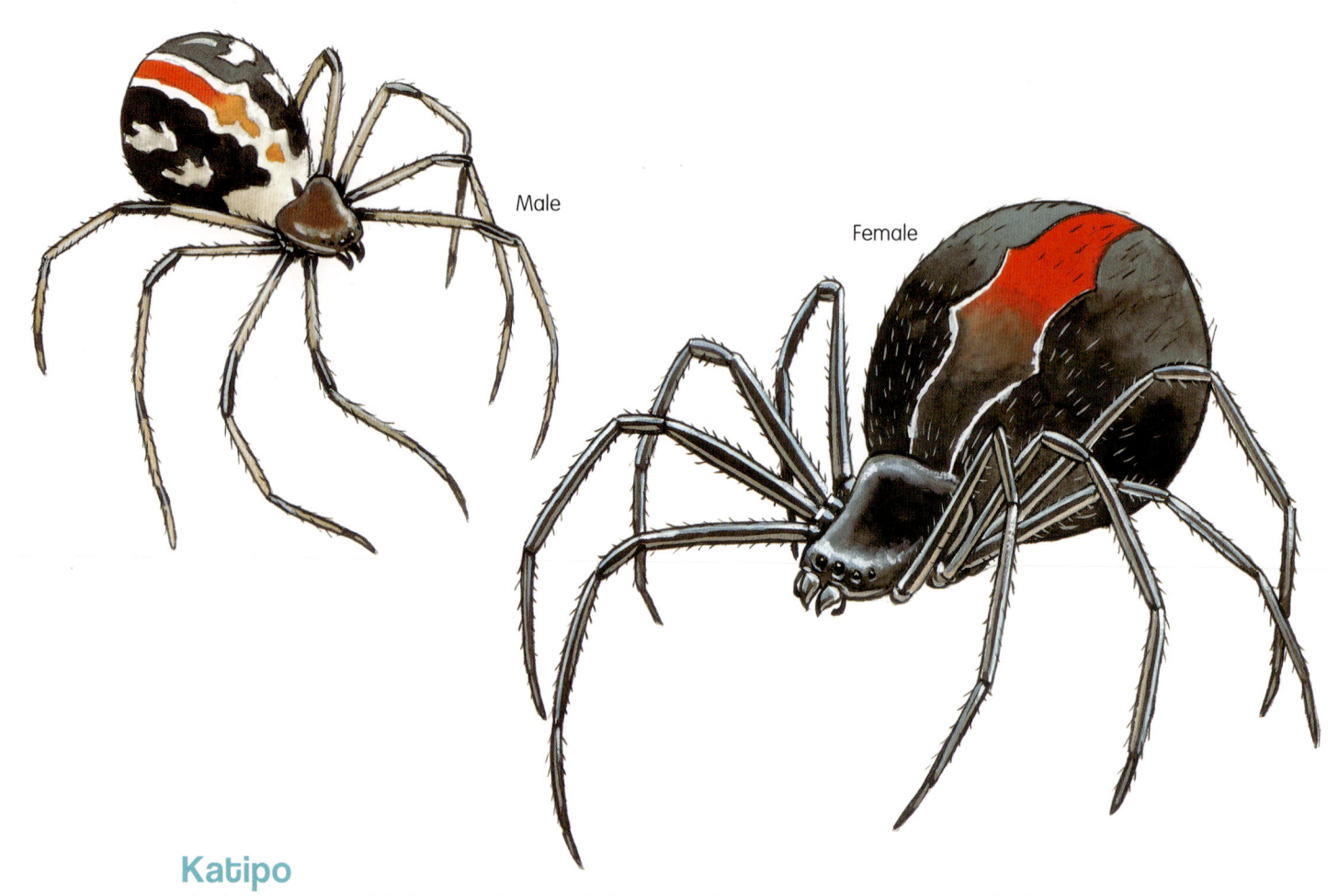

Male

Female

Katipo

The katipo is probably the most famous of all New Zealand's spiders, though it's unlikely that many ordinary Kiwis have ever seen a live one. It's a shy, secretive spider that lives in webs built at the rear of sandy beaches in the usual tangle of grasses and driftwood, where it catches other small ground insects, slaters and sandhoppers. It can even subdue the sand scarab beetle (page 77), which is many times its size.

The name katipo means 'night biter' or 'night stinger'. Only the pea-sized female can bite humans, and there are only two recorded deaths from her bite, both of which were over 100 years ago. The male is much smaller and cannot bite.

The katipo is easy to identify by the red marking on its back. There is an all-black katipo that can be found near some North Island shores, but this species is not especially poisonous.

ANIMALS • Spiders & Mites

Garden orbweb spider

This is the most commonly found spider of over 30 orbweb species in New Zealand. It measures about 1 cm in body length. The large, circular webs that are seen strung around the garden are usually the work of an orbweb spider of some type. These spiders hide during the daytime, but in late evening they can be seen on their webs, feeding, or sitting off to one side, with one leg in contact with the web in case some unsuspecting flying insect blunders into it, when the spider will rush out to capture it.

This spider is sometimes stung and carried away by wasps, which will take the paralysed spider back to their nest as food for their hatching young.

Grey house spider

This spider lives in tangled, zigzag webs, which are often seen under house weatherboards and around windows. The webs can become very untidy and unkempt, with bits and pieces of old, unwanted prey – such as fragments of insects' wings and legs – lodged here and there.

This 1.5 cm-long spider lives in a silken tunnel off to one side, and waits there for any disturbance in the web, caused by a blundering insect, and then rushes out to trap it.

The white-tailed spider (below) preys on the grey house spider by coming along and carefully 'tickling' the web with a leg, and then pouncing quickly before the investigating grey house spider realises that it's been tricked.

White-tailed spider

This is an unusual species, because it prefers to hunt and eat other spiders (see above), rather than the usual prey of insects such as flies and beetles.

It arrived from Australia in the late 1800s, and in recent years has gained a reputation for having a particularly nasty bite that results in a necrotic ulcer – a type of sore that is very slow to heal, or might even spread in the skin.

This reputation is apparently quite undeserved, for not a single case against this spider has been proven. So though its bite can hurt, it's no more dangerous to humans than most other spiders. White-tailed spiders are around 1.5 cm in length.

ANIMALS • Spiders & Mites

Tunnelweb spider

There are about 25 species of these spiders in New Zealand. They are large – usually about 2 cm in body length – and can deliver a painful bite, though their venom is not thought to be harmful to humans.

They construct webs under logs and stones, and in available holes and crevices in tree trunks and branches – such as in ponga ferns, where the small, webbed holes are quite plain to see. Inside, the spider lies in wait for insects or small creatures such as slaters to pass by, and then it rushes out to strike with its strong fangs.

The black tunnelweb spider also likes to eat the common garden snail (page 58), which it attacks and then grips with its fangs to prevent the dying snail from withdrawing into its shell.

Though most spiders live for only 1–3 years, tunnelwebs can live for over 10 years.

Black-headed jumping spider

Black-headed jumping spider & House hopper spider

There are between 50 and 100 species of jumping spider in New Zealand. Two that are often seen around the house and garden are the black-headed jumping spider and the smaller house hopper spider. Both are quite harmless and will jump onto an inquisitive finger. They have excellent eyesight, and can react very fast to possible prey within jumping range.

The black-headed jumping spider (1 cm long) will even react to its own reflection in a mirror, and posture aggressively. It can often be seen around cabbage trees and flax, and readily comes into houses.

The house hopper spider (5 mm long) also goes freely into houses to search for possible prey, though it's less obvious, because of its much smaller size and duller colouring.

Both spiders trail a fine 'safety line' of silk as they jump, so that should they miss their target, they can simply climb back up and try again.

House hopper spider

Cave spider

Cave spiders are some of the most ancient of all spiders, and the only ones protected by law. There are three species in New Zealand; the Nelson cave spider is the largest, with a leg span of around 15 cm.

The eggs are hung in a ball from the cave ceiling. When the spiderlings hatch, they often feast on each other, until only the half-dozen biggest and strongest are left from the original brood of 80 or so.

Once they are fully grown, these cave spiders are big enough to hunt and trap cave weta (page 87) for food.

ANIMALS • Spiders & Mites

Daddy-long-legs spider

Although this spider has venom glands, its jaws are too small to worry humans, so it is actually quite harmless. It catches its prey – such as small flies that become entangled in the web – by quickly and tightly wrapping it up in silken strands to restrain it, and then it sucks out the captive's body juices. This spider will 'vibrate' vigorously if it's disturbed.

The female spider can often be seen carrying a white ball of her eggs with her until the little spiderlings hatch. After they emerge, they sometimes hang upside down in a row, like a line of washing.

Water spider

The water spider is a true 'fisher' – it typically waits at the side of a slow stream, with front legs resting on or in the water, ready to pounce on passing prey such as insects and their larvae, or even small fish. Sometimes it will spread out, with all eight legs in the water, and it may even float gently along in the current. It can run across the water's surface, and 'dive' by walking around and down a partially submerged rock, taking a film of air with it to breathe. It can stay under for up to half an hour. Its body length is up to 2 cm.

Mites and their close relatives, the ticks, number about 30,000 species around the world. Most measure less than 1 mm in length. Some exist entirely on vegetation, or on decaying animal material, but most are parasitic on all sorts of animals – on land and in the sea – including insects, mammals, birds and reptiles. Many can pass serious diseases on to their hosts; and they can also be harmful pests in plant crops, and infest stored food.

Mites

There are thousands of species of mite in New Zealand. They come in a wide range of colours, including brown, red, blue and black. This group even includes the tiny mites that can live on human skin, in carpets and in our beds! They range in length from about 3 mm down to just over 0.5 mm. Most species are soft-bodied, to allow for swelling after taking in a host's blood.

95

ANIMALS • Tunicates

Also known as sea squirts, tunicates come in a great range of types and sizes. Some look like blobs of jelly attached to rocks and shells around the seashore, but larger species of these marine animals can take on different forms.

They can develop a primitive backbone, called a notochord, in the very young larval stage. Because of this, scientists group tunicates with the animals called chordates, which includes fish, birds, reptiles, amphibians and mammals (which, of course, includes ourselves).

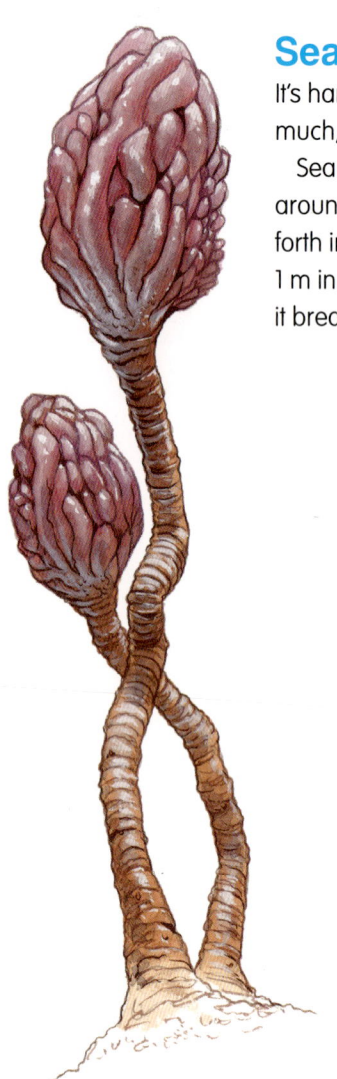

Sea tulip

It's hard to believe that this really is an animal, not a plant – and its name doesn't help much, either!

Sea tulips can be so numerous between low tide and deeper waters – especially around the South Island – that they form great underwater forests swaying back and forth in the currents. There are several species, and the largest can grow to well over 1 m in length. A sea tulip's siphons, through which it draws in and expels seawater as it breathes and feeds, are located in the main body at the top of the stalk.

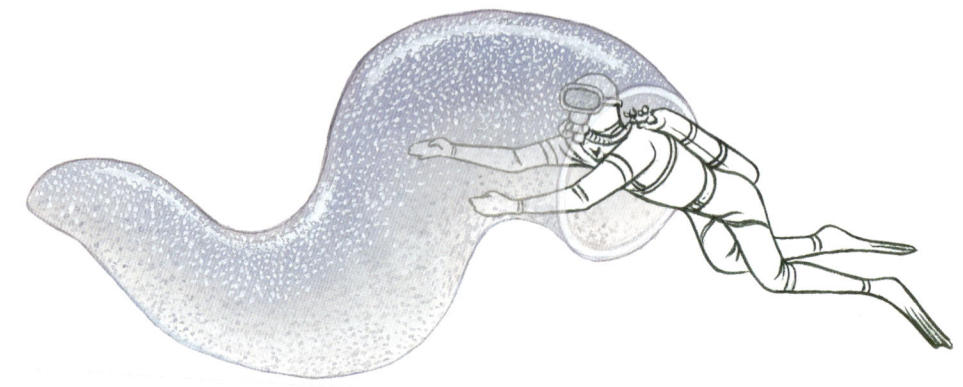

Fire salp

Some small tunicates, called salps, do not attach themselves to hard surfaces but swim free in the oceans. Some live singly, and others form colonies to create great jelly-like tubes, open at one end. The tiny individual animals work together to draw water in from the outside and expel it inside, so that the open-ended tube acts as a siphon to push the colony along. Some of these tubes, such as the fire salp, can reach several metres in length – wide enough for a diver to swim inside!

Sea squirt

These small creatures – usually just 1–2 cm across – come in a great variety of colours, textures and sizes. They can be seen as colourless blobs of jelly, wrinkled brown lumps and all shades of red and pink. They attach themselves to old shells, sponges or rocks. They have two siphons: one for drawing in water, which is sieved for food particles, and one for expelling the water again. If a sea squirt is given a slight squeeze, it will eject a jet of water from one of the siphons – hence its name.

ANIMALS • Fish

Fish were the very first animals with backbones and internal skeletons to appear, hundreds of millions of years ago. There are now over 24,000 known species around the world. Their size ranges from reef fish of just a few millimetres in length, to ocean giants of 14 m (and weighing 12 tonnes!).

There are three main fish groups: the jawless fish, which are the most primitive; the cartilaginous fish (such as rays, skates and sharks); and the bony fish, the most advanced group.

Most fish live either in salt or fresh water, but some can exist in both environments. A few species can even spend a considerable time out of water altogether.

The jawless fish – hagfish and lampreys – evolved some 500 million years ago, long before any other group of fish living today. They have no proper jaws, no developed fins, and have smooth, scaleless bodies. They also lack a true skeleton; instead, they have a simple backbone of cartilage – a flexible material that is not as hard as true bone. They feed by attaching themselves to host fish with their circular mouths, lined with rows of sharp teeth, and rasping away at the living tissue.

Hagfish & Lamprey

These creatures would certainly have to share the award for the least attractive fish in our waters.

The hagfish can reach 1 m in length. It is found in the seas all around the country, but is more common in cooler southern areas. The lamprey (kanakana) grows to around 60 cm in length and can be found in many streams and rivers when it comes in from the sea to spawn. A typical lamprey can consume about 1.4 kg of its host's blood and flesh during its lifetime.

Both fish have a good sense of smell and taste; but whereas the lamprey also has good vision, the hagfish is nearly blind.

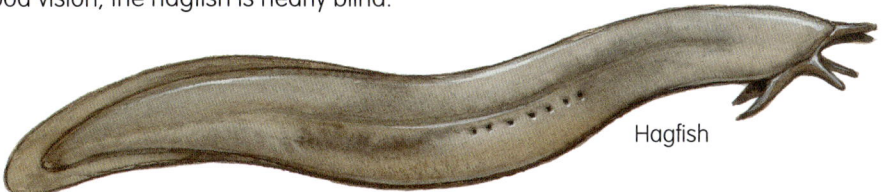

Hagfish

Lamprey

The cartilaginous fish have skeletons made of cartilage. Most have skin with hard, small scales that feel sandpapery. All are carnivorous and have specialised teeth that are continually replaced. This group includes sharks, rays and skates, and they total over 800 species around the world. Unlike most fish, they lack an internal swim bladder to regulate buoyancy, so must keep swimming to avoid sinking.

Rough skate

This the most common of the nine skate species in New Zealand waters. It is easily seen around the coast, gliding over the sand and mud seabed to hunt out small prey such as worms, crustaceans and small fish. It grows to a maximum of 1 m in length, and is named for the many horny prickles on its upper body.

Like other skates and rays, this fish swims in a 'flying' motion, using its wing-like body shape, and is capable of fast, sharp manoeuvres.

ANIMALS • Fish

Short-tailed stingray

This ray hunts for prey such as small fish, crabs and shellfish by searching through the sand and mud of the seabed. It crunches through heavier shells with its strong, fused teeth. But since its mouth is on the underside of its body, it never actually gets to see what it's eating!

In open water a stingray is not dangerous, but if taken by surprise in the shallows, it can lash out with its strong tail, which is armed with one or more sharp and poisonous barbs. These can cause considerable pain and damage to a predator, and are even deadly enough to kill juvenile orca (page 154) – the ray's main predator.

Some stingrays can reach 2–3 m in length, and they often hide half-buried in the seabed.

Eagle ray

The eagle ray lives in shallow waters around the North Island and the top of the South Island. It feeds by gliding low over the sandy seabed to search out crabs and shellfish, which it breaks open with its strong, chisel-like teeth. Some eagle rays use a 'dinner table' such as a rock or clear space on the seabed, where they carry their prey to break it up and eat it.

Eagle rays usually measure about 1–1.5 m across their fins, and their overall length can be as much as 2 m. As with stingrays, the barbs in the tail are quite sharp and carry a toxin.

Electric ray

Because of its ability to generate electric fields for defence and attack, it's thought that the electric ray can also use this facility to detect prey, such as shellfish, worms, crabs and fish, hidden under the sandy seabeds. Once close, the ray stuns or kills its victim with a strong discharge of electricity. It also uses this weapon to defend itself against sharks and large predators. The electricity is produced by special body organs that act rather like tiny batteries, storing the natural electricity generated by the movement of the fish's muscles.

The New Zealand electric ray grows to about 1 m in length, but some overseas species can reach twice this length and weigh up to 90 kg.

ANIMALS • Fish

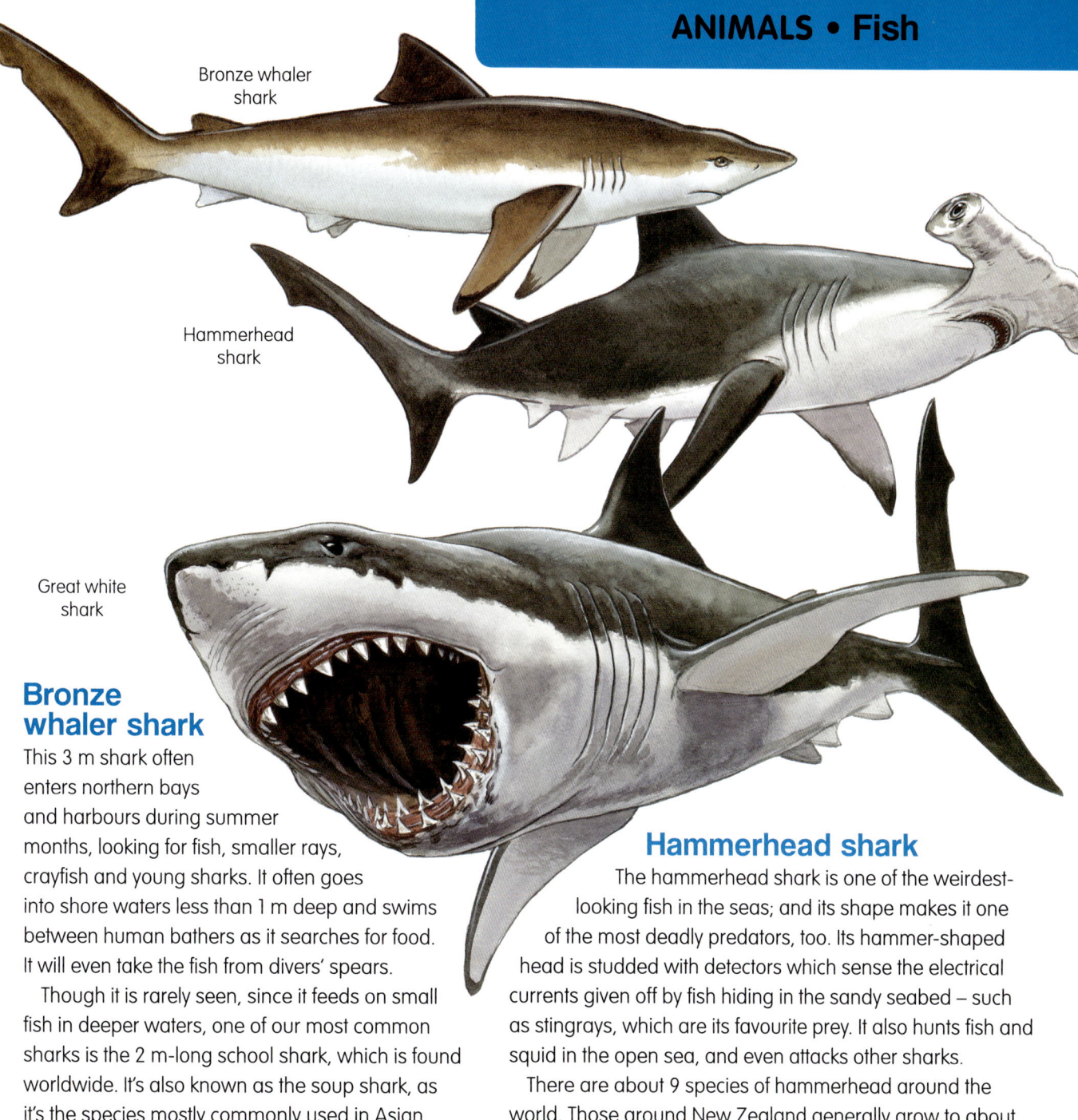

Bronze whaler shark

Hammerhead shark

Great white shark

Bronze whaler shark

This 3 m shark often enters northern bays and harbours during summer months, looking for fish, smaller rays, crayfish and young sharks. It often goes into shore waters less than 1 m deep and swims between human bathers as it searches for food. It will even take the fish from divers' spears.

Though it is rarely seen, since it feeds on small fish in deeper waters, one of our most common sharks is the 2 m-long school shark, which is found worldwide. It's also known as the soup shark, as it's the species mostly commonly used in Asian countries to make sharkfin soup!

The deep-dwelling pygmy shark is the smallest of all. It's just over 20 cm in length: about the width of this page!

Hammerhead shark

The hammerhead shark is one of the weirdest-looking fish in the seas; and its shape makes it one of the most deadly predators, too. Its hammer-shaped head is studded with detectors which sense the electrical currents given off by fish hiding in the sandy seabed – such as stingrays, which are its favourite prey. It also hunts fish and squid in the open sea, and even attacks other sharks.

There are about 9 species of hammerhead around the world. Those around New Zealand generally grow to about 3.5 m in length, though juveniles measuring about 1 m are more commonly seen. The largest hammerhead species can grow to 5 m and weigh well over 400 kg. These larger species can live for about 20–30 years.

Great white shark

The great white shark – or white pointer – is a regular visitor to our seas. It has excellent hearing, eyesight and sense of smell. Anything that moves in the water is a possible meal for this aggressive shark: other sharks and fish, dolphins, seals, squid, penguins and more. It will regularly dive as deep as 1200 m in search of prey.

The jaws are not fixed and hinged to the skull as in other animals; when this shark opens its mouth, powerful muscles thrust its jaws forward and wide to get a much bigger bite. The jaws are made of tougher material than the skeleton, which is why they can be preserved after death, while the rest of the softer skeleton decays quickly.

It grows to about 3–5 m, though some individuals can measure over 7 m, and weigh around 3 tonnes. Great whites can live for 30–40 years.

ANIMALS • Fish

Bony fish are the largest fish group of all, and are the most recently developed. Fossil records show that the first members evolved only some 160 million years ago. A typical bony fish has a gas-filled bladder within it, which allows it to control buoyancy. It has a lightweight but strong proper skeleton, which supports sometimes complex fin structures, for propulsion and precise manoeuvring.

The lateral line visible running down the sides of most fish is an area sensitive to movement and minute changes in water pressure. This allows the fish to sense its immediate environment, and to move efficiently when in large groups or shoals.

There are over 23,000 known species of bony fish around the world.

Long-finned eel

The long-finned eel and the short-finned eel spend most of their lives in freshwater habitats, but travel to the open sea to mate and spawn.

Once hatched, the young take about 2 years to reach New Zealand, by which time they are about 60 mm in length. These youngsters are known as elvers. They swim into the rivers in great numbers, and then make their way upstream. They are slow-growing fish, and it may take 30–40 years before they're ready to return to the sea.

The long-finned eel can grow to 1–2 m in length and weigh between 10 and 50 kg. The short-finned eel is usually about two-thirds the size of the long-finned eel and has a shorter fin along its back. It's also more a dull olive-green in colour.

These freshwater eels generally inhabit all sorts of water environments, and will even wriggle their way across wet ground to move from one stream to another. They are usually more active at night, when they swim about to hunt small animals such as snails, insects, larvae and small fish.

Moray eel

There are about 30 eel species living in our seas. Some of the largest are the moray and conger eels. These usually hide in small crevices and caves among reef rocks during the day, and emerge at night to hunt for small fish, crabs and shrimp.

At nearly 2 m in length, the mosaic moray is one of the most spectacular in appearance. Its skin patterning, which continues right inside its mouth, makes it hard to see against the reef background. Its near-transparent teeth are unusual because they are hinged. They can fold away if pushed back, but then lock in place when pushed forward by prey struggling in the eel's mouth.

The conger eel tends to be larger (over 2 m in length and weighing 20 kg) and is usually a plain grey-brown or grey-blue in colour. Despite its fearsome looks, the conger eel is not aggressive, though it will give a nasty bite if provoked.

ANIMALS • Fish

Giant kokopu

Koaro

Short-jawed kokopu

Banded kokopu

Inanga

Inanga whitebait

Whitebait

Whitebait isn't just one kind of fish, but a group name for the young of at least five freshwater fish species known as galaxiids. The young fish look much alike, but the adult forms are very different from one another. The largest of these is the giant kokopu, which can grow to over 50 cm in length. Three species are 25–30 cm in length: the koaro, short-jawed kokopu and banded kokopu. Smallest of all is the inanga, at just 80 mm.

Adults lay their eggs downriver, near the coast, and the hatched young are swept out to sea by the tides. After some months growing in the coastal waters, the young – by this time about 40–55 mm long – swim back into the rivers and streams. And here they are caught, as whitebait, by whitebaiters with their nets and traps. The young of the tiny inanga are usually the most plentiful of all these juvenile whitebait.

Galaxiids and their whitebait young are common at many locations around the country, but reach their greatest numbers along the West Coast of the South Island, where they are caught in their millions.

Fish that manage to make their way upstream choose different environments. The inanga and giant kokopu live in the slow and muddier waters of lowland marshes and waterways, while the other three species prefer the cleaner and faster waters of forest streams and rivers. These three fish will swim and clamber up steep and difficult waterfalls – even as high as 50 m – on their way to higher country.

All the galaxiids catch water insects for food, and they sometimes nuzzle into the mud or gravel for prey, or take food from the water's surface. Lifespans vary greatly – the tiny inanga usually lives for less than a year, while a giant kokopu may live for up to 20 years.

ANIMALS • Fish

Orange roughy

It's easy to see how this fish gets its name. There are several related species, and they are sometimes called sandpaper fish because of their rough body texture. They are usually about 20–40 cm in length and can live to an amazing old age – up to 150 years!

Orange roughy are found in various seas around the world and are a common catch in commercial fishing. They are a deep-sea fish, living at depths between 500 and 1700 m, where there is practically no light at all. But the orange roughy have no problem in finding food – they simply hunt down those small fish, squid and shrimps that have light-emitting organs on their bodies, making them easy to see in the gloom. Some scientists think that the special black lining to the orange roughy's mouth and stomach stops the light from eaten prey giving the roughy's presence away to other predators, such as larger fish, sharks and sperm whales, who all find the roughy a tasty treat.

John dory

With its great 'eye-spot' marking, it's almost impossible to mistake the John dory (or kuparu) for any other fish. It's common all around the world, and a favourite commercial catch. Its very flat body, about 40–60 cm long, enables it to approach its prey – nearly always other, smaller fish – quite closely without being detected. When within striking range, the John dory suddenly shoots its mouth out into a long tube-shape to snatch up the victim, which is often swallowed whole. Specially shaped jawbones enable it to extend its mouth in this way. The fish can change its colour patterns, too, to blend in with surroundings as it glides slowly along in search of prey.

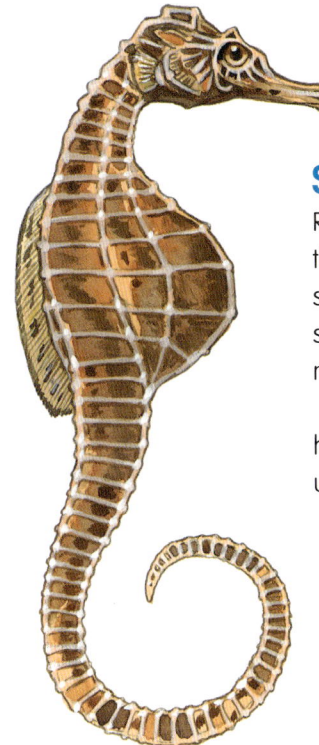

ANIMALS • Fish

Seahorse

Rock pools and shallow waters are home to quite a variety of small fish. One of the most interesting is the seahorse, which curls its tail around seaweed fronds to steady itself while it sucks up tiny animals from the water. To move, the seahorse simply uncurls its tail and swims slowly in its vertical position, nodding gently as it moves forward, just like a slow-motion horse.

The usual parenthood roles are reversed with this species: the female deposits her eggs in a special brood pouch on the male's abdomen, and he protects them until they hatch as miniature seahorses a month or so later.

With the tail uncurled, the seahorse can measure up to 25 cm in length.

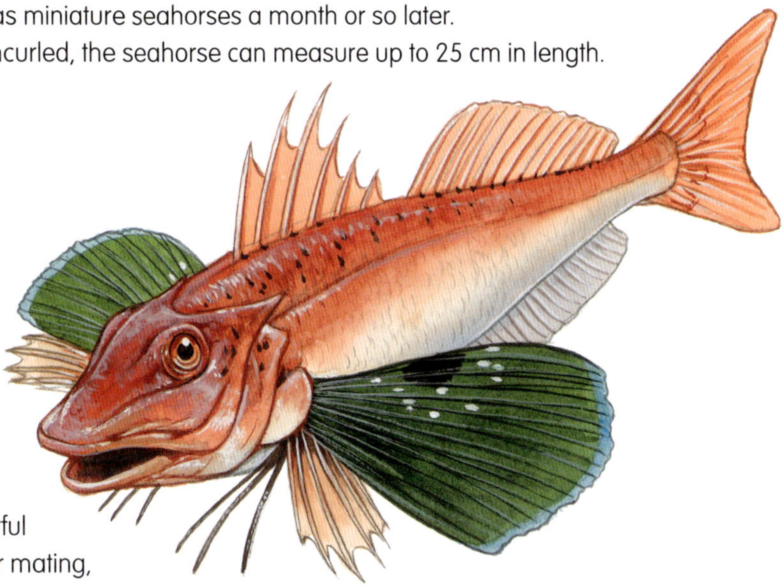

Red gurnard

The red gurnard uses the long spines on the front of its fins to poke around on the sandy seabed in search of worms, shellfish and crustaceans under the surface. On finding prey, the gurnard thrusts its bony snout into the sand to snatch it up. Its large and colourful fins can be spread wide to display to other gurnard for mating, or as a sudden 'flash' to frighten off predators.

The red gurnard is usually 25–40 cm in length. There are similar species found all around the world, though some are up to twice this size. It is a popular commercial fishing catch.

Fish are mostly silent creatures, but some species of gurnard elsewhere in the world can control the muscles around their swim bladder to produce deep grunting noises to keep in touch with one another.

Hapuku

The grim-looking hapuku is a member of a wide group of similar-looking fish commonly referred to as grouper. Hapuku can reach 1.8 m in length and weigh over 100 kg. Fish of this size may be 50 years old or more.

The hapuku feeds on crabs and small fish around the sea floor of reefs around 20–60 m deep. Although generally a leisurely swimmer, it can take off at great speed, with its powerful tail making an audible boom through the water at each beat.

The hapuku gets its name from its large body shape – puku means 'stomach' or 'belly'.

ANIMALS • Fish

Snapper
The snapper is common in waters around the North Island and upper parts of the South Island, though its numbers have fallen in recent years. It's a very robust fish, and not a fussy hunter; it will eat all sorts of small fish, crabs, sea urchins and worms. It has very well-developed teeth that are strong enough to crunch through the toughest of prey – even the shells of limpets and other shellfish.

Snapper are slow-growing fish that may live for 60 years or more; full-grown adults can reach over 1 m in length and weigh more than 20 kg. Most adult snapper are coloured a pinkish-grey with iridescent blue spots, though this fades with age to a darker, even-coloured grey.

Tarakihi
The tarakihi is one of our most important commercial fish catches. It usually grows to around 30–40 cm in length, though some 'old man' specimens can reach more than 60 cm and weigh more than 6 kg. Tarakihi feed by swimming head down over a silty or sandy sea floor, nuzzling out small animals that might be under the surface. The fish steadies itself in this position by angling its long pectoral fins downwards onto the sand, as a sort of tripod. The sand that gets 'vacuumed' up is filtered out through the fish's gills, and the small animals stay trapped in its mouth and throat to be crushed and eaten. These include worms, sea stars, sea urchins, shellfish and small crustaceans.

Lord Howe coralfish
This striking 20 cm-long fish is found in waters 10–30 m deep, where it nibbles at corals and other small animal colonies on the rocks. It has an elongated mouth, with lots of tiny brush-like teeth, and this helps it poke into cracks and crevices to catch up small worms and crustaceans.

Male and female pairs of coralfish usually bond for life, and make their home in a rocky cave or arch, where their striking markings can make them hard to see against the background of the colourful reef. If discovered, a coralfish can lock the spines on its fin upright, to deter predators from taking a bite.

ANIMALS • Fish

Sandager's wrasse

One of the most striking species, and most common around northern reefs, is Sandager's wrasse. This 45 cm-long fish can be a rather confusing creature, as it may change sex – from female to male – as it grows. The colour scheme changes, too. As a juvenile, the fish has yellow and orange stripes along its body; later, these break up into a more complicated pattern, until the final multicoloured scheme of the adult fish appears.

Sandager's wrasse has large, well defined teeth. It feeds on worms, crustaceans, shellfish and sea urchins on the sea floor, and will overturn small rocks and stones to get at any possible prey that might be hiding underneath. After dark, this fish often digs itself into the sand to remain hidden from any night-time predators.

Twister

There are more than 20 species of very small fish than can be seen in shallower coastal waters. Most are about 8–10 cm in length, and live for not more than 2–3 years. Most swim around the bottom of rock pools, and sometimes just rest on the bed, or hide at the sides and in crevices.

The 10 cm-long twister is one – it can be found in pools on all the zones of the shore, though it's more common lower down.

Mimic blenny

While most of these small fish eat tiny plants and animals such as crustaceans and the larvae of shellfish, the mimic blenny hovers patiently in the water until a larger fish swims within a metre or so, and then dashes in to nip off a small bit of flesh or a piece of fin. It will even swim with small groups of similar-sized but harmless fish, in order to sneak up on its bigger prey. It usually measures around 3–8 cm in length.

Variable triplefin

The variable triplefin is one of the most common of the smaller shore fish, and one of the largest. Though it's usually 10–12 cm in length, it can reach 20 cm in waters around the South Island. It's commonly found in the low-tide zone and below. The triplefin is large and sturdy enough to eat bigger prey, such as small crabs, shellfish and hermit crabs.

ANIMALS • Fish

Yellowfin tuna

Tuna are some of the fastest swimmers in the open seas, where they chase down and eat smaller fish and squid. The yellowfin tuna, which can be found in far northern waters in summer months, reaches speeds of up to 75 km per hour.

Fish are mostly cold-blooded animals, but many tuna can actually raise their body temperature slightly to make their swimming muscles work faster than those in other fish.

And tuna have another advantage; the swimming muscles of a 'normal' fish usually make up about 50–65 per cent of its weight, but for tuna they can account for 75 per cent or more. The yellowfin tuna can measure between 60 cm and 2 m in length.

Broadbill swordfish

The broadbill swordfish is typical of a group of large fish often referred to as 'game fish'. They're all keenly sought by anglers for their size and for the stiff contest they provide if hooked. Many will leap clear of the water, or 'tail-walk' frantically across the surface, in an effort to escape the line.

They have an upper snout that is elongated into a spear-like bill, and which may be slashed from side to side to kill prey – generally smaller fish and squid. The bill is sometimes used in a direct forward thrust for defence: large sharks have been found with a swordfish bill broken off in their side.

The broadbill swordfish can reach 5 m in length and weigh up to 650 kg. It is capable of swimming at almost 100 km per hour in short bursts.

Yellowbelly flounder

The yellowbelly flounder is a typical member of this strange-looking group of fishes. It begins its development from the egg normally, as a free-swimming juvenile fish. But it then goes through a stage where it begins to settle on its side on the seabed, and the eye on the lower side gradually moves to the upper surface. Some flounder species rest on their right side, but most – like the yellowbelly flounder – rest on their left side.

Flounder live partly buried in the sand or silt of the seabed, where they wait for passing prey, such as small crustaceans and small fish, which they catch by suddenly darting forward and upwards.

The yellowbelly can measure up to 50 cm in length.

ANIMALS • Fish

Black flounder
Though the black flounder can be found in coastal waters, it's most common in freshwater lakes and waterways all around the country. It feeds on crustaceans, insects, worms, small snails, and the organic material found in muddy lake beds.

The young flounder hatches from the egg and lives in the usual way as a free-swimming juvenile fish. But later it begins to settle on one side, and the eye on the lower side gradually moves to the upper surface of its body. Like most flounder in New Zealand waters, this fish rests on its left side, with its eyes on the right side.

Black flounder are usually 20–45 cm in length and weigh up to 2 kg.

Leatherjacket
The leatherjacket hardly ever seems to stop feeding, but nibbles away continuously with its sharp, small teeth on seaweeds, jellyfish, sea urchins, barnacles, sea squirts and especially sponges – even on the occasional scuba diver. Its body scales are reduced to horny points, which give the fish's body a rough, sandpapery feel. Leatherjackets can be seen in a wide range of colours, from grey, brown and green to near-white.

A very able but slow swimmer, the leatherjacket can move backwards as easily as it moves forwards. Its large dorsal spine can be erected and locked into position to deter predators.

Leatherjackets grow to around 35 cm in length and live for about 6 years.

Porcupine fish
This fish has a very good defence against predators: to eat it means certain injury and probable death. Its scales take the form of long, sharp spines, and if attacked it can inflate its body with water into a ball shape to make the spines stand out strongly. If a predator still tries for a bite, it will find that the spines and body tissues all contain a deadly poison.

The porcupine fish can grow to about 60 cm in length. It feeds on crabs, urchins and shellfish, which it breaks open with strong teeth that are fused together into sharp cutting shears – so sharp that the fish can easily bite off the ends of an inquisitive scuba diver's fingers.

ANIMALS • Fish

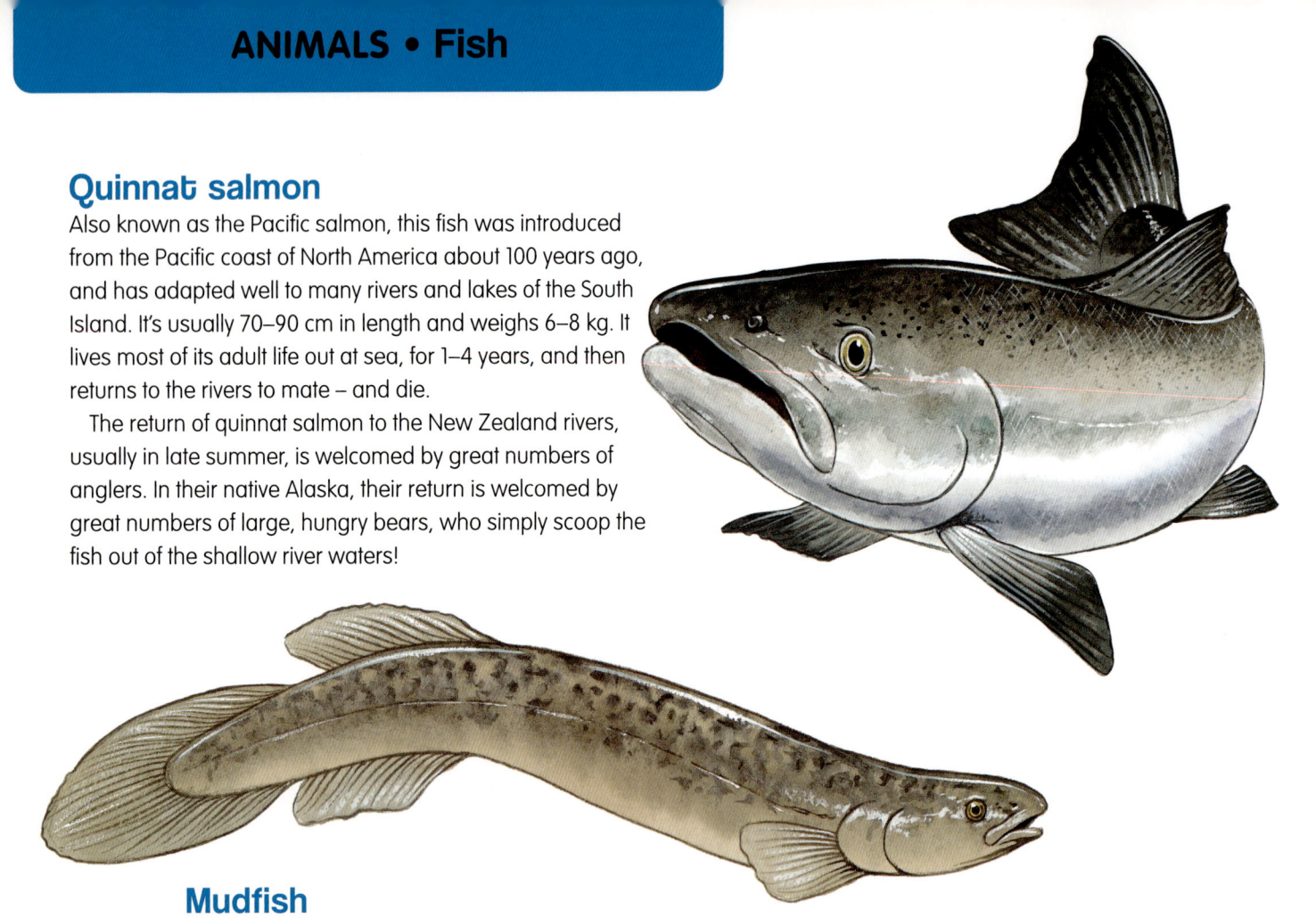

Quinnat salmon
Also known as the Pacific salmon, this fish was introduced from the Pacific coast of North America about 100 years ago, and has adapted well to many rivers and lakes of the South Island. It's usually 70–90 cm in length and weighs 6–8 kg. It lives most of its adult life out at sea, for 1–4 years, and then returns to the rivers to mate – and die.

The return of quinnat salmon to the New Zealand rivers, usually in late summer, is welcomed by great numbers of anglers. In their native Alaska, their return is welcomed by great numbers of large, hungry bears, who simply scoop the fish out of the shallow river waters!

Mudfish
The mudfish is a close relative of whitebait (page 101). There are three species of mudfish, all about 9–12 cm long.

They live in small swamps, bogs and muddy creeks, where they feed on small water insects and crustaceans. In turn, they are prey for many larger fish and eels.

In hot summers these watery places can dry up, but this doesn't harm the fish. They simply burrow down into the muddy bed to depths of 1 m or more. There they go into a state similar to hibernation – and can survive like this for up to 5 months. When water returns, they can instantly 'awaken' and dig their way out again.

Bully
Bullies are generally short, stocky fish about 7–15 cm long, though the giant bully can grow to 20 cm. They are found in streams, lakes and rivers, from coastal areas up into alpine regions.

They scour stony riverbeds for prey such as insect larvae and tiny crustaceans, and are capable of resting on rocks in fast-moving water by bracing their fins against the water pressure.

The male attracts a female by clearing all the dirt and algae from a small area of seabed. If the house-cleaning pleases the female, she lays her eggs in the chosen spot. The stickiness of the eggs helps to keep them anchored to the rocks in the rushing water. Once hatched, the young of most bully species migrate to the open sea, and then return when they are adults.

ANIMALS • Fish

Rainbow trout

Trout

Probably the most successful of all the introduced freshwater fish in New Zealand are trout. Two species were brought here in the late 1800s: the brown trout from Europe, and the rainbow trout from North America. Both are now quite common, especially the brown trout, which can be found in lakes and waterways throughout the country from the Coromandel Peninsula southwards. They look very similar, though the brown trout is plainer than its more colourful cousin.

Trout belong to the same family as salmon (opposite) and have a similar life history. Most species in this group migrate as young fish to the sea, where they develop and live for the greater part of their lives, then return to their home rivers to mate. Instead of this sea migration, some of the trout in New Zealand swim up lake tributary streams, and so remain in fresh water all their lives.

They feed on water insects, snails and crustaceans, and even on smaller fish. Trout will also rise to the water's surface to take flying insects, and this is often how anglers snare them on their lines.

Trout usually live for up to 4 years, weigh around 2.5 kg, and measure 50–60 cm in length – though some brown trout can reach well over twice this size.

ANIMALS • Amphibians

Amphibians are animals that spend part of their lives on land, and part of their lives in – or associated with – water. Invariably, the skin of amphibians is smooth, soft and unprotected by hair or scales. The skin is permeable to water, and although many amphibians have glands which keep the skin moist, they will 'dry out' if not in water or a damp environment. Many can breathe through their skin, which is often toxic to some degree.

Amphibians were the first true land animals, and appeared some 370 million years ago. They can claim several other 'firsts': they were the first four-legged creatures (quadrupeds), the first to evolve eyelids (to enable moistening of the eye, in air), and had the first proper tongues, which allowed food to be moistened and broken before swallowing.

There have been many amphibian forms in the past, small and large, but today the principal members of this group are newts and frogs. There are about 5000 species around the world.

New Zealand is home to several frog species, of which three are natives.

Archey's frog

Hamilton's frog

Hochstetter's frog

Archey's frog, Hamilton's frog & Hochstetter's frog

These three native species are quite unlike other frogs. They don't croak in the traditional way, but instead make a chirping noise if disturbed or handled. The life cycle is unusual, too. The female lays her large eggs usually on muddy ground under rocks and logs. The young pass through their tadpole stage while still within the egg, and then hatch out as tiny froglets; most other frog species have a free-living tadpole stage.

Archey's frog is the smallest, at around 4 cm in length. It's found around the Coromandel Peninsula and other North Island sites, in damp ground conditions.

Hamilton's frog is the largest of the three, at nearly 5 cm. It's found in Marlborough, and on a few offshore islands.

Hochstetter's frog is the most common of the three native species, and is the only one to be found near or in freshwater sites. Unlike its two relatives, it has webbing between the toes on its hind feet. It's mostly active at night, when it hunts freshwater crustaceans and insects. During the day, it shelters under stones or in damp ground crevices, in various locations in the upper North Island. It measures about 45–47 mm in length.

ANIMALS • Amphibians

Southern bell frog

The southern bell frog was introduced from Tasmania in the 1860s and is now very common in all kinds of freshwater sites throughout the country. It is also known as the golden bell frog, green frog or common frog. It usually measures 65–92 mm in body length, and the tadpoles can be even longer.

It comes out mostly at night to feed on aquatic insects and crustaceans, though it is sometimes seen resting and sunbathing on water plants in the daytime. Its call, a series of short harsh croaks, can often be heard on summer days.

The southern bell frog can be easily confused with another species from Australia, the green frog, which is now common throughout the North Island. This species is about two-thirds the size of its cousin and is similar in colouring, though slightly duller and less 'knobbly' in appearance.

Whistling frog

Southern bell frog

Whistling frog

The whistling frog was introduced into Westland from Tasmania in 1875, and is now found in many parts of the South Island and the lower North Island. It's a very adaptable animal and likes all types of water environments and situations from coastal regions up into alpine zones. It will often wander far away from water, but always returns to mate and lay eggs.

Similar in size to Hochstetter's frog, the whistling frog will eat just about anything smaller than itself, including insects, crustaceans, and even garden snails. It's mostly active at night, when it climbs trees, or explores the vegetation and the ground for prey, but will sometimes come out in the daytime just to bask in the sun. It can change its general skin colouring – browns, greys and olive-greens – to blend in with the surroundings.

It doesn't actually whistle; its call is a series of high-pitched *creee* chirrups.

ANIMALS • Reptiles

Reptiles evolved from amphibians about 340 million years ago. They have tougher, waterproof skin which is always scaly or horny. A reptile's legs support the body from the sides, rather than from underneath as with birds and mammals. This sprawled posture gives them a very distinctive side-to-side 'waddling' gait when they walk or run. Their eggs are better developed than amphibians' eggs, so they do not need moisture. These and other factors mean that reptiles are not reliant on wet or damp environments, as the amphibians are.

Some reptiles, however, such as crocodiles and turtles, have chosen to return to the water. Other main members of this group include tortoises, lizards, alligators and snakes. Past members include giant sea-dwelling predators and flying reptiles, and – most famously – the dinosaurs that existed many millions of years ago.

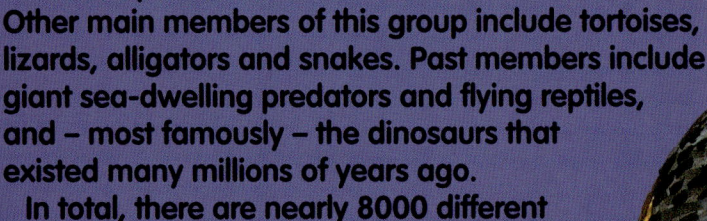

In total, there are nearly 8000 different species of reptile around the world today.

Yellow-bellied sea snake

Sea snakes don't live near New Zealand, but stragglers do appear in our waters from time to time – such as the yellow-bellied sea snake. This species is found in tropical waters all around the world. It reaches about 1 m in length and is quite dangerous.

Snakes such as this are usually from tropical reefs in northern Australian seas, where they prey on fish and eels. As a group, sea snakes are far more venomous than their cousins on the land. Some have a bite so poisonous that there is no known antivenom.

Sea snakes have special adaptations for a life at sea: their tail and much of their body is usually flattened so it can be used as a strong paddle for swimming. Their lungs are larger and longer than those of land snakes, allowing them to stay underwater for 2–3 hours at a time. The nostrils have a special scale-flap which automatically closes when the sea snake dives.

ANIMALS • Reptiles

Green turtle

Marine turtles are not very common visitors to New Zealand waters, but at least four species appear from time to time. The hawksbill and loggerhead turtles measure around 70–100 cm in length. Both feed on shellfish and crabs around reefs and rocky outcrops, and the hawksbill will also dine on sponges, jellyfish and seaweeds.

The other turtles are much larger. The green turtle can grow to 1.3 m in length and weigh around 300 kg. It's probably the most common of all the marine turtles and lives in tropical and subtropical seas all around the world. Juveniles eat crabs, molluscs, jellyfish and sponges, but as they grow they become near-vegetarian and prefer sea grasses, mangrove roots and leaves.

'Green' has nothing to do with the colour of the shell, but refers to the fact that the fat of the turtle's meat gives a green colour to green turtle soup!

Green turtle

Leatherback turtle

Leatherback turtle

The leatherback is the largest of all the marine turtles – it can reach 1.5 m in length and weigh up to 800 kg. It lacks the usual hard, horny-plated back of other marine turtles, and instead has a ridged back that feels like hard rubber or leather.

Leatherbacks feed mostly on jellyfish near the sea's surface, but can dive to depths of up to 1 km in search of prey. On deep dives they can hold their breath for up to half an hour. Like all turtles, the leatherback has no teeth, but instead relies on its sharp beak to catch prey and to crop sea plants. The throat is lined with lots of small, backward-pointing nodes or spines, which prevent prey from slipping back out again.

All marine turtles must return to the land to lay eggs. These are usually buried in the sands of remote beaches, but eggs and the hatched young are still prey for birds and other animals.

ANIMALS • Reptiles

New Zealand is home to over 40 species of gecko – a form of lizard. All have a grainy, loose skin. They have fixed eyelids, which means that they cannot blink and must clean their eyes with a flick of the tongue. Most gecko species around the world lay eggs, but New Zealand species give birth to live young. It's thought that many can live for up to 30–40 years. Green geckos are active by day, while those coloured grey-brown are mostly active by night. Most geckos feed on insects, spiders and small fruits.

   Geckos are the only lizards capable of producing a full range of vocal sounds; the name actually comes from the *gek-o* **call of a large Asian species. In some places around the world they are known simply as 'chit-chat lizards'.**

Gray's gecko
Most geckos prefer drier habitats, but a few can be found in wetlands. One of these is Gray's gecko, which lives around upper Northland and measures about 9.5 cm in body length (not including the tail). Instead of scurrying away if disturbed, this gecko will often 'bark' and lunge at the intruder, with mouth wide open to display its red tongue against its deep blue lower mouth. It is typical in appearance to the many species of green and green-patterned geckos around the country.

Forest gecko
This gecko lives in forests of the upper North Island and parts of the upper South Island. Its colourings and complicated body markings can make it very hard to see. Its body length can measure up to 9.5 cm. The mouth and tongue are usually in shades of bright orange and yellow. Though most brown and grey-brown gecko species are active in the night-time, the forest gecko can be seen in daylight, too.

   The smallest gecko in New Zealand is the pygmy gecko, found in the high grasslands and rocks of the Rangitata Gorge in the Canterbury foothills. Its body length is just 4 cm, which means it's barely 8 cm from nose to tail-tip.

Duvaucel's gecko
This gecko is the largest of all the New Zealand species, at over 16 cm in body length. It was once common throughout much of the country, but it was easy prey for rats and other introduced predators, despite being a large and robust lizard, and is now found only on a few offshore islands. It can live for 40 years or more. Its inner mouth and tongue are in shades of pink. Though mostly active by night, it will also forage on the forest floor in the afternoon, for insects and other small prey.

   The largest gecko ever found in New Zealand, and in the world, was the now-extinct kawekaweau. This giant measured 37 cm in body length, or 62 cm including the tail.

ANIMALS • Reptiles

As well as being much smoother-scaled, skinks are generally smaller than geckos – and they can blink, too. New Zealand is home to around 50 species.

Most species of skink and gecko can shed their tails to escape predators. The tail continues to twitch and writhe to distract the attacker while the lizard runs off. Although the tail can be regrown, it is always a little smaller than the original, and slightly different in pattern and colour.

Lizards such as skinks and geckos are the most successful group of all the reptiles. They first appeared around 300 million years ago, with little change in their appearance over that time. They now number about 4500 species around the world, of which nearly 2000 are skinks.

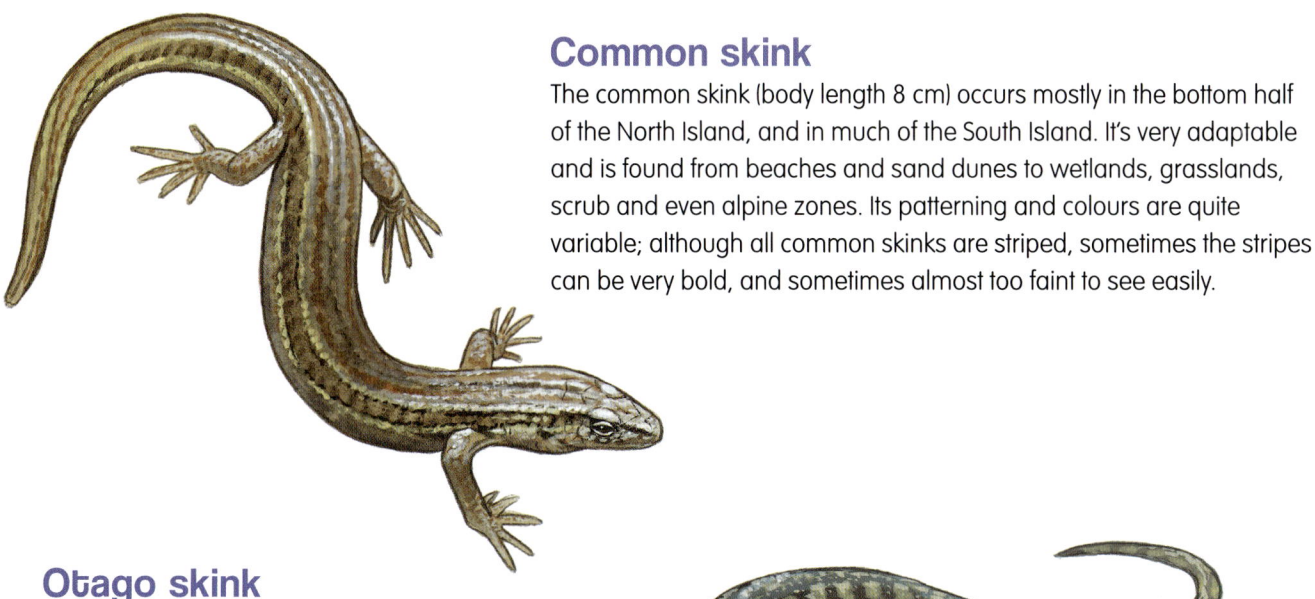

Common skink

The common skink (body length 8 cm) occurs mostly in the bottom half of the North Island, and in much of the South Island. It's very adaptable and is found from beaches and sand dunes to wetlands, grasslands, scrub and even alpine zones. Its patterning and colours are quite variable; although all common skinks are striped, sometimes the stripes can be very bold, and sometimes almost too faint to see easily.

Otago skink

This very strikingly marked species is found in various locations in . . . Otago! It favours rocky places in tussock and shrublands. It can measure up to 13 cm in body length and, with its long tail, 30 cm or more in overall length. As with many skinks, it likes to sunbathe on exposed rocks, between jaunts into the vegetation to hunt out insects, spiders and small fruits. It can live for up to 40 years.

This skink can also be found in family groups, with several generations living together.

Diving skink

This is the only native New Zealand skink to lay eggs, instead of giving birth to live young. It's also known as Suter's skink, or – yes, you guessed it – the egg-laying skink. It lives around rocky and stony shores in the upper North Island, and on many islands in the north. It's mostly active in the evenings and at night, but can be seen basking in the sun on warm rocks in the daytime. It forages around the shore and in rock pools for crustaceans and insects, and is a good swimmer. It measures around 12 cm in body length.

ANIMALS • Reptiles

Tuatara

Tuatara come from a very ancient line of reptiles indeed, and are unique to New Zealand. They have no close relatives anywhere in the living world. Reptiles are divided into just four groups: snakes and lizards, crocodiles and alligators, turtles and tortoises, and tuatara.

Tuatara have remained practically unchanged for some 200 million years. They managed to survive the mass extinctions that saw the end of the dinosaurs, and they've also weathered extremes of climates and environments – such as large and small ice ages and hot, tropical periods. The new, introduced predators of the last few hundred years have taken their toll, though – rats, dogs, pigs and so on have reduced tuatara to a tiny fraction of their once nationwide population. Tuatara are now mostly confined to several offshore islands around the country. Tuatara still number in many thousands, but a second species – Gunther's tuatara – which is very similar in size, colouration and habits, numbers only a few hundred individuals.

Tuatara have small teeth, arranged to be very efficient. They have one row on the lower jaw, and one on the upper jaw, and a third row in the roof of the mouth. The bottom row can interlock with the upper two in a shearing motion, so a tuatara's bite is certainly far worse than its bark – which is actually more like a squeaky croak.

Like geckos and skinks, the tuatara can shed its tail to confuse a possible predator, and then regrow it again. Tuatara are often seen with half-grown or misshapen tails and body scars from bites; many of these are the result of territorial fights with other males.

ANIMALS • Reptiles

Tuatara live in deep, long burrows – sometimes shared with a seabird, such as a sooty shearwater (page 118) – and come out at sunset to catch a passing skink or gecko, a spider, or insects such as weta and beetles. If particularly hungry, the tuatara may even take the eggs or chicks of its seabird flatmate. Although tuatara are essentially nocturnal, they will sometimes come to the burrow entrance in the daytime to bask in the sun.

The ridge of spines running along the tuatara's head, neck and tail are not rigid, but soft – the Maori name of tuatara means 'spiny-back' or 'peaks on the back'.

Male tuatara are usually much bigger than females. Though an average male weighs around 500 g, some older specimens can weigh well over 1 kg. Body length can be around 28 cm, and with the tail, large tuatara can exceed 60 cm in total length.

The female lays eggs only about once every 4 years or so, and the clutch of between 5 and 15 eggs, each 3 cm long, is buried in a nesting spot in the burrow. They take a year or more to incubate, and the resulting hatchlings can take about 12–13 years to reach maturity. Tuatara can live for 60–100 years, or even longer.

ANIMALS • Birds

Primitive birds first evolved from reptiles some 150 million years ago. These developed and diversified until direct ancestors of modern bird types were identifiable in fossil records by around 100 million years ago. Today, there are about 9000 species of birds around the world.

Though many other animal species are capable of flight, only birds have developed this capability to the highest level. They have lightweight but strong skeletons, feathered bodies and wings, and excellent vision.

Partly because of the lack of ground-dwelling mammals, and the number of flightless birds that evolved to occupy this ecological niche – a circumstance unique in the world – New Zealand has long been dubbed 'the land of birds'.

Royal albatross

The albatross is a member of a group of seabirds called 'tube-noses' because of the special tubed nostrils above the bill, which help to remove the salt from all the water that the bird takes in when catching surface fish and squid.

Albatrosses can spend months or even years at sea, before returning to land. Most have regular circuits that they follow around the southern oceans, as they glide and soar in their search for food. A single journey can cover 5000 km.

The royal albatross is one of the largest flying birds in the world, with a wingspan of over 3 m. It can weigh up to 9 kg and live for around 60 years. Although it can be seen all around New Zealand coasts, Taiaroa Head on the Otago Peninsula is the albatross's only mainland breeding site.

Sooty shearwater

There are many shearwater species all around our islands. They are mostly dark grey birds, though some have pale or near-white underwings and bodies. One of the most common is the sooty shearwater, also known as the muttonbird or titi. These birds live, breed and travel throughout New Zealand's seas and beyond, and probably have a population of many millions. They feed by diving steeply into the water to swim and catch small fish, squid and crustaceans. Like many of our seabirds and land birds, the sooty shearwater is a fully protected species, though a traditional Maori 'harvesting' of young birds is permitted each year. They live for about 15–20 years, and their body length is around 44 cm.

ANIMALS • Birds

White-faced storm petrel
This is one of the smallest of more than 20 species of petrel living around New Zealand's seas. Some can be nearly the size of the smaller albatrosses, but this petrel is only about 20 cm long – around the size of a blackbird – and weighs just 45 g. It can be seen in small flocks around our coasts, especially in northern waters. It has a very obvious 'fluttering', erratic flight, and often flits up and down near the water, with its feet dangling, while it searches for surface-dwelling fish and small crustaceans. During the winter months, and after breeding, these little birds will travel all the way to the coast of Chile and Peru in South America to spend some time in warmer climates.

Blue penguin
Penguins are found only in the waters of the southern hemisphere, and many different species breed and live around New Zealand and its southern islands. These birds long ago lost the ability to fly. Instead, their wings have developed into very efficient 'flippers' that allow them to swim through the water – often at great speed – to chase their prey.

The blue penguin or korora is the most common species in New Zealand waters, and is also the smallest at just 30–40 cm tall and around 1 kg in weight. It makes nests and raises chicks in all sorts of situations around our coasts: under houses, in the coastal bush, among rocks and on cliff ledges. It hunts for fish, squid and octopus, and can dive to depths of around 70 m. It can live for around 20 years.

Fiordland crested penguin
The Fiordland crested penguin or tawaki is a relatively rare species, with a population similar to the yellow-eyed penguin (next page). It's also a mainland shore-dweller – it usually nests in holes under tree trunks, or in rock crevices and caves, around the coasts of the lower South Island, especially Fiordland.

An adult stands around 60 cm high, weighs about 4 kg, and hunts for fish, octopus and squid in the southern oceans.

Many other penguin species breed and live around our southernmost islands, including the Adélie, chinstrap, rockhopper, erect-crested, Snares crested and emperor penguins.

ANIMALS • Birds

Yellow-eyed penguin

The yellow-eyed penguin or hoiho is found only in New Zealand waters. It's one of the rarest of all penguins, with a probable total population of some 5000 birds. At around 65 cm, it stands more than twice the height of the little blue penguin. It, too, nests on the mainland – mostly around Banks Peninsula, and on the coasts of Otago, Southland and Stewart Island. It is also found on several small, southern offshore islands.

Just like the blue penguin, this bird likes to come ashore regularly to roost and nest in vegetation and in hollows in the ground. These are often up to a kilometre or more inland. Hoiho do not nest in colonies, but make well separated nests, out of sight of other penguins. Nesting on land this way can make the eggs and the chicks vulnerable to predators such as ferrets, stoats, rats and cats, so various local and government bodies have introduced strict predator control measures to help ensure the penguins' survival.

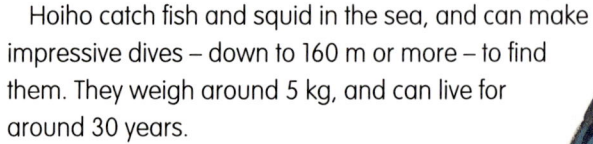

Hoiho catch fish and squid in the sea, and can make impressive dives – down to 160 m or more – to find them. They weigh around 5 kg, and can live for around 30 years.

ANIMALS • Birds

Australasian gannet
Famous breeding colonies of these birds can be visited at Muriwai (Auckland's west coast), Cape Kidnappers (Hawke Bay) and at Farewell Spit (the northern tip of the South Island). The very noisy colonies are a mass of close-packed, bowl-shaped nests made from droppings and seaweed.

The gannet hunts for food by making a shallow dive into the water for surface fish or squid. Often, it makes a high dive into the sea from 20 or 30 m, and can plunge into the water at speeds up to 145 km an hour. It can swim under the water to a depth of around 8 m to catch small fish such as anchovies, mullet, pilchards and small squid.

These gannets are around 30 cm in length and can live for up to 30 years.

Pied shag
One of the most common of the 12 species of shag in New Zealand, the pied shag or karuhiruhi makes its nest in trees around estuaries, shorelines and lakes in most of the country. The trees can suffer a great deal from the shags' heavy landings, sprawling nests and even the large amounts of shag droppings.

Shags dive to catch crayfish, mullet, eels, flounder and other fish, and can stay underwater for around 30 seconds. Afterwards they will perch on a rock with their wings outspread to dry out, as their feathers lack any waterproof oils.

The pied shag measures about 80 cm in length, and can live for about 20 years.

Black shag

Little shag & Black shag
These two shags are quite at home around inland waterways and lakes, and are common throughout the country. Both species make bulky, untidy nests in trees near their favoured waters, where they dive to search for fish, eels and freshwater crayfish, or to catch frogs. After several dives they must find a place to stand with their wings outspread to dry them off.

The little shag, or kawau paka, is about 56 cm in length and weighs around 700 g. The black shag, or kawau pu, is longer at nearly 90 cm and more than three times heavier.

Little shag

ANIMALS • Birds

White heron

The white heron or kotuku can be seen near the coast around much of the country, though it's quite a rare bird, with fewer than 200 individuals. It is by far the largest of all the heron species in New Zealand. Its overall length can be around 90 cm, and it can weigh close to 1 kg.

This heron nests in trees. It likes to hunt for food in swamps, wetlands and estuaries in various coasts around the country, especially on the West Coast of the South Island, and north of the Waikato. It will stand motionless or walk very carefully and quietly until it sees its prey – such as fish, frogs, mice and insects – and then lunge at it with its large bill. It is so fast in its strike that it can even take small birds such as the silvereye and the kingfisher.

The long white feathers of this bird were popular with Maori and early Europeans for decorations and hats. Because of the demand, the populations of this heron reduced rapidly, and in 1885 it was given legal protection to prevent further hunting.

Royal spoonbill

The royal spoonbill also builds its nest in waterside trees, or on raised islands, and feeds in similar situations to the white heron. This bird is slightly shorter than the white heron, but nearly twice its weight. It sweeps its unusual bill back and forth in shallow estuary waters to catch small crustaceans, insects, fish and frogs.

The royal spoonbill is originally from Australia. It began visiting New Zealand in the 1860s, but it was not until the 1940s that a breeding colony was established at the Okarito Lagoon in Westland. This is also where the white heron has its main nesting site.

ANIMALS • Birds

White-faced heron

The white-faced heron, also known as matuku moana, is the most common of all the heron species in New Zealand. It became established here from Australia in the 1940s and has now spread throughout the country, turning up around all kinds of coasts, in farmlands and pastures, wetlands, estuaries and even sewage treatment ponds. It will even appear in parks and gardens close to the coast. Its overall length is around 67 cm, and it can live for around 8–12 years.

This heron often finds food by standing in shallow water or on wet ground and raking the ground several times to stir up any small fish or other prey such as worms, mice and insects. It constructs flimsy, straggly nests of sticks in larger coastal trees, such as pohutukawa and macrocarpa.

White-faced heron

Reef heron

Reef heron

The reef heron is not very common, but can be seen from time to time along most rocky shorelines around the North Island. It can weigh around 400 g, with a length of 66 cm, and it can live for about 14 years.

The reef heron carefully stalks the water's edge to seek out fish, shellfish and crabs. It often holds up one wing as it walks, to shade the water and to cut out reflections. Because it always feeds near the water's edge at low tide, it can be seen out foraging at different times of the day – or even at night. It's rare to see this bird in freshwater locations.

It usually builds a nest of sticks and grasses inside caves or rock crevices, and even between the roots of trees in secluded situations. The nest is not abandoned after the chicks have hatched, but is maintained and added to each year.

Some reef herons will even enter colonies of other birds, such as terns, and steal food intended for chicks.

The general Maori name for herons is matuku, and the reef heron is known as matuku tai.

ANIMALS • Birds

Australasian bittern
This bird feeds mostly at night, tramping through the reeds of swamps and marshes to catch insects and freshwater crayfish. It will take bigger prey too, such as fish, eels, frogs and rats.

If threatened, the bittern 'freezes' with its bill pointed up in the air, so that its patterned feathers blend in with the surrounding reeds. Its call of *boom* can be heard more than 1 km away.

Bitterns are mostly solitary birds, and if a male strays into another's territory, they will fight and stab at each other with their heavy bills.

Bitterns can measure over 70 cm in length, weigh up to 1.4 kg, and live for 10–15 years.

Australasian crested grebe
This bird is found only on South Island lakes and waterways. It rarely leaves the water, and builds a floating nest that is attached to standing reeds. Chicks are often carried on a parent's back until they're able to fend for themselves. The grebe can make long dives – sometimes for up to a minute – in search of prey such as insects and fish.

The crested grebe can weigh around 1 kg and measure 50 cm in length. It earns its name from the ruff of feathers around its neck and the crest on its head. These play a part in the bird's impressive courting dance, which helps it attract a mate. Two grebes face each other in a display of head-bobbing, shaking and nodding, and then take off together in a near-frantic 'run' across the water's surface.

New Zealand dabchick
Closely related to the Australasian crested grebe, this small bird measures just 29 cm from bill-tip to tail-tip, and weighs about 250 g. It's not very common, but can be seen on lakes throughout the North Island. It spends all of its time on the water, only coming 'ashore' when returning to its nest, which is usually made from water plants and attached to standing reeds in the water.

Its lobed feet make it an efficient diver and swimmer, but a very awkward walker! During dives that can last 20–30 seconds, the dabchick hunts for its prey of insects, water snails, freshwater crayfish and small fish. Chicks are able to paddle and dive very soon after hatching – though they often ride on a parent's back.

ANIMALS • Birds

Mute swan

Mute swan & Black swan

These two swans are probably the easiest of all our freshwater birds to identify. Both were introduced into New Zealand in the 1860s. The black swan was brought here from Australia, and the mute swan from Europe. The mute swan is the slightly larger of the two species – it often weighs 10–12 kg, with a length of over 1.5 m. The black swan usually weighs much less, at around 5–6 kg.

The black swan is found on all sorts of lakes and ponds throughout New Zealand, and even in parks and farmland. The mute swan is less common, keeping to a small number of lake sites around the country. Both feed on underwater plants and waterbank vegetation. Mute swans will also eat crustaceans, insects and small fish, and even the occasional frog.

Both species can live for nearly 30 years, and they mate for life. A male swan is called a cob, and the female is called a pen. Pairs build a huge mound of reeds and other vegetation, sometimes as large as 1 m across, to raise their young.

Despite its name, the mute swan may *hiss*, *snort*, *whistle* and *honk* quite loudly! The black swan can also give a loud bugle or trumpet call.

Black swan

Canada goose

Introduced here from North America during the early twentieth century, probably for hunters to shoot, the Canada goose has quickly adapted to life in New Zealand. It has become quite widespread, especially in South Island high-country lakes. Many of these geese will move to lower-country lakes in the winter.

Canada geese eat water plants, and they like to eat grass, too. This is a problem for farmers, as large flocks – sometimes 2000 birds or more – will descend to graze on pasture lands and grain crops.

The Canada goose can measure up to 1 m in length, weigh well over 5 kg, and live for over 30 years. Its call is a distinctive *honk-a-honk*.

ANIMALS • Birds

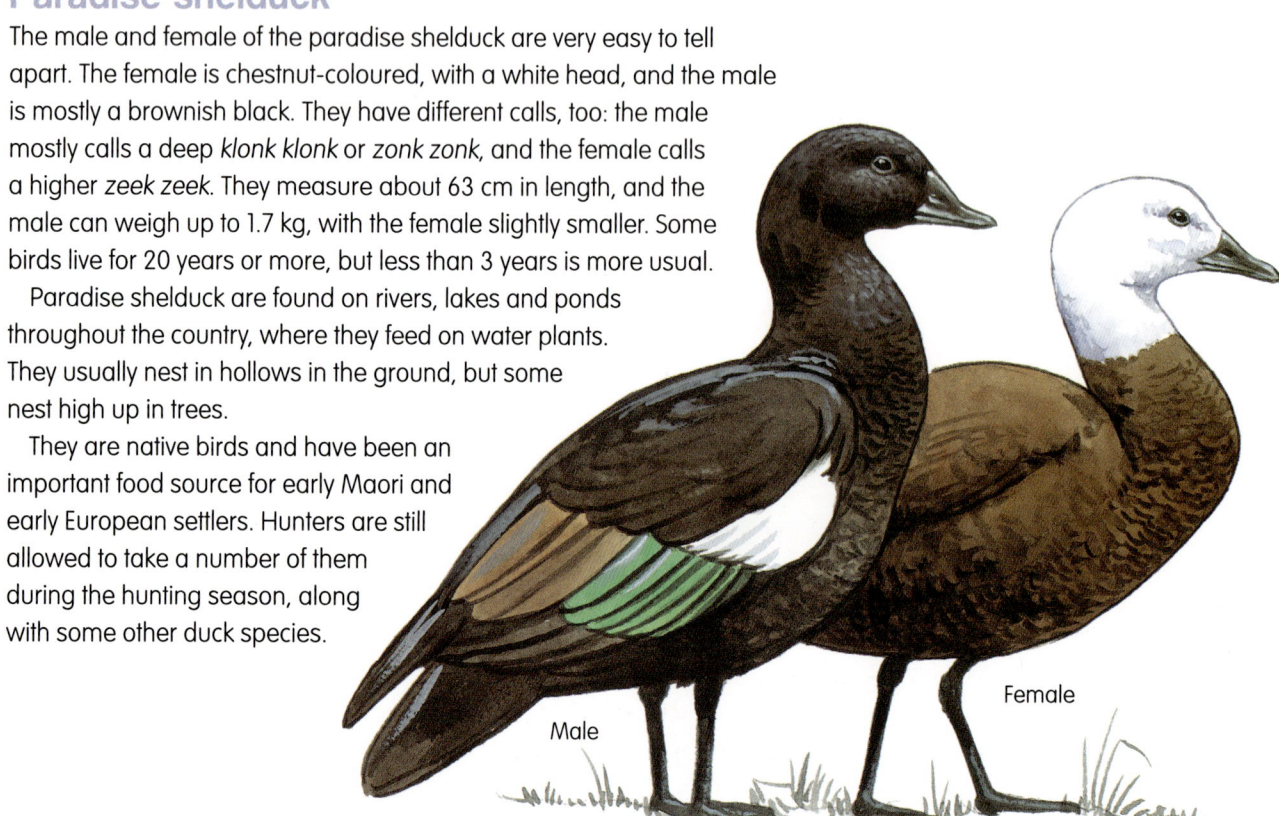

Blue duck

The blue duck lives in and around the fast, turbulent mountain rivers of central and western regions of the South Island and the central North Island. It takes water insects and their larvae by scraping them off the river rocks with its bill, the end of which is protected by a special tip of soft, black skin.

A pair of blue ducks will claim a 1 km-long stretch of river as their own territory, and retain it for most of their lives. Intruders are vigorously chased off.

When chicks are born, they already have large feet to help them adapt quickly to life in and around the rushing waters of mountain rivers.

The Maori name for this duck is whio, which comes from the male's soft, whistling call of *whee-oh*. The female duck just says *craak*.

The blue duck usually measures about 53 cm in length and weighs up to 900 g. It can live for about 13 years.

Paradise shelduck

The male and female of the paradise shelduck are very easy to tell apart. The female is chestnut-coloured, with a white head, and the male is mostly a brownish black. They have different calls, too: the male mostly calls a deep *klonk klonk* or *zonk zonk*, and the female calls a higher *zeek zeek*. They measure about 63 cm in length, and the male can weigh up to 1.7 kg, with the female slightly smaller. Some birds live for 20 years or more, but less than 3 years is more usual.

Paradise shelduck are found on rivers, lakes and ponds throughout the country, where they feed on water plants. They usually nest in hollows in the ground, but some nest high up in trees.

They are native birds and have been an important food source for early Maori and early European settlers. Hunters are still allowed to take a number of them during the hunting season, along with some other duck species.

Male

Female

ANIMALS • Birds

Mallard

The mallard was first introduced into New Zealand from Europe in 1867 and has now become the most common duck in the country. It's easy to spot in parks, estuaries, rivers and farms, and often becomes familiar with humans and tame enough to be fed by hand.

In places where these ducks are used to getting handouts, they will follow visitors in a quacking bunch and peck at ankles until they get fed. Their usual food consists of insects, freshwater snails, seeds and water plants. They can weigh well over 1 kg and measure around 58 cm in length.

Some mallards can live up to 26 years or so, but most live only for a couple of years.

Female

Male

Grey duck

The grey duck, or parera, used to be the most common duck in New Zealand, but since the arrival of the mallard, its numbers have reduced dramatically as the mallard has taken over much of the grey duck's usual habitat. Nowadays, the grey duck is mostly seen around the lakes and rivers of more remote regions.

The grey duck is very similar in appearance to the female mallard, but has a green panel of feathers (a speculum), where the mallard has a blue-purple panel.

Although some birds can live for 20 years or more, most have a life expectancy of just two or three years.

These ducks feed on the same insects, snails and plants as the mallard, and are of similar size, only slightly smaller.

127

ANIMALS • Birds

New Zealand shoveler

The long bill of this duck has comb-like edges, and together with its bristle-haired tongue, helps it sieve food from the water's surface. The menu includes seeds and small water plants, crustaceans, snails, worms and insects. The shoveler may appear in large numbers in lowland lakes and wetlands throughout New Zealand. It's a great traveller and can fly long distances between lakes. It's a fast flyer for a duck, too, and can top speeds of 80 km an hour.

The shoveler is usually about 38 cm long. The male bird (shown here) has a dark head and a red-brown chest, and the female is a plain grey-brown. These birds can live for about 11 years.

While other ducks call *quack–quack–quack*, the shoveler calls *took–took–took*.

New Zealand scaup

The New Zealand scaup (pronounced skawp) or papango is our smallest duck, at an overall length of just 40 cm. Its small size and 'rubber duck' profile make it easy to spot. It prefers large, deep lakes, rather than shallow lakes or rivers. Usually, the nest is built in dense reeds near the water, but sometimes scaup group together in larger colonies to nest and raise chicks.

The scaup dives to 3 m for crustaceans, water snails and plants, and can stay under for more than a minute. The chicks can dive and catch their own food within just a day or so of hatching.

The female scaup goes *quack*, but the male gives a high whistle of several notes.

Weka

This large, flightless bird is renowned for its inquisitive nature; it will investigate tents, huts and gear for food, and make off with anything it finds bright and interesting, such as items of cutlery, watches, compasses and so on. Its distinctive call is *cooeet*.

The weka's broad diet includes insects, worms, snails, rats, and even birds' eggs and chicks. This can make it a pest near conservation areas, where it raids the nests of other ground-dwelling birds.

It's quite rare in the North Island, but much more common in several South Island locations, especially in the northwest, and on some offshore islands.

It can measure 53 cm in length, and live for 15–18 years.

ANIMALS • Birds

New Zealand falcon
Though it's only half the size of the Australasian harrier, the New Zealand falcon, or karearea, is a much more aggressive bird and will even attack the harrier and other birds in flight – including the tui, the New Zealand pigeon and the Australian magpie. Some falcons will regularly check other birds' nests to prey on newborn chicks.

Mostly, the falcon hunts by watching the countryside from a high perch, and then launching into flight when ground prey – such as rats, mice, lizards and small birds – is spotted. It can reach speeds of up to 180 km per hour in a dive, and strikes with its claws, then makes the final kill with a bite from its powerful bill.

Once seen as a threat to farm birds, the falcon was regularly shot until it became a protected bird in 1970. It's seen around the central North Island and most of the South Island, except for an area of Southland and Canterbury. It can live for about 6–10 years.

Australasian harrier
This large bird of prey, also known as the swamp harrier or kahu, can be seen circling above farmland and scrub nationwide as it searches the ground for small animals such as rabbits, hares, rats and lizards. Having spotted prey, the harrier will swoop down to catch and kill its victim with powerful claws. It's also commonly seen on country roads, feeding on the carcases of hedgehogs and possums and other roadkill. Some will even go 'fishing' for fish and tadpoles. Younger harriers will hunt insects and small animals on the ground by jumping and pouncing.

When much of New Zealand was covered in forest, many centuries ago, there were not many harriers here, but their numbers have increased dramatically as much of the country has become open land, and with the arrival of more small prey animals such as rats and rabbits.

The harrier can weigh up to 850 g and measure 60 cm in length, and it usually lives for around 18 years.

129

ANIMALS • Birds

Takahe

This large flightless bird was once widespread throughout the country. It was regularly caught and eaten by Maori and by early European settlers – as was the North Island species of takahe, which is now long extinct.

The South Island species was thought to have become extinct, too, until the discovery of a small population living in a valley of the Murchison Range, in the South Island, in 1948. Although this population dwindled further, because of introduced deer competing for food, conservation programmes around the country have now almost ensured this bird's survival.

The takahe looks like a much larger version of the pukeko (opposite), and it's thought that both birds share the same ancient ancestor. A very substantial bird, it can weigh up to 3 kg and usually measures around 63 cm in length. It feeds on tussock stems and shoots, seeds and fern roots.

Takahe are very territorial, and some males will even rush to attack human intruders during the breeding season. Young takahe sometimes stay with their parents for up to 18 months and may help to raise younger chicks. Life expectancy is around 14–20 years.

ANIMALS • Birds

Pukeko

The pukeko is one of New Zealand's most distinctive birds. It can be seen in and around wetlands, on farms and parklands. Often, communities of several pairs are formed. They nest in the reeds and rushes around swamps and other wetlands, with several females helping to raise the chicks.

Pukeko can hold food – such as roots or raupo rushes – in one claw, parrot-fashion, while they strip the shoots with their strong bill. They're not fussy about their diet, which also includes insects, spiders, worms and frogs. They've learned that humans are also a good source of food, and will occasionally approach lunchers in parked cars for handouts!

Though they have strong wings, pukeko can be reluctant flyers and often prefer to walk from one spot to another.

The pukeko may sometimes be confused with the takahe, its distant relative, though it's plain, if the illustrations are compared, that the pukeko is more lightly built and has much longer legs. It weighs around 850–1050 g and measures around 50 cm in length, and can live for about 5–9 years.

ANIMALS • Birds

Spotless crake
If you hear the distant sound of a sewing machine running in the marshes, or the sound of an alarm clock running down, then it's probably the call of the spotless crake. Its calls also include a musical *dook-dook-dook* and a sharp *pit-pit*. But it's hard to see, as it's a very secretive bird indeed. It's most likely to be heard in the North Island, though it's also found at the very top and bottom of the South Island.

This bird scrambles and wades through the shallows deep within marshes and swamps to feed on insects and grubs, earthworms, snails and tadpoles. It emerges only very rarely, and flies mostly during the night.

It usually measures about 20 cm in length and weighs around 45 g.

Australian coot
The Australian coot is very easy to spot around the freshwater lakes of the North Island and the east coast of the South Island.

Its odd, head-bobbing way of swimming, and the shape of its bill, both show that it's not a duck, but actually a member of the rail family. Instead of webbed feet, it has wide lobes of skin on its toes. And it doesn't quack, but calls *kraak, kraak* instead. It can be aggressive when nesting or with chicks in company, and will noisily shoo away much larger birds – even swans – if they come too close.

The coot eats small water insects and crustaceans, and can dive underwater for the tastier shoots of some water plants. It's usually about 38 cm long and weighs just over 500 g. It can live for over 18 years.

Pied oystercatcher
The pied oystercatcher or torea can be seen in small or large flocks (sometimes numbering many thousands of birds) on the coast around most of the country.

Its long, stout bill is used to probe for worms and shellfish in the sand. It opens the shells by stabbing with the bill between the two halves and then twisting them open to get at the animal inside. Some birds are even strong enough to stab right through the shell. Small fish and insects are also eaten.

The variable oystercatcher is a close relative though it is slightly larger, and has less obvious 'shoulder straps', and sometimes all-black birds can be seen.

Oystercatchers can weigh around 550 g and measure 46 cm in length. They can live for over 27 years.

ANIMALS • Birds

Pied stilt & Black stilt

The pied stilt or poaka is a relatively recent arrival from Australia – probably during the early 1800s – and can be seen around estuaries, mudflats, wetlands and pastures throughout most of the country. It forages by wading through the water on stilt-like legs and probing the soft mud or sand with its long bill to seek out food. When inland, it feeds on water insects and worms; and on the coast it eats shellfish.

The black stilt or kaki is found only in New Zealand and is the rarest of all the world's wading birds. In the 1800s, it was common throughout most of the South Island and parts of the lower North Island. But then settlers brought changes to its habitat, along with pests such as cats and ferrets, and the bird's numbers tumbled to just 23 adults. The population is back up to around 100, but the species is still endangered.

The black stilt favours the shallows of shingle rivers and wetlands, where it digs around with its long bill for crustaceans, insects and fish.

The pied stilt weighs about 190 g and measures 35 cm in length. The black stilt is slightly longer and heavier. Both can live for 12–15 years.

Pied stilt   Black stilt

Banded dotterel

This small bird can be seen on many coasts around the country. It will run, stop, look, bob, run, and peck its way around the shellbanks and sandflats as it picks out small insects, worms and crustaceans. Sometimes it will tremble a foot on the ground, to bring out small creatures.

These dotterels often nest in hollows and depressions on the beach or riverbank, where eggs and chicks are sometimes easy prey for predators. Many of them nest on the wide shingle beds of South Island rivers, and then migrate to the North Island in the summer months.

Dotterels weigh just 60 g and measure around 20 cm in length. They can live for about 10 years.

Wrybill

This is the only bird in the world to have a bill that curves sideways – and always to the right. It uses this unique feature to poke and fossick around and under small stones for insect larvae, worms, beetles, spiders and crustaceans.

Most wrybills nest and breed around the wide riverbeds of the lower South Island, and then move to the harbours and shores of the upper North Island during summer months. They weigh 60 g, are about 20 cm in length, and can live for around 17 years.

ANIMALS • Birds

Spur-winged plover

A visitor from Australia, the spur-winged plover first began breeding here in 1932, and has now spread throughout most of the country. It can easily be seen on or near open-country pastures and riverbanks, and near seashores and lake shores. Nests with chicks have even been seen just a few inches away from the busy motorway traffic north of the Auckland Harbour Bridge!

The plover has a bony spur over 1 cm long on the front of its wing, which it can use as a weapon to defend its nest against predators such as the Australasian harrier and the Australian magpie. It feeds on the ground for grubs, caterpillars and earthworms.

Plovers weigh about 350 g and are around 38 cm in length. They can live for 12–16 years.

Turnstone

The turnstone is well named, for at every opportunity it flips stones, shells and seaweeds aside on the shore to uncover insects, worms and other small animals such as sandhoppers. It will even dig at the wet mud or sand between waves, to find small crabs and other crustaceans.

Turnstones weigh about 120 g, and are 23 cm in length. Their call, if disturbed, is a metallic *kititit*. They are seen in small or large flocks on many coastal sites around the country, where they arrive in great numbers from their breeding sites in the northern hemisphere. Many of the birds that migrate here nest in the tundra regions of Siberia and Alaska. They usually arrive in late September, and return to the north in March.

Bar-tailed godwit

This bird – also known as kuaka – can be seen in summer months, digging in the muddy waters of harbours and estuaries of the upper North Island, particularly in the Firth of Thames. It digs vigorously for crabs, shellfish and worms, sometimes with its head under the water as it probes with its long bill. It migrates here each year from breeding grounds in Alaska, Siberia and Scandinavia. It's the most numerous of the many species of migrating birds that are summer arrivals in New Zealand, with over 100,000 godwits regularly making the trip each year. The 11,000 km, one-week flight over the Pacific Ocean is made non-stop, without any sleep, food or rest. Younger birds often stay here for the winter, so there is always a small permanent, though changing, population. The godwits weigh about 350 g and measure around 40 cm in length.

ANIMALS • Birds

Black-backed gull
Also known as karoro, this is by far the largest and the most distinctive of New Zealand's gulls – its black back and wings make it very easy to spot. It's a great scavenger and seems capable of eating just about anything even remotely edible. It will look for food in estuaries and on shorelines, and will sometimes follow boats far out to sea. It feeds on shellfish, worms, insects and carrion (dead animals). The young black-backed gull is called ngoiro; and because of its mottled grey-brown appearance it is sometimes thought to be a different species of bird. This 'teenager' can seem awkward and clumsy when other birds are gathered around human beach visitors – ngoiro can usually be seen at the back of the bunch, wondering how to get some of the goodies on offer!

These gulls can live for about 28 years. They can weigh up to 1 kg and are about 60 cm long.

Red-billed gull
This gull, also known as akiaki, is very easy to see around the coasts, with its red bill and its distinctive noisy call of *scrark*. Like the black-backed gull, this bird will scavenge for food scraps in all sorts of unusual places – parks, rubbish dumps, supermarket car parks and so on, and of course is often seen flying or walking up and down the shore on the lookout for anything edible. It will catch and eat any fish (even dead and decaying ones washed up on the tide), shellfish, insects and worms.

It usually weighs up to 300 g, is about 37 cm long, and can live for about 28 years.

Black-fronted tern
Though most terns are birds of the sea and seashore, the black-fronted tern prefers to live around rivers – especially the waterways of the eastern South Island – while it is in its nesting phase. In the spring and summer, the bird is a common sight on the shingle and sand of Canterbury riversides. Unfortunately, the nests in these locations are easily damaged by sudden floods or by human activity. Rats and other predators will also raid the shingle beds to snatch up eggs or chicks.

Black-fronted terns roam the surrounding area, often in flocks, to feed on fish, insects and skinks. They will explore nearby ploughed fields to take up insects and earthworms.

The black-fronted tern is usually about 30 cm in length and weighs around 80 g.

ANIMALS • Birds

Rock pigeon

Rock pigeons were introduced into New Zealand by early European settlers, and can be seen in most towns and cities. They're common in the countryside, too, where they feed on insects and fruits. They'll also help themselves to new crops of barley, beans, peas and cereals.

They nest on any available ledge or niche on city buildings, and will also settle on rocky outcrops and in depressions in cliffs and banks. Nests can be a very odd assortment of materials – one nest found in Wellington was made almost entirely of bits of old wire!

These pigeons weigh around 400 g and are 33 cm in length. They can live for about 3–5 years.

New Zealand pigeon

This pigeon has several Maori names: the most common one is kereru, but other names include kuku and kukupa, which sound like the bird's call – *coo-coo*.

It likes to eat a wide variety of plant leaves, seeds and fruits, such as the berries of puriri, miro, tawa, taraire, karaka and nikau. The pigeon is the only bird capable of swallowing the larger types of berries whole, so it is important in helping with the dispersal of the seeds through its droppings.

Before becoming a protected bird in 1921, the pigeon was highly prized and was caught in great numbers by Maori for food and for its feathers, which were used in cloaks.

The kereru has been seen to take a 'shower' in the rain, by hanging over to one side from a branch to get its undersides wet, and then swinging over to the other side to complete the job!

Kereru weigh around 650 g and are about 51 cm long. Their usual lifespan is around 10 years.

Eastern rosella

This Australian bird became established in New Zealand after some escaped from cages into Auckland's Waitakere Ranges in 1910. Rosellas are now found around Auckland and Northland, with some isolated populations in Wellington, Canterbury, Otago and other locations.

Rosellas live in small groups, and usually nest in holes in forest trees and in the trunks of tree ferns. Though they occasionally eat insects, they mostly prefer plant food such as seeds, fruits and flowers – they even enjoy the seeds of the Scotch thistle.

The rosella's call is a loud *twink twink*, which can be heard called loudly by several birds as they chase through the bush in a flash of bright colour.

The rosella weighs around 110 g and is about 33 cm in length. It can live for 10 years or more.

ANIMALS • Birds

Kakapo

Before the arrival of humans, dogs and cats, the flightless kakapo was widespread throughout the country, but these days the population is probably less than 100 birds. It was given legal protection in 1896, and is now restricted to predator-free sanctuaries on offshore islands.

Kakapo feathers were prized by Maori for making capes and cloaks – perhaps over 10,000 feathers for a single cloak – and it was also caught for food.

The name kakapo means 'night parrot' and refers to the bird's habit of emerging from its daytime hiding place – among the rotten logs and fallen foliage in the undergrowth – to forage on the ground at night for seeds, shoots, leaves and roots.

Though flightless, the bird can still use its sizeable wings. It holds them out for balance as it clambers and claws its way up accessible tree trunks to feed; and they also help to slow its descent.

The kakapo is renowned as the heaviest parrot in the world, and is mostly solitary in its habits. However, when it comes time for the male to find a mate, he joins other males in constructing bowl-shaped scoops in the ground from where they each make booming noises through the night to announce their presence. These deep booms can be heard by females over 7 km away. After mating, the female leaves to construct her own nest for the eggs.

Kakapo can weigh over 3 kg and measure 63 cm in length. Like many parrots, they are long-lived compared with most other birds – kakapo can live for 30–50 years.

ANIMALS • Birds

Kea

Named for its call of *kee–aa*, this cheeky species of parrot has been reckoned by some to be one of the most intelligent of all birds, with its strongly inquisitive nature and its ability to solve complex puzzles.

Visitors to the high country of the Southern Alps can be both charmed and annoyed by the kea's behaviour: it likes to 'ski' down the corrugated iron roofs on huts; and it's likely to investigate any unattended camper's or tramper's equipment and take off with anything remotely interesting or edible – it will even strip the seal from a car windscreen or rip a sleeping bag apart.

The kea eats fruits, seeds, insects and carrion, and will greedily snatch up any unattended food around visitor centres and car parks.

Many tens of thousands of kea were legally killed by early settlers, as they were seen as a danger to sheep; but they have been a protected bird since 1986.

Kea can weigh up to 1 kg and measure 46 cm in length. They can live for 15–20 years.

Kaka

The kaka is a close relative of the kea. The two species are thought to have a common ancestor that came to New Zealand many tens of thousands of years ago. The North Island population and the South Island population adapted to different environments and gradually evolved into the two separate species that we see today. The kaka is now often regarded as a bird of the upper North Island, though there are substantial populations in the South Island, particularly the West Coast, and also around Wellington.

Besides being an able flyer like the kea, the kaka is a very good climber, and uses its feet and bill to clamber up and down tree trunks and branches when looking for food. It likes to eat various types of wood-boring beetles, such as the kanuka longhorn beetle, and will spend a long time tearing away rotten bark and wood to get at the grubs just beneath.

As well as insects and grubs, kaka eat nectar, fruits, leaves and shoots. And although they prefer to live in forest areas, they will sometimes enter gardens and parks during winter to feed on exotic plants. Kaka feathers were once much prized for making feather cloaks – up to 400 birds were required to make just one.

Though similar in length to kea at 45 cm, kaka are often less substantial, weighing around 500 g. Their lifespan is around 20 years.

ANIMALS • Birds

Yellow-crowned parakeet

The Maori name for this 25 cm-long bird – kakariki – means 'small parrot' and also 'green'. It was once common enough to be seen in flocks of tens of thousands, but its numbers have been dramatically reduced due to hunting and introduced predators. It can only be seen now in a few areas, such as on the West Coast of the South Island and in central North Island forests, where it hunts out insects, seeds and fruit to eat.

Some parakeets will chew the leaves of manuka and kanuka; these contain a natural insecticide, which they spread through their feathers to control lice. Parakeets reach a length of 25 cm and usually live for about 4–7 years.

Shining cuckoo

Like most other cuckoos around the world, the shining cuckoo, or pipiwharauroa, is an attractive bird with an unpleasant habit – it doesn't make a nest for its own egg, but lays it in the nest of another bird, usually the grey warbler (page 143). When the cuckoo chick hatches, its first instinct is to push any other chicks or eggs out of the nest, so that it has the place all to itself – and of course gets all the food and care. The grey warbler then raises the cuckoo chick as its own.

The shining cuckoo does not spend winter in New Zealand. Instead, it flies to islands around Papua New Guinea and Indonesia and then returns around September and October. It's about 16 cm long and lives for around 5–7 years.

Long-tailed cuckoo

This bird is seen mostly in the upper half of the North Island and western parts of the South Island. It's usually found high in the treetops, rather than low down near the forest floor. It's not a fussy eater; it feeds on insects such as weta and beetles, spiders, birds' eggs, skinks, geckos and sometimes other, smaller birds. It also eats berries and fruits.

Like the shining cuckoo, the long-tailed cuckoo never builds a nest for its own eggs, but lays them in the nests of other birds, such as the yellowhead or the brown creeper.

It spends the winter in islands of the south-western Pacific, leaving in March and returning to New Zealand in October. The cuckoos usually come back to the same site every year.

Though it's not a large-bodied bird – it weighs only around 125 g – the long tail contributes to an overall length of 40 cm.

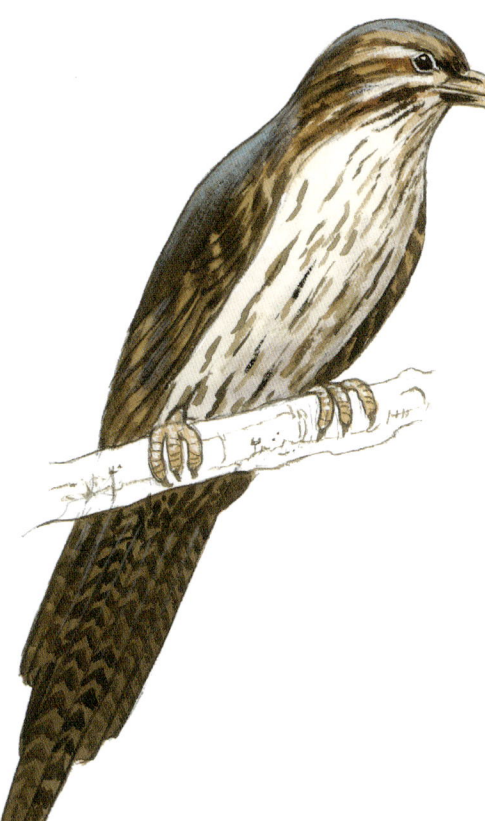

ANIMALS • Birds

Morepork

Maori named this owl ruru for the sound of its call, and Europeans called it morepork for the same reason.

Like most owls, the morepork prefers to hide by day and hunt by night. Its excellent eyesight and hearing, plus the soft feathers on the edges of its wings that help it to fly with hardly any noise, all combine to make it an exceptional hunter.

In many owl species, the skull openings for the left and right ear are of unequal size and shape, and are located asymmetrically on the head. This enables them to receive specific left and right sounds from their surroundings. This extra 'targeting' ability makes for greater accuracy in swooping and diving on their prey.

The morepork was one of the few native birds to prosper with the arrival of human settlers, who brought more small prey for the morepork to catch – mice, rats and several small birds such as the chaffinch (page 149). It also snatches up geckos, skinks, moths and other flying insects.

Moreporks generally weigh around 175 g and are 29 cm long. They can live for 6–10 years.

Little owl

The little owl is also known as the German owl or the brown owl. It was introduced into the South Island from Germany in 1906, when finches and sparrows were becoming too much of a problem on Otago farms – but it was soon found that the little owl much preferred to eat insects, spiders and earthworms!

Unlike most other owls, this bird hunts mainly in the daytime, and can be seen perched on posts and hedges as it keeps a lookout for prey. It will also walk and run around on the ground as it looks for food. If disturbed, it has a comical display of bobbing up and down, rotating its head to help judge the nearness of the intruder.

Little owls can live for about 10 years. They are 23 cm long and weigh around 180 g.

Kingfisher

The kingfisher or kotare can be found nationwide, but is more common in the North Island. In winter it moves to the coast, to watch for mud crabs (page 70) and other prey near harbours and estuaries. It also preys on insects, lizards, mice and small birds like the silvereye (page 147), and will even rob other birds of the earthworms they've caught.

It makes a nest in earth banks and cuttings. It begins by flying directly at the bank and striking it with its heavy bill. Once the hole is deep enough, the kingfisher will perch and start digging until the tunnel is about 10–20 cm long, with a wide chamber at the end.

Kingfishers can live for 10–15 years. They are about 24 cm in length and weigh about 65 g.

ANIMALS • Birds

Rifleman

The rifleman gets its name from its green plumage, which reminded early European settlers of the army's green-jacketed rifle regiments. The Maori name of titipounamu also refers to the bird's green colouring – just like pounamu (greenstone). The female rifleman is similar, but her colours are more olive and grey-brown – and no, she isn't called a riflewoman!

To feed, the rifleman hops and climbs up tree trunks in a spiral fashion to pick off any spiders, grubs or insects it can find there.

This is New Zealand's smallest bird: it weighs just 6–7 g (less than the weight of a $1 coin!), and is only 8 cm long from the tip of its bill to the end of its tail. The rifleman is found in many types of forest throughout the country, and lives for around 6 years.

Welcome swallow

Welcome swallows first arrived in Northland from Australia during the 1950s. They are now found throughout the country, except for the South Island's western coasts. They can be seen swooping and darting in open country, or over water, as they catch flying insects such as flies, moths and small beetles.

Swallows make a bowl-shaped nest from a mixture of mud and grass, usually in a protected place like the underside of a bridge or under the overhang of a house or garage. They weigh around 14 g and are about 15 cm long. Most live for around 5–6 years.

Blackbird

The blackbird is probably our most common bird of all and can be seen in lots of gardens and parks around the country. It likes to feed on the ground, scratching or flicking at leaves and grass as it searches for insects, earthworms, skinks and seeds. Its song is soft and tuneful, but its alarm call is a very distinctive *tchock, tchock*.

The blackbird sometimes 'sunbathes' by resting on the ground with wings outspread.

The male bird is black with a yellow bill, and the female is dull brown, with a light brown bill. Juveniles have dark speckles on their chest, and can sometimes be confused with the song thrush.

Blackbirds are up to 25 cm long and weigh around 90 g. Most can live for around 20 years.

Female

Male

141

ANIMALS • Birds

Song thrush
The song thrush was brought to New Zealand in the 1860s, and just like its close relative, the blackbird, it has now spread throughout most of the country.

It is often seen feeding on the ground, hopping or running along to search out insects. The thrush will stop and cock its head as though listening for movement, but in fact it's just having a better look at the ground. It searches for insects, spiders, fruits and earthworms. It also likes to eat snails, and will carry the shell to break it open against a handy stone to expose the snail inside.

The song thrush weighs around 70 g and is about 23 cm long. It can live for about 10 years.

Skylark
Brought into New Zealand by English settlers in the 1860s, the skylark is now more numerous here than it is in England! It can be heard throughout much of the country as the male bird soars high over open ground of all types, seemingly singing non-stop. He sings as he rises to heights of 30–100 m, where it hovers, facing into the wind, for 5–20 minutes. He continues to sing as it slowly circles back down again.

The skylark comes to the ground to feed on seeds, insects and their larvae, and spiders. Sometimes it also feeds on grain and on vegetable crops such as cabbages, peas and tomatoes.

Skylarks weigh around 38 g, and are 18 cm long. They usually live for about 8 years.

Fernbird
The fernbird, or matata, can be seen around the upper half of the North Island and in coastal areas of the South Island. It's usually heard rather than seen, as it likes to hide in the scrub and reeds around swamps and marshes. It doesn't often sing, but gives brief calls, such as *uu-tik*, *tchip*, *tcheong*, *zrup* and sometimes a row of chittering *clicks*. It's a weak flyer, and prefers to scramble through undergrowth stalks and vegetation to hunt for spiders and insects and their larvae. Some fernbirds of the far south will even perch on the backs of basking seals to catch flies.

Fernbirds have distinctive tails: the barbs of the feathers don't knit together well, which gives the tail a tattered and frayed look.

They usually measure around 18 cm in length and weigh about 35 g. They can live for about 6 years.

ANIMALS • Birds

Yellowhammer

Yellowhammers were introduced into New Zealand in the 1860s. They quickly became a nuisance for farmers and gardeners because of their preference for eating seeds; many of them were killed as pests. They also feed on spiders, insects and grubs.

Yellowhammers can be seen in all kinds of country, from alpine tussock to the exposed seashore, and they will visit gardens and parks, though of course they are most common in open country and farmland. Their song of *tintintintintink–swee* has sometimes been written down as 'a little bit of bread and no cheese'.

They weigh around 27 g and reach about 16 cm in length. They can live for 10 years.

Grey warbler

The grey warbler, or riroriro, is a native bird found nationwide. Its pretty, trailing song is often heard without the bird ever being seen, as it's reluctant to come out into the open and prefers the protection of foliage and shade.

The grey warbler builds a hanging, pear-shaped nest with a very small side entrance – all of which gives it good protection against rats, though not against the shining cuckoo (page 139), which sometimes lays its own eggs in the warbler's nest.

The grey warbler eats mostly insects and spiders, and will even 'hover' for a few seconds to snatch prey from hard-to-reach leaves and branches. It weighs 6.5 g and measures 11 cm in length. Its life expectancy is around 10 years.

Fantail

The friendly little fantail, piwakawaka, is one of the most common of our native birds, and is often seen and heard around gardens and bush walks as it follows human walkers to snatch up any insects that might be disturbed. It hardly ever feeds on the ground, but instead will catch insects in flight, or hover for a few seconds to pick them off leaves and branches. It also eats spiders, and fruit from trees. Some will even enter the house during the summer to look for flies, and then take a quick bath under the garden sprinkler.

Nests are tidy, cup-shaped affairs, usually built just a couple of metres from the ground. They are constructed from grasses, moss, bark and cobwebs, and often lined with hair and feathers.

All-black fantails can be seen in the South Island and around the Wellington region.

Fantails weigh about 8 g, and grow to about 16 cm in length (with the tail accounting for half of this!). Most live for 3–10 years.

ANIMALS • Birds

Brown kiwi

The kiwi is undoubtedly the best known of all New Zealand's birds, and the brown kiwi is the most common of five kiwi species. Brown kiwi can be found in forests throughout the country, but mostly in the upper North Island. There are two other brownish-coloured species. These are the rowi (upper South Island) and the tokoeka (lower South Island and Stewart Island). Two somewhat different species are the great spotted kiwi (South Island) and little spotted kiwi (both main islands). As you might suspect, they have spotted plumage and are of different sizes. Kiwi can be found in many habitats besides forests: in scrublands and swamps, on coasts, and even up into high-country tussock.

All kiwi populations of all the different kiwi types have been reduced from many millions down to some tens of thousands, as they have fallen prey to dogs, stoats, rats and other introduced animals, and also to forest clearances and hunters.

Kiwi nest in burrows and emerge at night to forage for food in the ground leaf litter. Snuffling along, they poke and probe the ground with their long bills – often burying its full length – to find and dig out earthworms. The bird's nostrils are located near the tip of the bill, which is a great help in finding hidden prey. They'll also eat insects, grubs, spiders and fallen fruits. The kiwi's shriek of *kiweee* is heard well after sunset, as the bird leaves the burrow.

Females are usually larger and heavier than males. The eggs they lay are some of the largest in the world (see caption next page). The hatched chicks can leave the burrow after about a week, and forage by themselves on short excursions. They gradually leave the burrow more and more, but they stay in the parents' territory for several months before finally departing.

Brown kiwi can weigh between 2.2 and 2.8 kg, and are 40–50 cm long. Most can live for 20–30 years.

ANIMALS • Birds

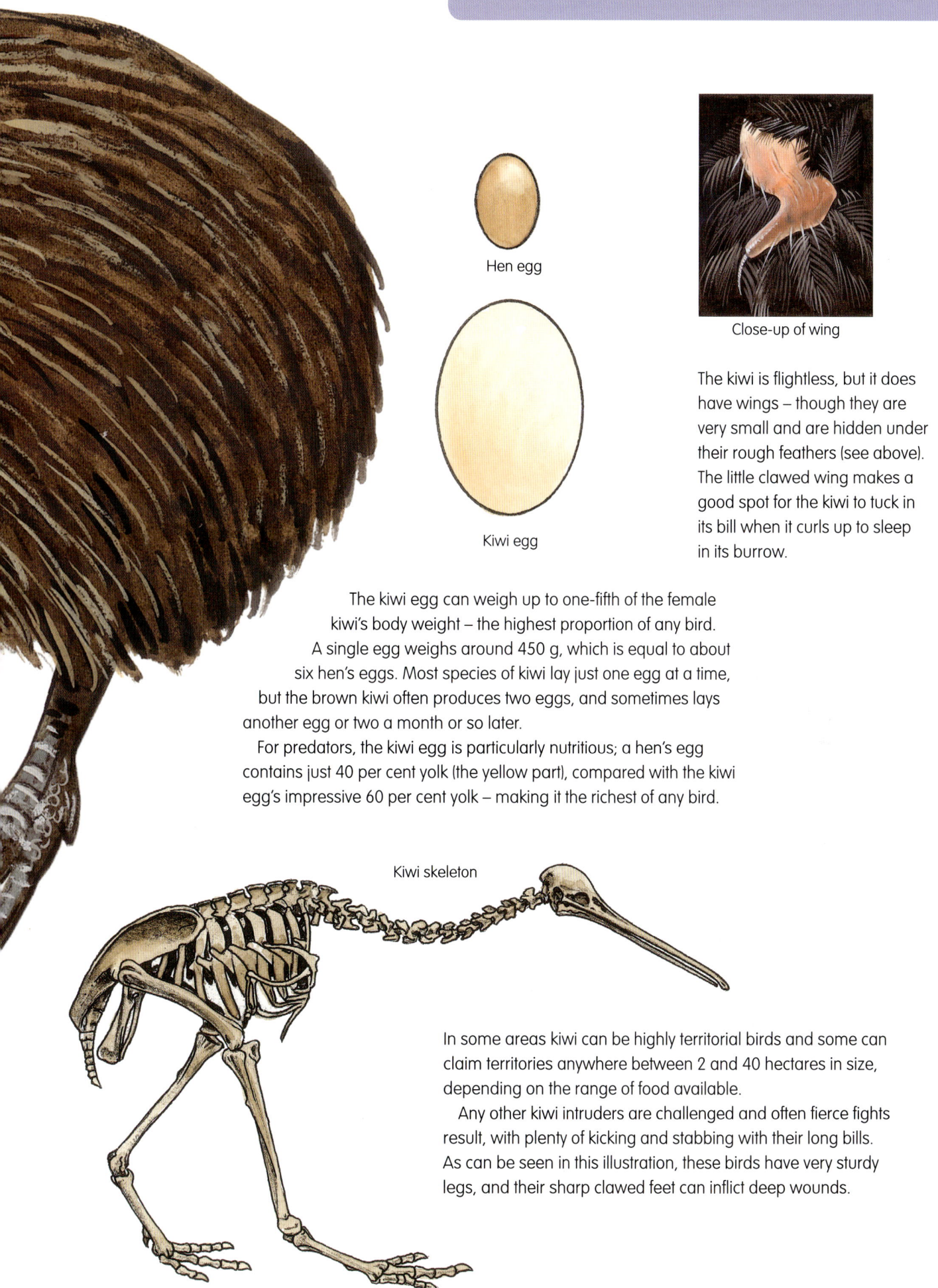

Hen egg

Kiwi egg

Close-up of wing

The kiwi is flightless, but it does have wings – though they are very small and are hidden under their rough feathers (see above). The little clawed wing makes a good spot for the kiwi to tuck in its bill when it curls up to sleep in its burrow.

The kiwi egg can weigh up to one-fifth of the female kiwi's body weight – the highest proportion of any bird. A single egg weighs around 450 g, which is equal to about six hen's eggs. Most species of kiwi lay just one egg at a time, but the brown kiwi often produces two eggs, and sometimes lays another egg or two a month or so later.

For predators, the kiwi egg is particularly nutritious; a hen's egg contains just 40 per cent yolk (the yellow part), compared with the kiwi egg's impressive 60 per cent yolk – making it the richest of any bird.

Kiwi skeleton

In some areas kiwi can be highly territorial birds and some can claim territories anywhere between 2 and 40 hectares in size, depending on the range of food available.

Any other kiwi intruders are challenged and often fierce fights result, with plenty of kicking and stabbing with their long bills. As can be seen in this illustration, these birds have very sturdy legs, and their sharp clawed feet can inflict deep wounds.

ANIMALS • Birds

Tomtit

The tomtit, or miromiro, likes to use a low perch in the forest to watch for insects, spiders and worms on the forest floor, and then dive down to snatch up its prey. Like other small forest birds, it often follows bush walkers to see what they might disturb, and it will sometimes land on their head or shoulders to get a better vantage point.

Some tomtits have been seen to wash their catch in a nearby creek before offering it to their chicks.

The tomtit's usual call is a simple *swee* or *seet*, but the male can declare his territory with a loud *ti oly oly oly oh*.

Tomtits weigh about 11 g and measure 13 cm in length. They can live for 10 years.

New Zealand robin

This forest-dwelling robin perches on low branches, and then swoops down to catch insects such as weta and beetles. It also eats worms and fruits. Sometimes it will stand on one leg and tremble the other leg among the leaf litter to encourage any concealed insects to move. Like the fantail and tomtit, the robin will follow walkers on bush tracks to snatch up any disturbed prey.

Though it's not a common bird, the robin (also known as toutouwai) can be seen in central North Island forests and on parts of the West Coast.

Robins weigh around 35 g, measure 18 cm in length, and can live for around 16 years.

Black robin

This bird is found only on the Chatham Islands, and its story is the greatest escape from extinction in recent times. Populations had dwindled, and completely disappeared in places, until by 1979 there were only five birds left, including the very last productive pair – 'Old Yellow' (the male) and 'Old Blue' (the female). Careful management by wildlife and conservation staff included the removal of eggs laid by Old Blue and given to foster birds to raise. This encouraged the bird to lay again, and gradually increased numbers, until they had reached a safer margin of over 200 birds some 15 years later, spread over several localities.

Though the life expectancy of these robins is only 5 or 6 years, Old Blue didn't have her first chicks until she was 9 years old. By the time she died at the age of 13, she had become a great-grandmother many times over.

These little birds weigh 22–25 g and are around 15 cm in length. They feed on weta, beetles, spiders, aphids and caterpillars. They hunt their small prey by hopping about on the forest floor, or flitting through the lowest branches.

ANIMALS • Birds

Silvereye
Though small numbers of these birds had arrived here from Australia on several occasions, it wasn't until 1856 that a flock large enough to establish itself arrived in Waikanae, near Wellington, in 1856, and the bird has since spread throughout the country. It's also known as the waxeye or white-eye, and Maori named the bird tauhou, meaning 'stranger'.

Like the tui and the bellbird, the silvereye has a brush-like tongue, which helps it take nectar from flowers. It also hunts for insects and spiders. It will quickly appear in suburban gardens if bread, fruit or sugar-water are left out on a bird table.

Silvereyes weigh around 13 g and are 13 cm in length. They usually live for 11 years.

Stitchbird
The stitchbird was once common throughout the North Island, but now it's restricted to just a few island sanctuaries. Its call of *t-zee* caused Maori to name it hihi, while to Europeans the call sounded like the English word 'stitch'.

Like the bellbird and the tui, the stitchbird has a brush-tipped tongue, which enables it to enjoy the nectar of flax, pohutukawa, rata and puriri flowers, as well as many others. It will also snatch up insects and spiders.

The male bird, pictured here, is strongly coloured, but the female is much duller in colour, though with the same white 'shoulder'.

Stitchbirds live for around 7 years. They weigh 30–40 g and can be about 18 cm in length.

Bellbird
The bellbird, or korimako, is named for its very pretty song, made up of 2–6 clear, bell-like notes. It sounds at its most attractive when several birds are singing together in the early morning.

The bellbird is common in forested areas all around the country, but rare north of Auckland and in much of Canterbury and Otago.

Like the tui and other birds on this page, the bellbird has a brush-like tongue, which helps it to take nectar from native and introduced plants. Males will chase off females from the nectar plants, so the female's diet is mostly insects and spiders.

Bellbirds weigh up to 34 g and are 20 cm in length. They can live for 8 years.

ANIMALS • Birds

Tui

The tui must be one of the country's most admired birds. It's certainly one of our most talented singing birds – often the first to start singing in the morning, and the last to finish in the evening. Sometimes it will even sing into the moonlit night.

The song is a series of clear, liquid notes, plus an amazing range of chuckles, coughs, whistles, twangs and beeps. It can imitate nearly any other bird's song, as well as a range of mechanical devices such as car alarms and phones. Its talent for mimicry was employed by Maori, who would keep tui caged and teach them to repeat lengthy human phrases.

The bird is a fast and noisy flyer; a notch in the wing feathers produces a whirring, fluttering sound in flight. It was once called the parson bird, on account of the two tufts of white feathers under its throat, which resemble a clergyman's white collar.

It can regularly be seen in forests, parks and gardens, especially where favourite nectar plants might be found – flax, kowhai, rata, rewarewa and so on. It will also eat fruits and insects. It's found nationwide, except for a few areas of Canterbury and Otago. The species has been legally protected since 1873.

Tui usually measure about 30 cm in length and weigh 90–120 g. They can live for 12 years or more.

ANIMALS • Birds

House sparrow

The house sparrow was first introduced into New Zealand in the 1860s and is now our most common city bird. It can also be seen in parks, gardens and farmland throughout most of the country, except for parts of the south-west South Island.

Nests are usually built in thick trees, or around houses – in gutters, under eaves and even in chimneys.

Sparrows eat seeds, cereal crops, insects and small fruits. They are great scavengers and are always on the lookout for easy pickings and scraps around cafés and supermarkets. They are smart enough to activate door-opening sensors to gain access to food stores.

The male bird can be easily identified by the black 'bib' on its front, and its stronger colouring, while the female has duller shades of brown and grey. Sparrows weigh about 30 g and are 14 cm long. Most live for 10–15 years.

Male

Female

Chaffinch

Introduced into New Zealand by settlers in the 1860s, the chaffinch has now spread to all parts of the country – to parks and gardens, farmland, forests and high into the mountains. This hardy little bird has even found its way to some of the subantarctic islands, including Campbell Island. It has become by far the most common of all the finch-like birds that have been introduced into New Zealand, which include the greenfinch, redpoll, goldfinch, yellowhammer and cirl bunting.

Chaffinches often shuffle about on the ground to hunt for insects and spiders and to pick up seeds and fruits.

The chaffinch is also known as the 'bachelor bird', because it has a habit of forming flocks of hundreds of birds of the same sex.

Its call is a simple *pink pink*, but its full song ends in a flourish that has been written down as *chip chip chip tell tell tell cherry-erry-erry tissi cheweeo*.

Chaffinches weigh about 22 g and are 15 cm in length. They can live for around 10 years.

ANIMALS • Birds

Goldfinch

First introduced by European settlers in the 1860s, the goldfinch is now found nationwide, and is more common here than it is in Britain. It eats insects and spiders, but mainly eats a wide range of seeds, even those from the prickly Scotch thistle. It frequents suburban gardens, orchards, farmland and open country. During winter, the goldfinch can be seen in large flocks in open countryside – sometimes the birds number in their thousands.

Its call is a simple *pee-yu*, but during summer the male sings a pretty *tswitt–witt-witt*.

The goldfinch weighs around 15 g and is 13 cm in length. Life expectancy is about 8 years.

Starling

Along with the song thrush and the blackbird, the starling has become one of our most common birds. It's reckoned that the starling might even be the most common bird in the world, with a global population of well over a billion! Some flocks seen in New Zealand may have contained over a million birds.

Starlings like to nest in available holes in trees, cliffs and in man-made structures such as chimneys and ventilation shafts.

When feeding on the ground, the starling will take snails, insects and spiders, and dig into the soil with its bill to search out grubs and worms. It can also snatch flying insects while in flight.

Starlings weigh around 85 g and are 21 cm in length. They usually live for 20 years or more.

Myna

The myna was introduced into New Zealand from India in the 1870s and has now spread throughout much of the North Island north of the Whanganui region.

It's a very bold and cheeky bird and can be seen strutting back and forth across sealed roads, just inches from passing traffic, as it searches for food such as grubs, insects, earthworms and fruits.

It's also very aggressive and will sometimes take over the nests of other birds by killing their chicks or destroying the eggs.

The myna is a good imitator of sounds and can copy lots of other birds' songs, as well as the rings of doorbells and mobile phones. In some countries, mynas are kept as pets and taught to speak human phrases, just like a parrot.

These birds weigh around 125 g and are 24 cm in length. They can live for about 12 years.

ANIMALS • Birds

Kokako
The kokako is a rather poor flyer and makes its way through the forest by scrambling, flapping and gliding through the trees and branches. It will eat foliage, flowers, fruits and insects, and usually feeds parrot-fashion – perched on one foot, and grasping the food with the other.

The blue-coloured folds of skin at the side of its bill shows that the kokako is a member of a group of birds known as wattlebirds, which includes the saddleback and the extinct huia. Its name comes from the main part of its song – *ko-ka-kooo*.

Kokako can weigh 230 g and measure 38 cm in length. They usually live for around 20 years.

Saddleback
It's easy to see where the saddleback gets its name – from the 'saddle' of orange-brown feathers across its back! Its Maori name is tieke.

Numbers of saddlebacks have fallen dramatically since the arrival of cats, dogs, rats and weasels, as these birds like to forage for food on the forest floor. They rummage noisily in the leaf litter for insects, and dig at rotten logs with their tough bills, which all makes them relatively easy prey for those introduced predators. Saddlebacks are now found mostly on protected offshore islands.

Fantails and other small birds will follow a feeding saddleback, eager to pick up any insects that it might stir up.

The saddleback can weigh up to 80 g and is 25 cm in length. The lifespan is about 17 years.

Australian magpie
This bird was introduced from Australia in the 1860s to help control insect pests on farms, but was soon found to be a very aggressive bird when protecting its nesting territory. It will attack other birds such as the New Zealand falcon and even the Australasian harrier, which is twice its size. Humans passing too close can also find themselves 'dive-bombed'. Magpies are quite common around the country, except on the South Island's West Coast.

Magpie nests can be strange affairs: in addition to the usual plant material, magpies will sometimes add lengths of string, pieces of china, cardboard, cloth and glass, and even barbed wire!

Magpies are certainly not fussy eaters; they'll take a variety of seeds, insects, spiders, snails, geckos, skinks and carrion. They can weigh around 350 g and are 41 cm in length. They can live for 20 years.

ANIMALS • Mammals

Though they were the last major animal group to come to prominence, mammals had their beginnings a very long time ago. They began to evolve from a particular reptile group (the therapsids) over 200 million years ago, and became fully separated over a period of 5–1 million years or so, with their own special features.

In these early times, when the dinosaurs ruled, many mammal species were small and generally nocturnal. But when the time of the dinosaurs came to an end in the great extinctions at the end of the Cretaceous period, some 65 million years ago, the mammals were free to expand and develop further.

One of the factors that allowed them to survive those extinctions was the ability to regulate internal body temperature (hence the expression 'warm-blooded'), despite changing conditions or environments, while dinosaurs and others were unable to cope with the planet's cooling periods.

In almost all species, mammals give birth to live young, which can be suckled and nourished by the mother. Mammals are all or partly covered with hair, which both insulates and protects, and have jaws that are hinged directly to the skull and equipped with specialised teeth. All have four limbs, although the evidence might be hard to see at times.

Although New Zealand has been home to species of land mammals in the prehistoric past, only bats have survived to the present day.

Lesser short-tailed bat

Bats are the only mammals to have developed proper wings and true flight. They hunt at night, using echolocation techniques for navigation and identification of flying prey. New Zealand has two species of bat – known to Maori as pekapeka – the long-tailed and the lesser short-tailed bat. A third species, the greater short-tailed bat, became extinct in the 1960s, when rats established themselves on its island home near Stewart Island.

The long-tailed bat can be seen in native forests throughout the country, but the short-tailed bat is comparatively rare and is an endangered species. It's found on Stewart Island, and in a few locations in the North and South islands. Of nearly 1000 bat species known around the world, only this bat forages on the forest floor for food such as beetles, cockroaches and weta. This makes it vulnerable to predators such as rats, cats and others.

The bat's wingspan is around 30 cm, but its body is little more than thumb-sized, and it weighs about 16 g. The bat usually lives for 6–10 years.

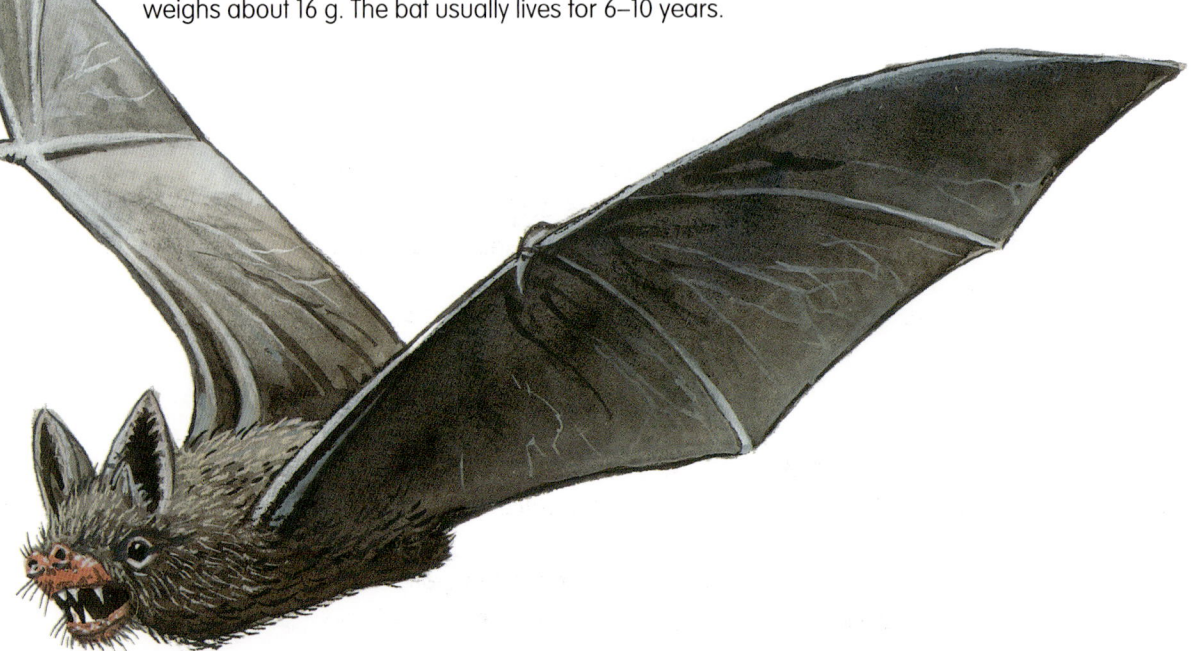

ANIMALS • Mammals

While most of the world's mammal species live on the land, there are many that have adapted to life in the seas.

Whales are by far the largest mammals of all. Early forms of whales had four limbs, but over time the forelimbs have developed into fins, and the rear limbs have reduced to just bone remnants within their bodies. Whales are divided into two main groups: those with teeth, which enable them to chase and catch larger prey, and those with comb-like baleen plates in their mouths to filter small food from seawater.

The toothed whales find their prey by echolocation. They send out sound signals, then receive and understand the reflected 'echo'. This allows them to identify different types and numbers of prey – and predators – from a great distance. The complex sounds that most toothed and baleen whales can make also allow them to communicate with each other.

The toothed whales make up about 90 per cent of all the whales in the oceans, and the smallest of these are the dolphins. There are more than 60 different species of dolphin around the world, and about 9 of these live in or visit New Zealand waters.

Hector's dolphin

Common dolphin

Dusky dolphin

Bottlenose dolphin

Common dolphin, Hector's dolphin, Dusky dolphin & Bottlenose dolphin

Most dolphin species chase and catch small fish and squid for food; some hunt in groups, and 'herd' their prey in order to surround and trap it. They use echolocation to find and identify their prey, and they can communicate with each other using a variety of complex sounds. All have well defined teeth – some species have as many as 100 or more. Life expectancy is usually 10–20 years.

The common dolphin is the most common species around the world. It's the most numerous species in New Zealand waters; sometimes several thousand can be seen travelling together. It grows to about 2.4 m.

Hector's dolphin is found only around New Zealand. At 1.4 m in length, it's one of the smallest and rarest of all the world's dolphins. A northern subspecies – Maui's dolphin – probably numbers only around 100 individuals.

The dusky dolphin is common in seas from the lower North Island to subantarctic seas. Large numbers, in pods (big family groups) numbering as many as 50 individuals, can sometimes be seen off the Kaikoura coast in wintertime. It usually measures just over 2 m.

At up to 4 m in length, the bottlenose dolphin is the largest of this group, and is the species usually seen performing in marine parks. Its apparently cheeky smile and playful manner have made it a favourite around the world.

ANIMALS • Mammals

Orca
Orca are the world's largest dolphins. They are also known as killer whales, partly because they are top predators and have little to fear in the seas. They hunt and eat just about anything of any size, including seals, turtles, dolphins, stingrays, sharks and other larger fish, and penguins. They will even form into hunting packs to attack the larger whales. Not even the great blue whale is safe from this ocean predator.

Orca have 40–50 peg-like teeth. These are used only for gripping and cutting, but not chewing – chunks of prey are swallowed whole. Orca can grow to around 9 m in length, weigh up to 10 tonnes, and live for about 80 years. They usually live and travel in groups of 2–40 individuals and sometimes as many as 100.

Long-finned pilot whale
Pilot whales can dive as deep as 500 m in the ocean at night to feed on deepwater squid, fish and octopus. They can remain submerged for up to 15 minutes at a time. Pilot whales may form very large groups – sometimes numbering several hundred individuals – and will often gather with other species, such as the bottlenose and common dolphins.

Though smaller whales like this are skilful swimmers and navigators, they regularly strand themselves on New Zealand's coast. Sometimes just a few whales strand; at other times there are dozens or even hundreds trapped ashore. Nobody really knows why this happens; perhaps a gently sloping beach confuses the animals' echolocation; or maybe a sick individual beaches itself and the others follow its lead.

Toothed whales such as this grow to around 5–7 m in length, weigh over a tonne, and live for 50 years or so.

Humpback whale
This species is one of the most recognisable of all the whales, and it's a regular visitor to New Zealand waters. It's found in oceans all around the world and travels great distances, moving from cold waters that are rich in food to warmer waters for mating and giving birth. Humpbacks are usually about 15 m in length and weigh around 25 tonnes. They are known for their 'singing', when they hang head-downwards in the water for 30–60 minutes as they go through a unique series of notes and sounds. These 'songs' may be for attracting females, or to claim territory, or just to detect other whales. The songs gradually change from year to year. Humpbacks are also well known for their habit of 'breaching' – leaping almost clear out of the water, and twisting about to land on their backs with a great splash. They may do this to clean parasites from their skin, or to create sound waves . . . or maybe just for fun!

ANIMALS • Mammals

Seals and sea lions are members of a mammalian group called pinnipeds. Over a long period of time, they have adapted to a life spent mostly in the seas, coming out onto land only to breed. They have developed sleek, torpedo-shaped bodies, with minimal hair, and limbs that have become powerful flippers. Most have layers of insulating blubber within their skin to help maintain a steady body temperature in cold seas. The blubber also helps with buoyancy. They have large eyes, and can close their nostrils and ears while underwater. Many can dive to 100 m or more, and remain underwater for an hour or longer.

New Zealand fur seal

There are about 9 seal species in our waters; the most common is the New Zealand fur seal. Although it was hunted to near-extinction during the late eighteenth and early nineteenth centuries, its numbers have now recovered to several tens of thousands.

Fur seals come ashore to breed at many coastal locations around the South Island and parts of the lower North Island. Small groups will come ashore all around the country for a doze and a laze in the sun. They are very efficient swimmers and can chase fish, squid and penguins at speeds up to 40 km per hour.

The male fur seal (125 kg) is larger than the female (40 kg) and can measure up to 2 m in length. Fur seals can live for 15–20 years.

Hooker's sea lion

This is the only sea lion in New Zealand waters. It comes ashore to breed on our southernmost islands, though individuals and small groups sometimes beach around the lower South Island for some rest and relaxation. Some will even travel up to a kilometre inland to find a comfortable spot. Weighing up to 450 kg, the sea lion is a much bigger animal than the fur seal, and also hunts for bigger prey. As well as fish and squid, it will also prey on seabirds and penguins, and even on the pups of fur seals and elephant seals. Sea lions can live for up to 25 years.

Southern elephant seal

This is by far the largest member of the seal family. The females reach 500–800 kg in weight, but the males can grow to an immense size – up to 4 tonnes in weight and over 6 m in total length. They live and breed all around our southernmost islands and can sometimes be seen ashore around the South Island coast. The males are very aggressive. They spend a lot of time arguing and fighting among themselves, and roaring through their great, enlarged snouts, as they try to control and dominate their chosen group of females. The elephant seal's roar can be heard over 1 km away! Though elephant seals are awkward on land, they are very strong swimmers; they can hold their breath for up to a couple of hours as they dive for fish and squid to depths of nearly 1000 m, and swim at speeds up to 25 km per hour. These great seals can live for nearly 25 years.

Index

A
abalone 60
Adélie penguin 119
air cushion weed 22
akiaki 135
algae 22
alligators 112, 116
allosaur 9
American cockroach 91
amphibians 8, 110
ankylosaurs 9
ants 82
aphid 82, 89
Archey's frog 110
arrow squid 65
artist's porebracket 19
Asian paper wasp 82
Australasian bittern 124
Australasian crested grebe 124
Australasian gannet 121
Australasian harrier 129
Australian coot 132
Australian magpie 151
Australian paper wasp 82

B
backswimmer 85
banded dotterel 133
banded kokopu 101
barnacles 67
bar-tailed godwit 134
beach slater 68
beech 40
bellbird 33, 147
birds 118
bivalves 48, 53, 56
black beech 40
black cockroach 91
black field cricket 90
black flounder 107
black fly 81
black pine 28
black robin 107

black shag 121
black stilt 133
black swan 125
black tunnelweb spider 94
black-backed gull 135
blackbird 141
black-fronted tern 135
black-headed jumping spider 94
bladder kelp 24
blue butterfly 74
blue damselfly 83
blue duck 126
blue penguin 119, 120
blue pinkgill 19
blue swamp orchid 39
bluebottle 45
Bluff oyster 55
bony fish 97, 100
bottlenose dolphin 153
breadcrumb sponge 44
brittle stars 47, 49
broadbill swordfish 106
bronze whaler shark 99
brown creeper 139
brown kiwi 144
brown owl 140
brown pine 28
brown trout 109
bull kelp 24
bully 54, 108
bulrush 43
bumblebee 82
by-the-wind sailor 45

C
cabbage tree 36
cabbage white butterfly 74
cake urchin 50
camouflaged anemone 46
Canada goose 125
cape fern 26
carpet star 48
cartilaginous fish 97

cat flea 91
cave spider 94
cave weta 87, 94
celery pine 29
centipedes 72
chaffinch 140, 149
chinstrap penguin 119
cicada 88
cinnabar moth 76
cirl bunting 149
clematis 36
cnidaria 45
coat-of-mail shell 64
colossal squid 66
columnar barnacle 67
common basket stinkhorn 20
common cat's eye shell 22, 61
common cockle 56
common crayfish 69
common dolphin 153
common flax 33
common frog 111
common jellyfish 45
common kelp 24
common octopus 64, 69
common rock crab 70
common scallop 55
common sea urchin 24, 50
common skink 115
common stick insect 90
common swimming crab 70
common wasp 82
conger eel 100
conifers 28
Cook's turban shell 60
coral fungi 20
coralline turf 22
cosmopolitan ground beetle 78
crabs 70
crane fly 80
creek fern 26
crocodile 9

crown fern 26
crustaceans 67
crustose lichens 21
cushion star 48
cycads 8

D

daddy-long-legs spider 80, 95
damselfly 83
dark top shell 60
dead man's fingers 47
devil's darning needle 83
dinosaurs 9
diving beetle 79
diving skink 115
dobsonfly 83
dusky dolphin 153
Duvaucel's gecko 114

E

eagle ray 98
earthworm 51
earwig 91
eastern rosella 136
echinoderms 48
electric ray 98
elephant weevil 79
eleven-spotted ladybird 78
elvers 100
emperor penguin 119
erect-crested penguin 119

F

fan coral 47
fan mussel 53
fan scallop 55
fan shell 55
fantail 143
feather star 49
fernbird 142
ferns 25
finger sponge 44
Fiordland crested penguin 119
fire salp 96
firebrick star 49
fish 97
fishbone fern 26
flapjack weed 23
flatworm 51
flax 33
flax snail 58
forest gecko 114

freshwater crayfish 69
freshwater limpet 59
freshwater mussel 54
freshwater shrimp 68
fructose lichens 21
fungi 18

G

galaxiids 101
garden centipede 72
garden orbweb spider 93
garden slater 68
garden snail 58, 94
gastropods 58
geckos 114–15
German owl 140
German wasp 82
giant cave weta 87
giant centipede 72
giant crab 71
giant dragonfly 83
giant eagle 10
giant ichneumon fly 79
giant kokopu 101
giant moa 11
giant squid 66
giant weta 86
giraffe weevil 79
Gisborne cockroach 91
globe sponge 44
glowworm 80
golden bell frog 110
golden sand sedge 33
goldfinch 149, 150
golfball sponge 44
gorse 14
grasshopper 89
Gray's gecko 114
great white shark 99
greater short-tailed bat 152
green frog 111
green lettuce 23
green plant hopper 88
green rock crayfish 69
green turtle 113
green vegetable bug 84, 88
green waxgill 19
greenfinch 149
green-lipped mussel 54
grey duck 127

grey house spider 93
grey warbler 139, 143
ground beetle 78
groupers 103
gum emperor moth 76
Gunther's tuatara 116

H

hagfish 97
Hamilton's frog 110
hammerhead shark 99
hapuku 103
harakeke 33
hard beech 40
hawksbill turtle 113
heart urchin 50
hebe 42
Hector's dolphin 153
hen and chickens fern 26
hermit crab 71
herringbone fern 26
higher plants 32
hihi 147
Hochstetter's frog 110
hoiho 119
honeybee 37, 81, 82
Hooker's sea lion 155
horse mussel 53
Hottentot fig ice plant 32
hound's tongue fern 25
house centipede 72
house hopper spider 94
house sparrow 149
housefly 81
huhu beetle 77
huia 13
humpback whale 154
hururoa 53
hydroids 45
hypsilophodonts 9

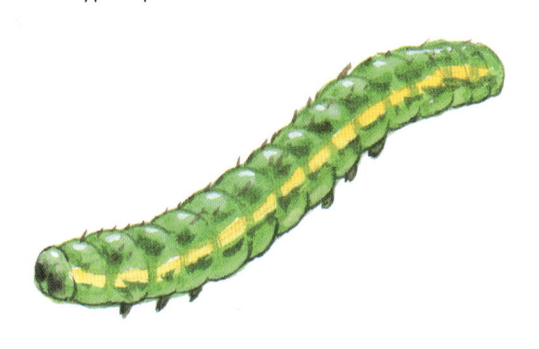

157

I

ice plant 32
inanga 101
insects 73
isopods 68

J

Japanese spider crab 71
jawless fish 97
jewel squid 65
jingle shell 55
John dory 102

K

kahikatea 28
kahu 129
kahukura 74
Kairaru 30, 31
kaka 138
kaka beak 35
kakahi 54
kakapo 137
kakariki 139
kaki 133
kanakana 97
kanuka 34, 90, 139
karaka 38, 40, 58
karearea 129
karengo 23
karoro 135
karuhiruhi 121
katipo 92
katydid 89
kauri 30–31
kauri snail 59
kawakawa 37
kawau paka 121
kawau pu 121
kawekaweau 114
kea 138
kereru 28, 136
kidney fern 25
kiekie 35
killer whale 154
kina 50
king crab 71
king's pouch 20
kingfisher 140
kiokio 26
kiwakiwa 26
kiwi 11, 144–45

kiwikiwi 26
koaro 101
kohekohe 40, 58
kokako 151
korimako 147
korora 119
kotare 140
kotuku 122
koura 69
kowhai 35, 39
kowhai ngutukaka 35
kuaka 134
kuku 136
kukupa 136
kuparu 102

L

ladder fern 26
ladybirds 78
lamprey 97
large dog cockle 56
large shore crab 71
large spotted mud whelk 61
laughing owl 12
leatherback turtle 113
leatherjacket 107
leech 52
lemon tree borer 77
lesser short-tailed bat 152
lichens 21
limpets 59, 60
little black mussel 54
little owl 140
little shag 121
loggerhead turtle 113
long-finned eel 100
long-finned pilot whale 154
long-tailed bat 152
long-tailed cuckoo 139
Lord Howe coralfish 104

M

magpie moth 75, 76
mallard 127
mamaku 25, 27
mammals 152, 153
manamana 26
manawa 32
mangrove 32, 61
manuka 35, 36
Maori ice plant 32

margin weed 24
matai 28
matata 142
matuku 123
matuku moana 123
matuku tai 123
Maui's dolphin 153
mayfly 84
megalosaurs 9
millipedes 72
mimic blenny 105
miro 28
miromiro 146
mites 85, 92, 95
moa 11
modest barnacle 67
molluscs 53
monarch butterfly 73, 82
moray eel 100
morepork 140
morning star shell 56
mosquito 80
mottled brittle star 49
mottled sand star 49
mouku 26
mountain beech 40
mountain daisy 43
mountain flax 33
Mt Cook lily 42
mud crab 70, 140
mud snail 63
mudfish 108
mute swan 125
muttonbird 24, 118
myna 150

N

native bush cockroach 91
Nelson cave spider 94
Neptune's necklace 22
New Zealand dabchick 124
New Zealand falcon 129
New Zealand flax 33, 58
New Zealand fur seal 155
New Zealand honeysuckle 37
New Zealand pigeon 28, 136
New Zealand praying mantis 90
New Zealand robin 146
New Zealand scaup 128
New Zealand shoveler 128

New Zealand vegetable bug 84
ngoiro 135
nikau 41
northern rata 38

O
octopus weed 24
olive beadlet anemone 46
orange porebracket 19
orange roughy 102
orca 98, 154
ostrich foot shell 61
Otago skink 115
oyster borer 62, 67
oyster thief 22

P
Pacific oyster 55
Pacific salmon 108
packhorse crayfish 69
paddle weed 24
palm-leaf fern 26
papango 128
paradise shelduck 126
paradox 159
parera 127
parson bird 148
passionvine hopper 88
paua 60
pea crab 54
pekapeka 152
penwiper plant 43
pepper tree 37
peripatus 52
petipeti 45
pied oystercatcher 132
pied shag 121
pied stilt 133
pikopiko 27
pingao 33
pink paua 60
pinnipeds 155
pipi 57
pipiwharauroa 139
piupiu 26
piwakawaka 143
plicate barnacle 67
poaka 133
podocarps 28
pohutukawa 34, 38
pond skater 85

ponga 25, 27
porcupine fish 107
Portuguese man-o-war 45
praying mantis 90
puawhananga 36
pukeko 131
pupu mai 60
pupurangi 59
puriri 41
puriri moth 41, 75
putangitangi 126
pygmy gecko 114
pygmy shark 99

Q
queen scallop 55
quinnat salmon 108

R
radiate limpet 59
rainbow trout 109
ram's horn shell 65
rangiora 43
rata 30, 34, 38
raupo 33
raurenga 25
red admiral butterfly 74
red beadlet anemone 46
red beech 40
red gurnard 103
red rock crab 71
red rock crayfish 69
red-billed gull 135
redcoat damselfly 83
redpoll 149
reef heron 123
reef star 48
reptiles 112
rewarewa 37
rifleman 141
rimu 29
riroriro 143
rock oyster 54, 55, 62
rock pigeon 136
rockhopper penguin 119
rough skate 97
rowi 144
royal albatross 118
royal spoonbill 122
ruru 140

S
saddleback 151
sand dollar 50
sand louse 68
sand scarab beetle 77, 92
sand star 48
Sandager's wrasse 105
sand-binder sedge 33
sandfly 81
sandhopper 68
sandpaper fish 102
sauropods 9
scarlet fly cap 18
school shark 99
screw shell 62
sea egg 50
sea lice 68
sea slug 63
sea squirt 96
sea star 48–49, 50, 54, 57, 60, 61, 62
sea tulip 96
sea urchin 24, 48, 61, 62
seahorse 103
shield fern 27
shining cuckoo 75, 139, 143
shore earwig 91
short-eyed mud crab 70
short-finned eel 100
short-jawed kokopu 101
short-tailed stingray 98
silver beech 40
silver fern 27
silver paua 60
silvereye 140, 147
skinks 115
skylark 142
slaty sponge 44
snakeskin chiton 64

159

snapper 104
snapper biscuit 50
Snares crested penguin 119
soft coral 47
song thrush 142
sooty shearwater 117, 118
soup shark 99
South African praying mantis 90
southern bell frog 111
southern elephant seal 155
southern rata 38
speckled anemone 46
speckled whelk 61
sperm whale 66, 102
spider crab 71
spiders 92
spinosaurus 9
spiny murex 62
spirorbis 52
sponges 44
spotless crake 132
spotted top shell 60
spur-winged plover 134
stalked barnacle 69
starling 150
steelblue ladybird 78
stick insect 90
stink bug 84
stitchbird 147
stone crab 71
stonefly 84
sundew 34
Suter's skink 115
swamp harrier 129

T

takahe 130
Tane Mahuta 30, 31
tanekaha 29
tarakihi 104
tarbosaurus 9
tauhou 147
tawa 37
tawaki 119
tawera 56
Te Waha o Rerekohu 34
ti kouka 36
ticks 95
tieke 151
tiger beetle 78
tiger centipede 72
tiger moth 76
titi 118
titipounamu 141
titoki 41
toheroa 57
tokoeka 144
tomtit 146
torea 132
totara 29
toutouwai 146
tree ferns 8
tree weta 86
triangle shell 56
trough shells 56
trout 69, 109
trumpet shell 61
tuatara 116–17
tuatua 57
tube worms 23, 52, 56
tube-noses 118
tufted millipede 72
tui 33, 148
tun shell 62
tunicates 96
tunnelling mud crab 70
tunnelweb spider 94
turban shell 60, 61
turnstone 134
turret shell 62
tusked weta 87
tussock 43
tussock ringlet butterfly 75
tutoke 27
twister 105
tyrannosaurus 9

U

univalves 58

V

variable oystercatcher 132
variable triplefin 105
vegetable sheep 42, 43
veined slug 63
velvet earthstar 21
velvet worm 52
Venus shell 56
Venus' necklace 22, 61
vigilant mosquito 80
virgin paua 60

W

wandering sea anemone 46
wasps 82
water boatman 85
water spider 95
wattlebirds 151
waxeye 147
weka 128
welcome swallow 141
wharariki 33
whau 38
wheel shell 60
whio 126
whistling frog 110
white heron 122
white pointer 99
whitebait 101, 108
white-eye 147
white-faced heron 123
white-faced storm petrel 119
white-tailed spider 93
winged bush cockroach 91
woodlice 68
worms 51
wrybill 133

X Y

yellow-bellied sea snake 112
yellowbelly flounder 106
yellow-crowned parakeet 139
yellow-eyed penguin 119, 120
yellowfin tuna 106
yellowhammer 143, 149
yellowhead 139

Z

zigzag shell 56
zigzag weed 23

160